PAPERBOY

A Dysfunctional Novel

Bob Thurber

Casperian Books

This is a work of fiction. All the characters and events portrayed in this book are either fictitious or are used fictitiously.

PAPERBOY. Copyright © 2011 by Bob Thurber. All rights reserved. No part of this book may be used or reproduced in any manner whatsoever without written permission except in the case of brief quotations embodied in critical articles or reviews. For information address Casperian Books, PO Box 161026, Sacramento, CA 95816-1026.

Front cover illustration by SMT Design.

www.casperianbooks.com

ISBN-10: 1-934081-31-0
ISBN-13: 978-1-934081-31-0

To speak the truth is a painful thing.
To be forced to tell lies is much worse.
— Oscar Wilde

– 1 –

In the dream I'm riding this red Schwinn Stingray Fastback—26-inch wheels, nubby tires, high-rise handlebars. Very cool bike. Same model Jack & Harry's Hardware sticks in the window every Christmas. Same candy-apple red, same slick nail-polish shine.

I've got my name stenciled in gold across the chain-guard, two chrome-wire baskets mounted saddlebag style, and another deep basket bolted to the handlebars. All baskets are full, heaped with newspapers, each paper neatly tucked and tri-folded and secured by a green rubber band. I've still got my dirty canvas bag looped across my chest, but it's empty, a useless sack. I wear it just to remind people what I am, and to advertise the name of the newspaper.

There's no traffic—the only cars in sight are parked in driveways—and I'm cruising down the middle of this smooth, black asphalt street, riding the centerline, barely pedaling as I reach and toss. A throw to my left, a throw to my right. Every house is a customer and I work in a regular snap rhythm. All my tosses are perfect. Each paper travels in a high arc, then lands soft, dead center on each porch's welcome mat like it was placed there by careful hands. People open their doors, look down in amazement. Everyone smiles and waves.

I pedal and throw, working steadily but never frantically, delivering two hundred newspapers in less than an hour. The street ends in a cul-de-sac with newly constructed homes and I cruise the circle, looking at the pretty empty houses, deciding which one I'd like to buy and give to my mother for Christmas. I hit the brakes, skid into a half spin, and come to a dead stop. I take out my green book and a stub of pencil and place a checkmark next to every customer's name, confident I haven't missed a single one.

Then I turn the bike around and head for home, traveling the road I came, passing the same houses, the same lawns. Some of my customers are still waving, but my baskets are empty now, except for one last tightly tucked newspaper, which is for my mother. The empty canvas bag flaps behind me catching the wind like a flag as I pedal, pumping hard, my ass high off the seat, chest forward, my hair streaming.

What I want to ask, what I need to know, is there a place like that, a street that peaceful and serene, a route so straight and effortless outside of dreaming?

– 2 –

Friday, May 2, 1969—I wake up hard in the dark, no idea which room I'm in. Our apartment only has three, so any guess is a good one. I wake up afraid, which is nothing new. The air tastes dry and thick. The darkness has an oily blue tint. A radiator is hissing, but I can't get a fix. My hair is damp, my T-shirt soaked. I'm sweating like I've got a fever, and when I shift onto my side, checking to see if maybe I've wet myself, something prickly presses against my neck. I turn slowly, carefully. A pink curler, barely visible, is wrapped tight against my mother's ear. It's big as a roll of quarters. Above her head I find the windows, two rectangles of gray cut into the slanted ceiling. I map the room. Everything is reversed. I'm in the big bed, covered by a sheet. My mother breathes in whispers and moans.

Where's Kelly, I wonder. On the couch? I hold my breath and listen. I wait for some sound that will tell me my sister is on my rollaway cart at the foot of the bed. You can't breathe on that mattress without the cheap wire frame squeaking like an early bird. How did I end up here? What time did I fall asleep? Did Mom carry me to bed?

I hear slippers sliding across the linoleum—Kelly's up, searching the kitchen for food. But it's only my mother grinding her teeth between short wheezing breaths. Curled slightly, clutching her pillow, she's the length that I am. She shifts her hold on the pillow, slides a knee up until it bumps my thigh. She's way past the middle, taking up more than half the bed.

I lift the sheet off and pinch the top of my shirt away from my chest. Why is it so hot? Why am I in bed with my mother? Why is the radiator hissing? It's May. In six weeks school lets out for summer.

I'm about to get up when I remember where Kelly is and how long she's been there, locked up in a room far, far away. I do the math. I work out the number of weeks, then days. Seventy-seven. It seems longer than that. I figure out what day it is, what day it will be. Saturday, May 3rd. My sister is coming home. Mom is signing her out. That thought makes the room cooler, the air easier to breathe. I close my eyes and try to get back to dreaming.

My mother grinds her teeth like she's chewing gum in her sleep. The radiator whispers "psst, psst." I try counting sheep, but Kelly's face keeps popping up. I miss her too much. Thinking about her makes my head hurt. Sometimes, in school, I drift off, like I'm asleep with my eyes open. So maybe I'm crazy, too.

My whole body aches remembering the last time, that special feeling, a warmth better than any other. It's such a strange and sudden happiness, one so brief and special, I'm sure it isn't allowed. Not for kids. Not for me. It's something meant for grownups. Adults only. And I'm pretty sure you're supposed to be married. I feel like I've been stealing money; not the little I pinch on my route every week, but filling my pockets with big handfuls from the church's collection plate.

A noise makes me jerk—a siren, a cat? Maybe it's a baby crying. A little girl. I open my eyes and stare at the blue-tinged darkness above my head and I try to imagine the room my sister's sleeping in, if there are bars on the windows or any windows at all, and I listen for the sound of traffic, for the squawk of early birds, for some sign of morning.

My grandmother used to say, "A new day always forgives you, unless it's raining and you wake up in jail."

– 3 –

Saturday, May 3, 1969—It's May and it's snowing. Huge flurries, like the ashes that float up from the backyard when our landlady, Mrs. K, burns rubbish. We're three floors up and the view looks like Christmas, which is nuts. Summer starts in three weeks. The radiator valve is hissing steam, so I'm careful where I put my elbows. My mother works as a waitress now, but back when she pressed shirts in a dry cleaner's she got a nasty L-shaped scar from not watching where she put her elbows.

I'm eating Froot Loops from a mixing bowl, sitting on the windowsill—eating them dry because the only milk we have is lumpy Carnation's Instant. I'm looking across at the Marshall house, hoping to see Patty Marshall parading in her underwear. Patty used to babysit Kelly and me a few years back and now she goes to junior college. I haven't seen her in a while. This morning there's a light on in her bedroom and the shade is at half-mast. Patty has nice breasts, and I'm hoping a glimpse of them, even in a bra, will take my mind off my life, but the snow is wrecking my view.

It's a freak storm, a total surprise with no warning from the weatherman. The forecast called for heavy rain. Two guys on the radio are explaining the unseasonable temperature with jokes and excuses. Their booming voices make them sound like a couple of smart-ass jerks. I've already got the storm figured out. Some idiot blew up the sun. Some Russian general pushed the wrong button and launched one of their million missiles, or maybe NASA misaimed one of our test rockets. Either way, the sun is gone and we're now engaged in a nuclear shootout. It's the end of everything. Batman and Superman aren't coming and James Bond doesn't have a trick up his sleeve to save us this time. In a week or a month, we'll all freeze to death, just like in that Twilight Zone episode where the pretty lady is burning up with fever, dreaming the sun is baking the world dry, when really the Earth has dropped out of orbit, is hurtling further and further away from the sun, rapidly turning into a big ball of ice.

One of the radio men mentions how the Apollo 10 astronauts, who are scheduled to take off in a couple of weeks, might be better off with Eskimo parkas and skis instead of pressure suits and space helmets. Then the first guy gets dead serious and predicts the temperature will gradually climb and all the snow will turn into rain. He promises a downpour.

I stop thinking about moon rockets and exploding suns and start worrying about my route. Sam takes Saturday mornings off unless the track is open and the horses are running. He leaves Huey in charge of the newsstand through most of the weekend. Huey is a freak, a burn victim, and a mess of ruined flesh. Pinkish scars cover his face and neck, and he's short a couple of fingers on a claw-shaped right hand. He looks sort of a like a wrinkly old pig that got into a fight with a pack of hyenas. Otherwise, he's a nice guy, though not too smart. My mother says you don't need to be a genius to stand on a street corner selling newspapers. I'm hoping Huey remembers to set forty-five aside and keep them dry for me. On Saturday the bundles arrive early, usually by ten, and I generally finish by noon, then walk back to the corner to meet up with Sam and pay my weekly bill. But I'll start my route late today.

– 4 –

By ten o'clock the roof and side yard of the Marshall's house are white. There's not a ton of snow, but I bet if it were a weekday, the radio announcers would be reading a list of school closings instead of telling stupid jokes. This is just a waste, a waste of good snow. From the bathroom my mother tells me to dig my boots out of the closet. I tell her it's not sticking. "Better bring your sister's boots, too," she says.

"She won't need them. Weatherman says it's changing to rain."

Her voice becomes a screech. "Don't start with me, Jack. Not today." She's jumpy because of the snow, and pissed because she's missing a Saturday breakfast shift. Saturdays are good tip days at the Blackstone Diner. I'm sure she told Rocky, who owns the place, that she's having her hair done or attending a funeral, or some other nonsense. Despite the snow, we have a mission. My sister has been locked up for seventy-seven days in Emerson Children's Hospital, on a ward with mental patients. Today we are going to get her. She's coming home, though I don't know for how long.

Mom comes out of the bathroom in a blue dress that she sometimes wears to church. She uses the phone to request a Royal Taxi to take us to the hospital, then she fiddles with her hair, which she wears high and heavily lacquered with Spray Net. She paces and smokes half of a cigarette while I take my time getting dressed. I'm still buttoning my shirt when she calls me a slowpoke and tugs me toward the sink. She turns on the faucet. She wet-combs and parts my hair, something she hasn't done the entire school year.

"What are you doing?"

"Hold still," she says.

I squirm and do a little dance and she squeezes my chin, which is badly broken out, pink and raw with half a dozen new pimples. "You're hurting me."

"Keep your head up and your mouth shut."

I stop struggling while she scoops my bangs into a wave, then pats it down with her hand. I twist away and touch the top of my head. I trace the part with my fingers. "No, I don't wear it like this."

"Today you do," she says.

– 5 –

We wait for the taxi in the downstairs hall where the radiator is always ice-cold because our landlady, Mrs. K, thinks heating an empty hall is a waste of money. Mom folds her arms across her bulky coat and presses her back against the door of the storage closet that cuts beneath the curved stairway. There's a new padlock on the storage closet's door, put there by Mrs. K. I've tried to pick it twice, once with a bobby pin, once with a screwdriver, but it's not a cheap lock. I could use a hammer and bang my way in, or borrow Grandpa Rudy's hacksaw, but there's really nothing I want except to look around. The storage closet holds our junk—Mom keeps Christmas decorations and old clothes and toys she paid good money for in it, and it's where I used to keep my bike until it was stolen. And it's where Mom once found Kelly naked to the waist, smoking Lucky Strikes that she had stolen from Grandpa Rudy.

Mom shifts her position, bumps the door, rattles the lock. "You forgot your boots," she says, and I shrug. For the next minute I listen to the sound a cold hallway makes.

Then a horn blares and she pulls on the heavy door. But it's just a car, just a neighbor. She stands there, looking foolish, with the door half open, letting the cold in. Snow slants down beyond the porch awning. The street looks slick and wet but it's still black.

"It's really coming down now," she says.

I think about my sister, how she'll look, how she'll act. It's been seventy-seven days. Mom says Kelly's not right in the head, but I guess she's better now. I grip the banister's railing, bending forward, all my weight on my heels, and pretend I'm rope-climbing a steep cliff.

"You must be pretty excited," my mother says.

I act like I don't understand. I grunt and shrug, then pull myself up a step. In heels my mother is a full six feet. On the second stair I'm a couple of inches taller. "Excited about what? Riding in a taxi?" I say like I'm a complete idiot.

She frowns and looks at her shoes which are a darker blue than her dress, though they match her pocketbook perfectly. She looks nice, almost pretty, like we're headed for church. I pull myself to the next stair wishing it was Sunday and I didn't have to do my route. "Don't act up now," she says. "And when you see your sister, make sure you give her a big hug. This has been hard on her, hard on all of us."

I want to say, "It's your fault. You locked her up." For weeks, every time she's mentioned Kelly, I've kept those words ready. I want to say, "You ruined everything, you old witch."

I roll those words around in my mouth, hanging onto the rail, waiting for her to look at me. When she looks, I'll let go. But she unsnaps her purse and busies herself, searching inside. I wonder if she has enough money to pay for the taxi. I watch her lips to see if she's counting. In a minute, another horn sounds. My mother snaps her bag shut. "That's him. That's our ride," she says, and we go out together.

– 6 –

One of the pretend games Kelly and I used to play when we were little was "Away in a Manger," based on the hymn she'd learned in church choir. Kelly acted out the part of Mother Mary and I got to be Baby Jesus.

Away in a manger, no crib for a bed,
The little Lord Jesus laid down his sweet head.

Even though I was pretending to be a newborn, Kelly said I was allowed to speak. Not because it was her game and her rules, but because I was Jesus, the son of God, a kind of superbaby who'd been born with secret, magical powers.

The stars in the bright sky looked down where he lay,
The little Lord Jesus asleep on the hay.

I remember one time we played "Away in a Manger" in the parlor when our mother was out, but the real manger was the storage closet under the stairs on the first-floor landing.

We pretended the emergency flashlight was a campfire and left the door open a crack to let a little air in. Behind boxes of Christmas decorations and clothes that no longer fit, I stripped down to my underwear and wrapped myself in an old sheet. Then I fake-cried and complained and fussed about everything and nothing, while my sister tried to shut me up and make me go to sleep. She held my head in her lap and hummed lullabies, rubbed and patted my back, but none of that worked. The only way to shut me up was for Kelly to tell me a story. And the stories she told had to be very old; authentic tales that the real Mother Mary might have told to her son, the real baby Jesus, right after he was born in a filthy, stinky manger alongside cows and camels and sheep in the little town of Bethlehem.

The cattle are lowing, the baby awakes,
But little Lord Jesus no crying he makes.

The trick was that Kelly couldn't just make some story up with people shooting guns or crashing cars off cliffs or dropping bombs from airplanes because none of that stuff had been invented yet. So she told stories she had learned in Sunday school from Mrs. Brown and other teachers, stories about fierce battles and holy wars, about brutal men charging on horseback or camels or elephants.

Sometimes we played Adam and Eve. Instead of using an apple, Kelly and I took turns taking bites from one of the sour pears from the tree in the Red Cross parking lot.

– 7 –

A black-and-white taxi aligns itself with the front gate. On the white door is a gold crown with the phone number painted underneath. I scramble down the walkway ahead of my mother, leaving her to stagger on her thin heels. The door handle is caked with snow. I climb into the back seat and leave the door open for her. I scoot all the way over. The driver turns his head but I look at my feet. Mom pushes the rear door closed then gets in front with the driver. She introduces herself with a three-finger handshake and a toothy smile. "How do you do? My name's Rita. That's my son, Jack."

The driver mumbles something, but the windshield wipers drown him out. My mother, still smiling, quickly negotiates a flat price, up and back, so that once we get going the man doesn't engage his meter, which is disappointing, because there isn't much to look at from the back seat of a taxi.

Snow rushes against the windshield as we drive. Flurries big as corn flakes stick to the side windows. "How about this weather," the driver says. "Is this something?"

"Nuts," says my mother. She shifts in her seat every few minutes. She seems nervous, almost scared. I wait for her to tell the driver that she used to work for Royal as a dispatcher before Kelly and I were born, but she makes no mention.

– 8 –

At the side entrance of Emerson Childrens Hospital Mom gets out and leaves me with the driver. She hurries inside to sign for my sister's release. I watch the door she went through, wondering how long it'll take. The driver shuts off the wipers, but the engine is still going. "Who's sick," he says after a minute.

"Nobody," I say a little too quickly. Then I think what a crappy answer that is to give to a cab driver trying to make polite conversation in a snowstorm. "My sister had a nervous breakdown." I don't look at him. "But she's okay now."

"Oh," the driver says.

When I do look up, his eyes are in the rearview mirror. He wrinkles them but I can't tell if he's smiling or just squinting. Then his eyes drop from view as he touches a lever on the dashboard. The heater hums louder. I turn my head and stare at the door my mother went in. When I'm sure the driver isn't watching, I practice kissing the cold glass, leaving overlapping lip prints that look like a flower.

– 9 –

When I was twelve, I tried to teach myself how to kiss by using my sister's bride doll. She was four feet tall with moveable arms and legs, though her elbows and knees didn't bend. Her name was Betty. She had a human-sized head, crystal blue eyes with lids that closed, rosy cheeks, and a red, tulip-shaped mouth. Her mouth didn't open but her lips were full and pouty with a deep crevice between them. I would lift her veil and tilt her head back, then slide my tongue in the gap of her pretty mouth. I really liked how her eyes would slowly close and at a certain angle became slits with the tiniest sparkle of crystal blue in them, like I was driving her wild. I never closed my own eyes when I kissed Betty. The first time I caught her watching me undress I pushed things further, posturing her arms and spreading her legs, sucking at her mouth while I humped like a savage. I kept rubbing until a rush of warmth filled my belly. I thought I had wet myself. I didn't know what else it could be. I didn't know anything. I was such a stupid kid.

– 10 –

While I'm waiting for my mother to spring Kelly from the nut house, I take out my unbreakable twenty-five-cent comb and work at my bangs until they cover my forehead. Then I rake across the side part, back to front, front to back, until I destroy it. The driver watches me do this, his eyes banded across the rearview.

This is my second unbreakable twenty-five-cent comb from Lee's Barber Shop. New combs are kept on a cardboard display above the cash register, each in a brown vinyl sleeve imprinted with Lee's address and phone number. When Lee sells a comb and removes one of the sleeves from the card, it's immediately replaced by an actual-size picture of itself. At the top of the display, in bold print above a detailed drawing of a man's neatly groomed head, it reads: "Lifetime Guaranty against Breakage."

I had to work very hard with a pair of pliers, twisting and bending, until the first comb snapped. When I brought the two pieces in, Lee couldn't have looked more surprised. "That's a first," he said. "Never had one come back before."

Then he cut my hair as usual—short in the back, buzz-clipped above the ears, cropped to the eyebrows. He asked about my mother, whom he used to date. He asked if I wanted my hair left wet or dry and I said dry. Then he charged me one dollar and when I handed it over, he told me to make sure I said hello to my mom. "She changed her number again," Lee said. Then he handed me a new comb in a brown vinyl sleeve, no questions asked. I've decided against breaking this one out of respect for the man.

– 11 –

The snow looks gray and wet. I can't tell if it's falling faster or slower. I close my eyes and pull in a couple of deep breaths, but I get so dizzy I have to open them again. Wind sweeps most of the taxi's window clean, but the inside is hazed from the heat. I swipe at the glass with my coat sleeve, clearing a peephole. I try to focus on the light above the door of the hospital.

Now and again, between bursts of static, the voice of a woman dispatcher asks the driver if he's available for another fare. He says he's not. He gives his location. She calls him Bill. After some more static she asks about the road conditions. "Not good," Bill says.

Even though it's a woman's voice, I pretend the dispatcher is Houston calling. I'm in a space capsule looking down at the surface of the moon. I'm supposed to land, but I'm low on fuel. There's no air and my eyelids are dead weight. I rest my head against the seat and fall into a dream of Kelly and I in puffy coats trying to catch snowflakes on our tongues. Then we're digging in the plowed heaps against the fence in the church's parking lot. The plow truck leaves the snow packed dense and good for building. We work to create a huge fort in no time at all. Then suddenly, it's summer and hot, and everything starts melting. An inch of water streams around my sneakers. Our fort turns gray and slushy. But my sister keeps working, digging like a maniac, tunneling until I can't see any part of her. I squat down and yell into the hole. I tell her it's not safe. "This is not a good idea," I say. "The weather is all wrong." Then Mom is calling us to supper, half her body out the window, her voice louder than a screeching bird.

A blast of cold air startles me awake. A girl is huddled on the seat beside me, a small red suitcase between us. She's not fat, not at all, but she's too thick to be my sister. Her hair hangs like a dark veil. My mother slides into the front and closes her door. The driver starts the engine.

I look at Kelly who is bent forward, hiding behind her hair. "Hey," I say.

Mom turns around, sticking her elbow over the top of the seat. "She's not talking."

"Not to you, I'm not," Kelly says.

My mother's mouth drops open. She appears genuinely shocked. "Oh, good. I thought they cut out your tongue." She hollows her cheeks and blinks at me. "Go on. What are you waiting for? Give your sister a hug and tell her you missed her. No point both of you being rude."

I can feel sweat tickling the back of my neck, dripping beneath both arms.

"I didn't bring them up to be bad-mannered," she tells the driver. "It's not my fault they've got their father's stubborn streak. He was a Southerner, a no-good rebel. Why aren't you talking to your sister?" she says to me.

"What? I said hello."

"Well, maybe she's lost her hearing," Mom says. "They've got her all drugged up and acting like a zombie. Kelly?" she says, snapping her fingers twice. "Can you hear your brother?"

Kelly leans forward, clutching her knees, keeping her face down. Her hair is a lot longer than I remember. And she's stopped biting her nails, because they're almost as long as my mother's nails.

The driver shifts the taxi into reverse. The wipers start swishing. Mom puffs a breath and shakes her head. She's close enough to slap us both, one, two. She won't whack us in front of the driver, I don't think. She closes her eyes. "Hold on a minute, please. Don't go anyplace." Her voice is tight.

Here we go, I say to myself. *Or rather, here we don't.* The driver pumps the brakes. He seems confused. The car lurches then slides a few inches sideways. I can feel a knot in my stomach, big as a fist. I look over at Kelly and think, *Don't be stupid. Say something nice or she'll drag you back inside by your hair.*

"I've got all the time in the world," Mom says.

Kelly raises a hand and sweeps hair away from her face like she's peeking from behind a curtain. The nail on her middle finger is longer than the rest. "Hi Jack." I can't see enough of her face to tell if she's smiling.

"There," my mother says, twisting to face front. "Was that so damn hard?" Her shoulders relax. "I apologize for that," she tells the driver, who shrugs and starts us moving.

The taxi bumps along. The moment we pass through the gate, Kelly picks up the suitcase. She holds it on her lap like a dinner tray. I think she's trying to turn to get a goodbye look at Emerson. Instead, she scoots over and leans her shoulder into me. Her hair tickles my cheek as she kisses beneath my mouth, just missing my lips. She grabs me above the elbow, squeezing, more for balance than anything, then tilts her head, offering her cheek in an obvious request for a return kiss. I check the front, scan the rearview, then give my sister a dry peck on the cheek. She pulls away, sits up straight. "Nice hairdo," she whispers, staring at the dome light, slowly raking her nails over the spot I kissed as though scratching at a mosquito bite.

– 12 –

Our TV died in February, the night before Valentine's Day. No smoke, no fire. Just a sudden stink like a match burning a pencil eraser, then—snap crackle pop!—the screen went dark, the picture was gone.

It was an old set, a '66 Zenith in a blond wood cabinet. According to Zenith's slogan "the quality goes in before the name goes on," but that TV had acted up since day one. The reception was never as sharp as our old Philco black-and-white. Despite a dozen service calls and repeated adjustments, the color remained slightly off. People's faces, particularly close-ups—more noticeable on men than women—took on a blue-green tint so that every actor, dead or alive, appeared less than healthy.

Mom bought the Zenith because it was on sale, the salesman was charming, the store was willing to finance, and the slick blond finish matched her coffee table almost exactly. Even after the picture tube died, she continued to make the weekly payments, and every Saturday she waxed and polished the slick wooden cabinet.

One Saturday Kelly came home a couple of hours late from choir practice; her eyes were heavy and she smelled funny, kind of like cat piss, only sweeter, and a little bit like burned popcorn. She seemed to be in a pretty good mood until she plopped down on the couch, then she began to sulk. She asked me why Mom was wasting her time polishing the dead TV. I didn't say anything and Mom didn't answer right away. She sprayed Lemon Pledge across the screen then buffed with an old sock. Then she told Kelly that the TV was a good piece of furniture and needed to be taken care of.

Kelly laughed. "Yeah. One that doesn't do anything."

Mom squeezed her lips together and breathed through her nose, never a good sign. "What would you like it to do?"

"I'd like it to work," my sister said. "I'd like to turn the F-ing thing on and see a picture."

"Watch your mouth, missy. I don't like that word."

"I didn't say any word. I said F-ing."

I got ready to move. I was too close to Kelly. If Mom charged and swung, I might catch a slap not meant for me.

"What do you want me to do," Mom said. "The picture tube is shot." She sounded more tired than angry. "Nothing I can do about it right now."

"Get it fixed," Kelly said. "Take it back to the store and make them fix it."

"It's not that simple," Mom said. She looked at me and I looked away. "Do you know how much a picture tube costs?"

"No," Kelly said. "And I don't care."

"You going to pay?"

Kelly ignored this.

"You got a rich boyfriend I don't know about?"

Kelly bumped my elbow, but not on purpose. She folded her arms across her chest. "Why should I pay? It's not my dumb TV."

Mom went back to polishing the Zenith. "You're right. It's not yours. It's my TV that I paid for and I'm still paying for it. And if you're not going to fork over the money for a new picture tube, then I think you should shut up and mind your own business."

"It's pretty stupid to polish a TV that doesn't work." Mom went over a spot she had already polished twice. "It's retarded," Kelly said. Mom looked at the can of Lemon Pledge like she was reading the label. "You're polishing junk," Kelly said.

"Shut your trap!"

I found out later that Kelly had skipped choir practice and smoked dope with the Shelton brothers, so maybe she didn't know what she was doing. Perhaps she didn't care. When Mom charged at her swinging the can of Lemon Pledge, Kelly fought back. She blocked Mom's arm with her own. The can went flying. Mom whacked Kelly on the side of her head and my sister slid off the couch onto the floor. The smart thing to do would have been to curl up in a ball, but Kelly sprang up swinging. She landed two quick punches, one to my mother's ribs, the second dead center in the stomach. I'd never seen anyone punch my mother before. It wasn't pretty. My mother folded, clutching at her midsection. As she went down, my sister rose up.

"Don't hit me," Kelly said. "No more hitting." Then she lined herself up and slapped Mom right in the face. The sound made me jump. I staggered back as though I'd been struck.

Mom groaned, then she sobbed, clutching at her midsection with one arm, holding her face with her other hand. She did that for five or ten seconds then picked up her can of Lemon Pledge and left the room. "That's the last time you do that," she said.

Kelly stood frozen for a moment, glaring at nothing.

"You'll see. You'll find out," my mother said.

Kelly paced in a small circle. "Fine," she said. She stood by the dead TV and glared at me. "Pay attention. You're my witness."

"Leave me out of it," I said.

Kelly cupped her hands beside her mouth, "I hereby renounce my allegiance to the queen. I will not be tortured. I will not be suppressed. I will not be silenced."

"Stop it, " I said.

"Let it be known to everyone that from this day forward, I shall defy, oppose, resist, and if need be, take up arms against her great cruelty."

"Shut up," I said. "You'll make it worse."

"You shut up. What could be worse than this?"

"Go ahead. Yap away," my mother said. "I'm listening. Keep it up, missy."

My mother seldom addressed us by our real names. Kelly was "Missy" and I was "Mister." As in "Mind your own business, mister."

My sister plopped herself into Mom's chair. She put her head down and hid her face behind her hair. I got up and walked toward the TV. I thought pacing the room would help, that it might take some of the electricity out of the air, but mostly I was trying to mind my own business. "I hate her so fucking much," Kelly hissed.

"I heard that, too, missy. Keep it up. You're one strike away from having a can of black pepper poured into that filthy mouth of yours."

"Good," Kelly said. "Feed me pepper. I don't care. You can choke me to death and I'll still hate you. I'm going to turn sixteen soon. Then you can't control my life anymore."

"My house. My rules. You don't like it, move the hell out."

Kelly threw open the door. I expected her to slam it behind her, but she didn't. She made as much noise as one person can make running downstairs. I went out into the hall and looked over the railing. She was nearly at the bottom. "Where are you going?" I said.

She stopped moving, her hand on the rail. She waited a three-count before looking up, sort of like an actress awaiting her cue. "Tell Mom she wants a war, we'll have a war. I'm not taking her shit anymore. Fuck her."

"Come back up. Don't make it worse."

She moved down a step, then another. "No. This is a war now. Pick a side, Jack."

I heard the downstairs door close. I didn't go to the window to see which way she ran. I went back into the parlor and looked at the dead Zenith. The blond wood shone like glass. After a minute, I went into the kitchen. I found my mother by the sink pressing a wet dishtowel to her face. "I'm not going to live like this," she said. "I won't do it." She dabbed at her face then looked at the towel as if expecting to see blood. "What was she screaming about in the hall?"

"She wasn't screaming."

"What did she say about me?"

"Nothing," I said.

She stared at me with her mouth open. Her cheeks and forehead looked like she had a sunburn and I could tell by her eyes that she was trying really hard to keep from crying. "Which way did she go?"

I shrugged because I hadn't looked, and my mother narrowed her eyes like she had caught me lying. "I think she's sorry," I said.

Mom tossed the washcloth at the dish rack. "Sorry as a sorry Christmas is what she's going to be. Go put the chain on the door in case she tries to get back in."

That dumb argument, that ugly fight, those two punches, and that one hard slap, all those things marked the beginning of the end for Kelly. Of course, I could have prevented the battle. I could have stepped between them and shielded the blow. I so desperately wanted to be a hero, but at every opportunity my timing was off.

– 13 –

We're zipping along on Interstate 95 making good time when the snow changes to a mix of ice and hard rain that rattles the taxi's roof and peppers the windows. The windshield wipers are flying but the view becomes a blur, like we're traveling underwater. Above the heater's hum, the tires make a loud whooshing noise. My mother pulls in a short, sudden breath. Or maybe it's the driver clearing his throat. Either or, it's the first sound out of anyone since we left Emerson's parking lot.

I look at the stone statue that is my sister: a dark figure of a girl hidden by her hair. I stare out the window and try to relax. I imagine walking my route in this shit. Most of my customers won't care if they get their paper a couple of hours late on a Saturday, but a bunch will complain if their paper arrives sopping wet.

The driver slows our speed. A truck rumbles past. I ask my mother for the time. She moves her head a little but doesn't answer, so after a few seconds, I ask again. "I'm not wearing my watch," she says, which is an absolute lie because I saw her slide it onto her wrist before we left the house.

"I need to know the time, Ma."

"Not right this minute, you don't. We'll get there when we get there. Settle down and let the man concentrate on his driving."

I look at my sister who is wrapped up, hugging herself like she's chilled to the bone. I'm sure she's listening, but I can't tell if she's peeking behind her hair.

"It's ten to noon," the driver says.

My mother shifts in her seat. "There. Satisfied now?" She brings out her compact and flips it open. She whispers something to the driver as she dabs the little pad around her mouth and smoothes it over her cheekbones. She puts the pad away and moves the compact so that it is angled toward the back seat. I see one of her eyes in the mirror. I glance at the rearview, and sure enough, the driver's eyes are staring too.

"Your brother's a working man now," my mother starts. She shifts the mirror and her eyes slide out of view. "Tell Kelly about your paper route, Jack."

I bring one knee up onto the seat and lean my elbow on the suitcase. "I've got a paper route," I say.

Behind her veil of hair, Kelly says, "Lucky you."

"Fifty customers," my mother says. "All downtown. He delivers to City Hall, the fire station. Don't you, Jack? He brings the mayor his paper. The mayor. Isn't that something?"

"Not on Saturdays," I say. "City Hall is closed on Saturday."

"Morning or afternoon," the driver says.

"All day, I think."

"The paper," he says. "Morning edition or afternoon?"

"I deliver *The Times*," I say. "They only print one paper a day."

"You don't deliver *The Journal*?"

"No, sir."

"I don't think I've ever read *The Times*. That's the thin paper, isn't it?"

I don't answer.

My mother snaps the compact shut. "He's making good money. Aren't you, Jack? Tell your sister about all the tips your get."

"Tips are important," the driver says.

"You're not telling me anything," my mother says.

"I bet the mayor is a good tipper," the driver says.

"The mayor doesn't pay me. His office sends the money directly to *The Times*."

"I bet they don't even charge him," my mother says. "Free papers."

"He pays," I say. "Everybody pays. Sam says his office sends a check."

"Does he include your tip?" the driver says.

"I don't get a tip from the mayor."

"You might want to look into that," the driver says. "Something doesn't seem right there."

"You should ask Sam about it," my mother says. "Do you know Sam?" she asks the driver. "Sam the paper man?"

"Sam the who?"

"Sam the paper man," my mother says, her voice going higher. "You must know Sam. Everybody knows Sam. Downtown Pawtucket. He's got a newsstand in front of the Industrial Bank."

"Oh, yeah. The burned guy," the driver says.

"That's Huey," I say. "Sam doesn't have any burns."

"Poor, poor Huey," my mother says like a song. "He's so nice. That man's got a good heart. He's always smiling."

"He doesn't smile that much," I say. "And he's not always nice."

"You don't know what you're talking about," Mom says. "He's a good man with a good heart. That's a miracle considering what he's been through."

"If that's not Sam," the driver says, "then who's Sam?"

"Huey works for Sam," my mother says. "Poor Huey."

"What happened to him?" the driver says. "Chemical fire? Car accident? He looks like someone threw acid in his face."

"He fell into a burning trash barrel," my mother says. "Head first. Ten, twenty years ago, I think. He was drunk, I guess, and he lost his balance. He fell into the rubbish barrel and he's a big man, you know. Wide. So I guess he couldn't get out. They found him with his feet in the air."

The driver says, "No shit," and takes a hand off the wheel. He touches above his ear. "Drunk, huh?"

My mother nods. "Doesn't drink anymore, though. Not a drop."

"Small wonder," the driver says. "Feet in the air. Jesus." The rain is easing up so he reduces the speed of the wiper blades. "He must have been pretty drunk."

"Personally, I've got no use for drinkers," my mother says. "A man likes a beer now and then, I don't mind."

"I like a beer. Maybe two," the driver says.

"I have no use for a man who boozes it up every night of the week."

"Two's generally my limit," the driver says.

"My husband was a whisky drinker. Out the door he went."

"I don't blame you. No, ma'am," the driver says. Then he says, "So you're divorced?" and my mother nods. He changes his grip on the steering wheel. "Same here. Well, almost. It's a long story."

Kelly moves her hands up over her ears. She holds them there, flat like earmuffs. She turns her face to me, smiling in a funny, crooked sort of way. She rolls her eyes like a magazine model trying to peek at the pages stacked behind her. I usually like it when anybody smiles at me, but this one is almost creepy. She might simply be out of practice. Both my mother and sister don't smile enough. I know Kelly's back teeth are bad, three missing adult teeth that the dentist pulled out last year, so she can't chew very good on one side, but her smile is still pretty. Her front teeth line up straighter than mine. She brushes more than I do. It's only when she yawns or laughs really hard that her mouth looks bad. I've never sat in a dentist's chair. Kelly said it wasn't fun. Mom says they charge an arm and a leg. I remember a lady from the dentist's office called up every week until the bill was paid.

– 14 –

The last time my sister and I rode in a car together was the limo ride from Baxter's Funeral Home on Broadway over to the cemetery on Armistice Boulevard. That was June 5th, 1968, the day of our grandmother's funeral. Kelly wept quietly and my mother sobbed loudly during the entire ride. I cried some too, but mostly on the inside.

I remember they wore identical hats with little veils and plain black dresses and I sat between them facing Grandpa Rudy, who rode with his back to the driver, fanning himself continuously with a laminated prayer card imprinted with my dead grandmother's name. Rudy's tie looked comically small and his huge belly strained against the buttons of his sports jacket. I kept waiting (and hoping) for the middle button to pop. He is an enormous man, close to three hundred pounds, but he didn't quite take up the entire seat and there was plenty enough room for me to squeeze in beside him.

I sat facing him for two reasons: one, if I rode backwards I'd get carsick. And two, I would have much preferred it was his body traveling in the hearse up ahead.

During my lifetime, my grandparents had never once been in the same room with one another, and if you ever mentioned one to the other, they would pretend they hadn't heard. My aunt Sally had not invited Grandpa Rudy to her wedding. And there had been some talk about excluding him entirely from Grandma's funeral. In the end, Mom threw such a fit about Grandpa having every right in the world to ride along in the limo, that my aunt yielded and rode in her own car with her new husband, my new uncle, Peter.

A short time after we put Grandma in the ground, the radio informed us that senator and presidential candidate Robert Kennedy had been shot in the head after giving a speech in California. The assassin, a man named Sirhan Sirhan, had been captured at the scene. In the news report, recorded during the struggle, a reporter kept yelling: "Get the gun, get the gun, break his thumb if you have to."

Although it wasn't made clear if Sirhan's thumb had actually been broken, my mother claimed such ugly behavior was entirely unnecessary. "Kennedy or no Kennedy, gun or no gun, that poor man is innocent until proven guilty in a court of law."

I thought that a remarkably kind and merciful statement for a woman who regularly beat her own children and had once almost broken my thumb.

– 15 –

One time when I was twelve and a half, Kelly was on the couch writing in her diary and I was belly down on our mother's bed reading a trashy romance novel that I'd found hidden in a hatbox. On the paperback's slick cover was a red-haired woman wearing a green dress and high heels. She was sitting on a desk cross-legged, showing a lot of thigh and cleavage. It was just a drawing but it had a lot of detail. You could see the top of one of her stockings, and one of her shoes looked like it was about to fall off.

I couldn't put the book down. The story told how the woman, a legal secretary named Rita, kept drifting from one job to another, but her movie-star looks and tight dresses kept getting her into trouble, usually with the boss' wife or a coworker's wife or a client's wife, and even though Rita had sex with all these men, she still got her pretty ass fired. Mom's name is Rita, and though she doesn't have the hourglass figure of the lady on the book, she does have nice legs and a pretty face. She can't type or take shorthand, but she's a pretty good waitress, and she used to work as a dispatcher for Royal Taxi and later for a short time as a phone receptionist, which is pretty close to being a secretary.

My plan was to read the whole book cover to cover before my mother got home. Then I'd put it back in its hiding place. But after forty pages, I had to stop. The pressure hurt so bad, I couldn't stand it. In the bathroom with the door closed, I unbuckled my jeans and pushed them down. I stared at my underwear and I got afraid. My penis stood straight out and I felt like I had to pee really badly. Some mornings I woke up stiff but this was different. When I tried pointing the tip down at the toilet, the base hurt and my heart beat faster. I figured I had cancer or rickets or polio or maybe rigor mortis. I pulled my pants up enough so I could walk and waddled into the parlor to show Kelly. I explained about the book, how all I was doing was reading.

She was sitting with her legs crossed, writing. She didn't appear shocked or even surprised. She closed her diary and said, "You did the right thing coming to me."

– 16 –

My grandmother died in her sleep in the early morning of June 2nd, 1968. We're sure it was morning, because Kelly was living there and later reported that Grandma was still alive, talking to herself, well after midnight. Six times in two years my sister had run away from home and gone to stay with Grandma for a day or a week, but this time she had been ordered to move in and sleep on the couch. She hadn't been to school in a month. Once a week Mom sent a note excusing Kelly due to a "continued family emergency." Every Friday I had to hunt down all her teachers and pick up her lessons, a ton of homework.

Kelly was allowed Sundays off, the afternoon and evening, when my aunt Sally would drive down and spend the day, give Grandma a sponge bath, then make dinner and try to get the poor old woman to eat. Sometimes my mother would pop in and help in some small way, but mostly Kelly had to watch over Grandma day and night like a babysitter watches a child, except Kelly wasn't getting paid. Getting paid was an issue for Kelly. Money. Compensation. Fair wages. My aunt promised a little something when the whole thing was over. We didn't know what that meant. Grandma showed no signs of getting better. She had become an imbecile. She couldn't be trusted to wipe her own ass.

On the morning of June 2nd, 1968, Kelly woke up and went to the bathroom. When she came out the sun was a dome on the flat roof of the glass place next door, so there was enough light streaming in, enough for Kelly to see that Grandma was pasty and blue.

"Brain hemorrhage," the doctor said.

That night Kelly moved back home. The little something from Aunt Sally turned out to be almost nothing—ten bucks in a thank-you card. Slave wages, if you ask me. My sister had been living there four weeks, working around the clock. Do the math. Slave wages and a ton of homework in exchange for watching her grandmother die. I would have gone nuts, too.

– 17 –

Soon as the driver pulls up to the curb, Kelly shoves her door open, swings her feet out, and takes off. She leaves her suitcase. My mother looks at me like I did something, then hands the driver a few bills. They're folded up tight so I can't tell how much, but there must be a good tip in there because he says, "Thank you, thank you very much. And God bless you."

Rain is trickling down, but Kelly waits by the fence, her face in the rosebushes, as casually as if the sun were shining. My mother gets out of the cab, crouching like an old woman, like the rain is fire. She moves past Kelly and up the walkway to the porch steps. The driver says, "You want help with that?" but I don't answer. I avoid his eyes as I drag Kelly's suitcase off the seat and close the door. The rain is ice-cold. I carry the suitcase up the walkway and onto the porch, where my mother holds open the heavy door as she waves wildly to the driver.

"What a nice guy," she says. "Why can't I ever meet a man like that?"

I'm tempted to say, "You just did," but I bite my tongue.

We climb the stairs single file—Kelly first, Mom in the middle. None of us hurry. I imagine our neighbors have their ears to their doors.

"Home again, home again," Mom says when we reach the top landing. She fits the key into the lock, then swings the door open and waves Kelly in. "Go on," she says to me.

As I bump past, she grabs for the suitcase. "Everything in here needs to soak," she says.

Kelly heads straight for the couch. She throws off her coat, plops down onto her back, and swings her legs up. Her shirt looks too tight.

Our apartment is three rooms (parlor, bedroom, kitchen) aligned in a row. I've only been gone a couple hours, but everything seems smaller, tighter. My mother carries the suitcase through the bedroom and into the kitchen. I look at my sister. Her eyes are closed, her perfect nose pointed at the ceiling.

"TV working yet?"

I shake my head though she can't see me. "Mom called someone to fix it," I say, though I'm not sure if that's true.

"She's probably lying," Kelly says. The soft line of her mouth seems to conceal a smile. "At Emerson," she says, "they've got a huge TV." She holds her hands two feet apart. "Big set. Color. Good picture. I'm going to miss that."

"What was it like?" I say. "Living there?" But what I really want to know is whether there are bars on the windows, locks on the doors, and if she told anyone there anything about me, about us.

Without opening her eyes, Kelly punches her fists upward and stretches her arms into a great yawn. "Pretty nice, once you get used to it. No one lies to you. It's one of their rules. No lying allowed."

– 18 –

The newspaper is sixty-five cents a week. That's the subscriber's price, which *The Times* prints right on the front page in tiny type beneath the masthead. It's hard to see, but it's there. So sixty-five cents is the amount I'm supposed to collect from each customer, not including tips. Out of that I pay Sam forty-five cents, which means I make twenty cents a week for each subscriber, not including tips. I don't know how much Sam has to give to the newspaper. I bring the paper right to your door, six days a week, for twenty cents. I deliver in the rain and the snow and the heat, for twenty cents. Not including tips. I haul forty-five papers but one is extra, so I can sell it in case somebody asks. If I don't sell it, and most days nobody asks, I can just bring it home. Sam only charges me for forty-four.

Forty-four customers times twenty is $8.80 a week, not including tips. That's what I should earn, minimum, every week, if you do the math right. With tips, even lousy tips, I should bring home about ten bucks a week. Easily ten. With decent tips more like twelve. Or fourteen. But let's use ten as a conservative estimate. Okay. The route takes two hours. Six days a week times two hours a day is twelve hours. If I earn ten bucks for that time, I'm making eighty-three cents an hour: barely half of minimum wage. Slave wages, Kelly calls them.

But I'm a kid, right? What are my options? Shine shoes? Tried it. Mow lawns? Done that too. Try steering a push-lawnmower through knee-high grass. Shovel snow out of some old lady's driveway? Tried and failed. The competition is fierce, and people expect you to have your own shovel. So I suppose I should be happy to pocket ten bucks a week for doing little more than walking city streets, going in and out of buildings, climbing up and down stairs.

But here's the thing. I don't make ten. I never collect more than six or seven dollars above what I'm supposed to turn in. Nevertheless, every Friday I hand over ten to my mother. My weekly bill for the forty-four customers is $19.80. That's the amount I'm supposed to hand over to Sam each Saturday. So far the most I've ever turned in for any week is $16.01.

Every Saturday when I pay my bill, I'm short a few dollars. One week I was

34

short $8.78 and Sam flipped. His eyes got big and his face turned so red I thought he was having a heart attack. He wrote the amount in his book, added it to my total, which is a fast-growing negative number. Every Saturday I'm short. Every week the amount I owe Sam increases. And every week he asks me twenty questions, then shakes his head and gives me a speech. It's always the same speech, how he can't figure out where the money is going. I don't tell him about the ten I give my mother, or the money I spend feeding myself at Times Square Diner.

I'd give the route up, but my mother says I can't. She says if I quit that would make me a quitter and quitters, she says, grow up to be nothing but losers, plain and simple. I know she counts on the ten I hand over. She uses it to buy milk and bread and eggs and sometimes as part of the rent. Last week I told her I couldn't keep giving her ten, because I'm falling too far behind on my bill. "Sam wants his money," I told her.

"Too bad for him," she said. "He's a rich, old Jew with a house and two cars and his own business. And a snotty wife who goes to the beauty parlor every week. What's ten dollars to him one way or the other?"

— 19 —

Up until my grandmother died in her sleep and the whole world turned upside-down, Kelly had always been the good one, the quiet one, the smart one. She seldom got in trouble, did all her homework, pulled As and Bs, and was always reading books she hadn't been assigned to read. My report cards contained Cs or C minuses, usually with a D or two, and once an F mixed in, and some notation from the teacher, a scribbled excuse for my failures: "Bad work habits," "Doesn't apply himself," "Mr. Fisher needs to buckle down and catch up with the class." I never buckled down, never applied myself, and I've never caught up. But year after year I still get promoted, so I don't think I'm stupid.

Before our TV's picture tube died, I had established a solid frame of reference on stupidity. I understood Gomer Pyle was a dangerous idiot who wouldn't last five minutes in Vietnam. *Mayberry R.F.D.* was boringly stupid without Andy and Opie or Barney. *Family Affair* was spoiled-rich-kid stupid. *Gilligan's Island* was somebody-please-kill-this-guy stupid. *The Beverly Hillbillies* was backwoods stupid. *Bewitched* was magically stupid. *My Three Sons*, which had been a good show until the boys grew up, turned *Father-Knows-Best* stupid. *Ironside*, a detective show my mother called "nothing but Perry Mason in a wheelchair" was paralyzed-from-the-neck-up stupid. And *Green Acres* was a half-hour of watching a snobbish New York lawyer and his crazy Hungarian wife trying to grow corn in Hooterville.

Except for *Ironside*, all those shows used a laugh track to fool you into thinking an audience was sitting right there, laughing their asses off. Kelly says TV people do that to let you know when a joke had been made, though telling anyone when to laugh is plain bad manners.

Most days I treated school like a dumb TV show that I had to appear in—against my will and for no paycheck. And it wasn't even my show. I didn't have any friends there and I didn't try to make any. After school I walked downtown and hung around the corner newsstand until the papers arrived. Then I did my route and went home.

Kelly had a dozen friends, but she wasn't allowed to bring them home anymore. Now and then, after school, she went off with one of them, then wouldn't show up until dark. Mom whacked her repeatedly for not listening, missing meals, making her worry, almost calling the cops, though I don't think Mom knew that Kelly's closest friends were boys, usually a year or two older, known troublemakers with established reputations as bullies, vandals, and thieves. A couple of them had already quit school and gotten factory jobs.

Far as I knew, only one—Patrick McHale, ninth grade—ever received the official rank of steady boyfriend, and only for half a summer; though another kid, Chucky Richardson, who some of the kids called Sledge because he was as big as a man and could grow a full beard in a week, did make Kelly ache with longing, miserable self-pity, general bitchiness, and nonstop tears, after he suckerpunched the principal in the left temple (a clean, direct shot reported as an instant knockout), after which no one, not even Kelly, saw or heard from Chucky Boy again.

Late one night, while our mother was on a date with the mailman, my sister twisted on the bed, sobbing and wailing in anguish over Chuck's disappearance, and when I asked what the big freaking deal was (because the kid was a thug, a punk, a loser), she jumped off the bed and charged at me. She stuck her nose in my face and screamed I was a rotten, thoughtless, uncaring, insensitive, retarded, little bastard who didn't understand a goddamned thing about real love. Most of which was true.

— 20 —

Except for Mrs. Lennon in the first grade, all my teachers call me Fisher, or Mr. Fisher, which is polite but dumb. And I pretty much hate when they do, because my mother calls me mister when she's in a bad mood. Most of the kids just call me Fish. A few tough guys refer to me as Fish Head. Or Fish Breath. Or Tuna Breath. Though I never eat seafood, especially tuna (not because of that thing with the dolphins, just because it once made me throw up), and I've told them that.

One kid punched me square in the face for telling him that. I never saw it coming. He knocked out one of my baby teeth, then threatened to throw my body in the Blackstone River if I squealed, so I blamed the bruise on running headfirst into a parking meter. I didn't care about the tooth, but my grandmother gave me a dollar and said it was from the tooth fairy. She used to call me Jack, or Little Jack, but she's dead.

On the rare occasions when someone does address me by my first name, I almost instantly fall in love with that person. Not love like I want to marry them or anything. It's hard to explain. I only know the warmth and affection I feel, the surprise and thrill at hearing my name. God, I love that feeling. Some days, most days, just about every day lately, I miss my grandmother so much I could cry.

– 21 –

I'm standing around like an idiot waiting to load up for my route. The sun is shining on the cars and store windows, and everything seems horribly bright. Huey is bullshitting with a woman who keeps taking baby steps toward the street while sneaking glances at her folded newspaper. Huey works up a lot of spit when he talks. Whitish foam gathers at the sides of his mouth. But he has his drool rag out and he's moving what's left of his tongue okay. I kneel in his fat shadow and count five papers at a time until I make a stack of forty-five.

The woman escapes across the street without looking back and Huey waves to her with his yellowed rag. He tells her to have a nice day. Then he comes over. "What's the matter with you?"

"Nothing."

"Why the long face? Something happen?"

"Nothing except my grandmother is still dead and my aunt moved to Sacramento and my sister just got out of a mental hospital."

"Oh," Huey says.

I spread my sack out, ready to load. Huey folds his handkerchief in half then in half again. I need him to check my count before I can go. "Which part of Sacramento," he says, and I shrug.

– 22 –

The route takes me a couple of hours, except on Fridays, when I have to stop and collect. Then it takes me three. Sometimes more than three.

I start at City Hall (three papers there, one to the mayor's office), except on Saturday when City Hall is closed. Then I do the fire station next door. The fire station is never closed because the firemen take turns sleeping there. Next, I deliver to seven small houses along Roosevelt Avenue, then across the street to the Carol Cable Company, then up Blackstone Avenue to a few tenement houses, then left onto St. Mary's Way (thirteen customers on that dirty, crowded, narrow, one-way street), up Exchange Street to Jack & Harry's Hardware, the credit union (except on Saturdays), the furniture store, the locksmith, the post office, the print shop, the G&T Tavern, Ray Mullin's Music store, the nursing home, the hearing aid dealer, up High Street to Roy's Plumbing and Heating Supply, then four papers to two nice apartment houses, and finally to my last stop, the white Victorian atop Blackstone Avenue, where I leave the new paper on the stack of old ones. (The next day it will still be there, though some of the pages will be wrinkled.)

Forty-four papers. Forty-five counting the extra.

When I first took over the route from a fat kid named Rusty, I had sixty-nine customers. Seventy papers, counting the extra, which is a lot of weight even on a Saturday when the papers are thin. By the end of my second week I had fifty-nine customers. After a month the number dropped to fifty, and now it's forty-four. Not my fault.

People moved without telling me, whole tenement houses emptied. One weekend I lost seven customers, all of them on St. Mary's Way. I didn't know, so I kept delivering their papers. Other people took them, I suppose. I don't know. I kept delivering papers to empty houses, then got stuck owing their bills. I told Sam nobody told me anything and I didn't think that was very fair.

"Fair," he said. "You want to talk about fair? You've lost twenty-five percent of your customers in two months. Every Saturday you're short a few bucks more. What in hell is going on?" He talked about trust, he talked about Huey. Then he accused me of stealing from him, robbing him blind, and I had to concentrate very hard to keep from crying.

I owe Sam a lot of money, so he has reason to be upset with me, but when someone moves without paying their bill, I shouldn't get stuck.

— 23 —

I'll admit I've been jittery, waiting for the other shoe to drop. Kelly says nervous breakdowns run in our family and someday I'll have one too. If this is mine I'm sure it's not a complete collapse. For months Kelly predicted she'd be first, the first to go—because she was older, and gave Mom more trouble.

"Me, then you. Just watch."

She claimed that with Grandma dead and Aunt Sally in Sacramento, Mom would find a way to get rid of us both. So I've been watching, weighing my mother's side-glances, the tone of her remarks, even her good behavior, all the time waiting for the second half of my sister's prediction to come true.

The whole time Kelly was locked up, I came home every day expecting to find strangers waiting—undercover cops or a social worker, or a couple of bulky guards from the Sockanosset Training School for Boys. Do they handcuff you, I wondered, and throw you in the back of a paddy wagon like a sack of dirty laundry? Strap a straight jacket on, no questions asked, like they did to Tony Curtis in *Houdini*? Or will they ask me to come along peacefully and without a fuss?

Some days, coming up the stairs, I stare at the door of our apartment like I've got X-ray vision. I see strangers waiting on the other side, my mother serving them coffee. I see them waiting and I know what's coming, but I keep moving toward the door. I imagine when it happens I'll cry and beg my mother to change her mind. ("Too late," she'll say. "You had your chance!") And other times I imagine I put up a good fight, a fierce battle, landing head punches and groin kicks, then escaping out the back door and down the stairs. I cut through the hedges to the Marshall's yard, then up and across the Red Cross parking lot, over the rail and down the embankment to the highway, then I run like there's no tomorrow. I move faster than the cars.

And other times I think I'll just go along with them, because what's the use, where I am going to go? My grandmother is dead and my aunt moved to Sacramento. Where am I going to hide?

If Kelly's guess is right, and I think it might be, I'm done. I'm next. I'm dead meat waiting for the butcher's hook to haul me away.

42

– 24 –

When she was thirteen and I was eleven, my sister pushed me off a twenty-five-foot retaining wall at the edge of the parking lot of the First Congregational Church. I landed face-down in the asphalt lot below, what was then the patient parking area of William C. Cunningham, MD.

According to Kelly, Dr. Cunningham's nurse was on the scene in a matter of seconds. The woman went right to work, checked my vital signs, summoned the doctor, then looked up at my sister who was standing at the edge gazing down. "What happened," the nurse said.

"He fell," Kelly said.

I fractured my skull on impact, jarred my brain, and was far from conscious at the time, so I'm not a good witness, and to this day I have no memory of the fall, or of anyone pushing me. What I do remember is I had been hunting bad guys, climbing the rocky embankment with my fingers pointed like pistols, dodging enemy fire right before the lights went out. It wasn't until she had returned from her seventy-seven-day stay on a mental ward that she admitted to the push.

"Are you sure," I said.

She traced a finger across her heart and said she was one hundred percent certain she'd given me a two-handed shove, then she demonstrated by standing behind me and placing her palms flat on my lower back. She said she had discussed the incident in some depth with her psychiatrist, a man called Dr. Rob. So I asked her why.

"Because I was trying to kill you," she said.

"No," I said. "Why mention it to a stranger?" The rule in our house was: what happens in the family stays in the family. Kelly knew this better than anyone.

"I had to tell him something," she said. "They want your life story. After I admitted to pushing you, Dr. Rob wrote something on his pad, then we spent my next two sessions discussing my anger and resentment toward you for being the baby of the family."

"Did you talk about Mom?"

"A little. Not much. He didn't like that she used to beat us."

43

"What about Grandma?"

"Yes. About when she died, mostly. And Aunt Sally, too."

"Grandpa Rudy?"

"Only when I had to."

I grabbed my canvas bag and looped the strap over my shoulder. I was already running late. I opened the door but I didn't go through it. "I'm not a baby," I said.

"Relax. It wasn't an insult."

"I'm nothing like a baby."

Kelly smiled, showing just the tips of her teeth. "Dr. Rob might argue with you. It's the family dynamic. Once the baby, always the baby. Nothing against you personally; it's just the way families work."

"I don't think you pushed me. I think I slipped. Mom says I'm clumsy."

"Believe me, I pushed you."

"Because I was the baby?"

"Probably. I don't remember what I was thinking. But that's the story I told Dr. Rob, which made him sort of happy. He perked right up, made lots of notes, called my admission an act of responsibility. A breakthrough. You score enough of those and after a while they stamp you good as new and push you out the door."

"But you didn't hate me, not really. I mean you don't know why you pushed me."

"Nope, and I'd rather not dwell on it. The past is the past. My focus is on the future."

"What are you going to do?"

"Fix my life, starting today. Right this minute. And the good news is I'm going to help you fix yours too, brother dear."

"My life is fine," I said.

"Dr. Rob would say—"

"Fuck him. I don't care."

She giggled. "He looks sort of like Festus on *Gunsmoke* without the limp. Or the cowboy hat."

"I'm going," I said.

"Though one time his foot fell asleep during a session and then he couldn't stand on it."

"I'm probably already in trouble." I wiggled my fingers in a goodbye wave. She blew a kiss off the tips of her fingers the way Italian people do. I shut the door behind me.

"Bring me back something good," my sister said from inside.

"Like what?"

I heard her slide the chain on the door. "Surprise me."

– 25 –

Our rooms line up, one after the other. The apartment is a narrow box. When every door is open, you can look from the front hall straight through to the back hallway and see the window where our mother hooked her clothesline. In 4th grade, for Show and Tell, I made a model with a shoebox. I cut the cover in half and put in two cardboard walls: parlor, bedroom, kitchen. In red Magic Marker I wrote "My Home" on the outside of the box. I used a steak knife to cut flaps for doors. I made little furniture with Play-Doh, used a pencil-sharpener TV, built a bed out of a Cracker Jack box with a handkerchief for a sheet, a folded Kleenex for a pillow. My sister had a dollhouse stove and sink that I borrowed. They were too big but good enough. I didn't cut windows, just drew them in with a black crayon, one with a crescent moon, one with a dome of rising sun. And I left out the bathroom, though I did cut a flap for its door. "You've got two back doors," some boy said. I didn't correct him.

"Where's your room?" Mrs. Pearl said.

"Where does your sister sleep?" one girl asked.

"Do you all sleep in that little bed?" said another.

"Is this really your house?" asked a boy with a lisp.

Mrs. Pearl saw my face, which felt like I had sunburn. She looked at me through her glasses, then put her hand up like a traffic cop. She ordered everyone back to their seats. "Show and tell time is over," she said. "Everyone, take out your geography book and turn to page thirty-nine."

— 26 —

Before Mom locked Kelly up, my sister slept in the big bed. Her on one side, Mom on the other, a pillow set vertically between them. I slept in a crib until I was almost seven. It was a tight fit. When I stretched my legs, my feet touched one end and my head bumped the other, so I used to sleep curled up, with my knees tucked, my neck bent. I wasn't a thumb sucker like Kelly, but I used to hug my pillow like it was a human form.

The bar of the crib used to slide up and down but the mechanism broke so my mother hammered half a dozen nails into the wood to secure it to the frame and when that didn't hold, she put in eight screws. From that point on I had to perform a balancing act over the rail, like a trapeze artist climbing out of a cage.

Now my bed is a rollaway cot from Sears. The frame is made of cheap aluminum and the mattress, which has a tag that says Deluxe, is thin, just a two-inch pad of white foam that sits on a wire grid that looks like it's made of straightened coat hangers, but it's a lot better than a crib. Every morning I fold the thing up and clamp the giant hook that holds the two halves together, then I wheel the cot against the wall so that there is room to move around.

Every night the wires press up through the foam and leave tic-tac-toe lines on my ass and thighs. When I roll over in my sleep the grid squeaks and rubs against the frame. Some nights, when I'm restless or kicking in a dream, Mom wakes me and tells me to stop making so much goddamn noise. But I don't think there's really any way to stop myself from rolling over in my sleep. One night I didn't wake up fast enough and she threw a shoe at the wall above my head. "Out," she said. "Take your pillow and go sleep on the couch."

I never mind spending the night on the couch. Sleeping in the parlor is like having my own room. I slept there almost every night while Kelly was locked up. I don't know where I'm supposed to sleep now.

– 27 –

I'm not a brainless idiot, but what does any kid know about anything? No one ever told me about the birds and the bees, so back when I was thirteen, I knew less than anyone. After four months of rubbing myself two or three times a day, something terrible happened. Instead of a dry shudder and a warm tickle, I squirted white pus all over my belly and it scared the holy shit out of me. Every bone and muscle in my body was shaking and I could feel my heart banging inside my chest. When the shivering stopped, I felt like I had pulled a muscle. I could feel the burn in my belly. My vision was wobbly and unreliable. For almost a minute I thought my eyeballs were going to tremble their way right out of their sockets. My pee hole was still oozing, but barely. The pus was obviously coming from something broken inside of me, a ruptured tube, a busted vein, something no doctor could fix without giving me sleeping gas and cutting me open.

I spent about thirty minutes just examining the goo, rubbing it between my fingers. Some of it was thick and bumpy but most of it was like milky water. I decided it was blood, some sort of white blood coming from some wound I'd torn open, probably my liver or a kidney. Maybe my appendix. All night I went in and out the bathroom, checking for more white blood, glad that the wound had at least stopped bleeding. I tried to convince myself I was still okay, because the squirt hadn't lasted more than a few seconds, and there really wasn't very much pus, just a couple of spoonfuls, though I knew something had changed because I felt different.

I hoped it was a small wound that would heal like knuckle scrapes and paper cuts do. But I couldn't stop shaking, couldn't relax for a minute, imagining the pus building up inside. How long before it filled my stomach, flooded my lungs, drowned my heart? Should I stick my finger down my throat and make myself vomit? My eyes hurt from staring, my head wouldn't stop pounding. I didn't want to go to bed, certain I would die in my sleep.

The next day, I walked downtown to the library. I told the librarian I was doing a science project for school and needed a book on adolescent development. She led me to a shelf and left me there. I got the whole scoop. I wasn't dying, no damage done. Just puberty, a word I'd heard Dave the crossing guard use a hundred times.

I read all about semen and spermatozoa. Semen, from the Latin, meaning "seed."

There was stuff about nocturnal emissions (wet dreams), which explained the dirty looks and one hard slap my mother gave me after changing my sheets. I wanted to take the book home and read more, but I didn't have a library card so when I was sure no one was looking, I slipped it under my shirt. It wouldn't be stealing if I brought the book back in a week or two. The lady who showed me where the book was wouldn't even know it was missing. I looked around. Another librarian was stacking books right behind me. I watched her lift a book off her cart and check its number. I wondered what she got paid for being a librarian, probably more than minimum wage.

I stood up to leave. The weight of the book caused it to shift and drop a little lower, I got ready to run. But then I thought how some other kid who didn't know anything might need to use the book before he had a nervous breakdown and jumped into the Blackstone River. Plus, it was still raining, coming down hard, and the book might get ruined, then it would be worse than stealing and they'd lock me up for destruction of public property. No book was worth going to Sockanosset for. So I dug it out of my shirt, dropped it on a table, and walked out into the pouring rain. Halfway home, a police siren went screaming by. I watched the flashing lights and I'd never felt so innocent.

– 28 –

Sam says the numbers don't add up. He means my numbers and he's right. I'm buying too much junk from the vending machines in the cafeteria at Carol Cable, and feeding myself every other day at Times Square Diner, plus slipping my mother her ten bucks every week, but I'm not really making anything. The change in my pocket is never my money. It's always Sam's and there's never enough to pay my weekly bill. I should quit. Quitting would be easy. All I have to do is not show up anymore, though Sam knows where I live and might come get me. Every day on my way downtown I think about quitting. I pretend I'm just out strolling, no place to go. Then I arrive at the corner, talk to Huey, load up, and go to work.

Monday, Tuesday, Wednesday, Thursday, Friday, Saturday.

It's only two hours. About two. Some days it takes me three. When I first got the route it took me four because I kept getting lost, plus I dragged my ass. The weight was too much. The strap cut into my collarbone. Now I understand the faster I go the sooner the bag loses weight.

Sam wants me to take on a Sunday route, but I can't see that happening. "Good money," he says. "Good tippers, Sunday people."

What he doesn't say is that Sunday papers weigh well over a pound; they get delivered to the newsstand in bundled sections throughout the week—junk and comics first, then classifieds and features. Front-page news and the sports section print last—and at the crack of dawn Sunday, you have to insert the sections, build your own papers before you load up. They don't pay any extra for that.

"Sunday route would help you catch up on your bill," Sam says.

And he's probably right. But why should I get another job to pay for the one I have now? Who wants to work every single day of the week? Get up every Sunday before the sun, on my only day off? For what? I tell Sam it is out of the question because my mother makes me go to Sunday school before church.

"If you hustle your ass you'd be done in plenty of time for church," he says. "Plenty of time."

I explain how before Sunday school I have to go to Bible class, though that isn't

49

true. I don't think there is a Bible class. Sam might think so, too. He makes faces at me like he makes sometimes at Huey. I owe Sam a lot of money, I don't even know how much. But that's not my fault. I'll pay him in time unless one of us drops dead before then. Meanwhile, I work the route. I don't quit, I don't complain. Each day I learn more than I earn. Things are going to get better.

– 29 –

Dean Martin, our third-floor neighbor, is not the same Dean Martin who played Matt Helm in *The Ambushers* and *Murderers' Row*; he's not the singing host of *The Dean Martin Show,* or the former straight man of the Martin & Lewis comedy team (until their regrettable breakup in 1956). This Dean Martin lives on the other half of the third floor and works the graveyard shift at a gas station that never closes, not even on Christmas. He wears the same oily blue work pants every day and has a line of black grease around his fingernails. He brings his beer home by the case—Narragansett, bottles. He smokes Pall Mall's, which Kelly says he steals from the guy who loads up the gas station's cigarette machine. She claims Dean is forty-something but my mother says he's not that old and served two years overseas.

When Mom says "overseas," I'm pretty sure she means Vietnam, but Dean has a round belly and looks too out of shape to ever have been a soldier. He's lived next door almost a year now and works crazy hours, sometimes not coming home to sleep for days. Mom says he's divorced and not very friendly, and once he came into the Blackstone Diner with a colored girl, but he's a good tenant who always pays his rent on time.

Sometimes, when it's wicked hot, Dean leaves his door open and when I come up the stairs I see him sitting in his T-shirt and oily blue work pants drinking a Narragansett. He doesn't have a couch. He sits in a big, brown upholstered chair in front of his portable TV which he keeps in the middle of the room with the back of the set toward the door so I never see all of him, usually just his white socks crossed at the ankles, or his beer bottle tilted toward his head. I can't tell by the back of his TV if the set is color or black and white, or what kind of reception he gets.

One afternoon I stood right outside his doorway, staring at the back of his TV, looking for a manufacturer's label, anything that might tell me if it was a good TV. I couldn't find anything, but I kept looking until he peeked around the side of the TV at me. He stared at me like I was doing something wrong, so I said, "What are you watching?"

He said, "None of your business. Get away from the door. You're blocking the air flow."

But there wasn't any breeze and I wasn't breaking any law standing in the hall, so I stayed put.

After a minute he said, "Hey. Are you deaf, retarded, or both?"

I should have said, "It's a free country," or "You don't own the hallway," or something that a retard, especially a deaf one, wouldn't say. But he didn't wait long for an answer. He got up, bottle of Narragansett and burning cigarette in the same hand, and he came around the back of the TV. He didn't move very fast and I didn't run or back away. I tried not to look scared, though I think I was. He shook his head at me, then almost fell over when he kicked the door shut.

I told Kelly about that incident just days before Mom brought her to the nut house. Kelly said Dean acts like that because he doesn't like people spying. "And because he's hiding the body of a dead girl in his bedroom closet. Want to know her name?" she said.

I told her she was making that story up.

"Girl Scout's honor," she said, flashing the peace sign instead of the Girl Scout salute.

"You're not a Girl Scout."

"Still counts," she said.

52

– 30 –

On the shelf of our closet my mother has two shoeboxes full of old photographs but only one of my father and it is not a good one: a grainy black and white of a tall, thin man in a dark suit standing ankle-deep in a pile of leaves beside a picket fence. He's hatless, holding, not wearing, a Fedora, standing in the shade of a broad, black tree. In the top right corner of the photo a forward-sloping branch shows a few leaves still clinging. The edges of the leaves are so sharp, so well defined, that I imagine the photographer—who might have been my mother—was actually aiming the lens there, going after a picture of the leaves, and the rest of the image, including my father, just snuck in.

Mom keeps that photo inside a plastic sandwich bag, separate from the rest, but Kelly went through both boxes one day and it wasn't there. A week later I found it during a pillow fight, and I studied it for an hour using a magnifying glass and the emergency flashlight we keep on the fridge. I showed the picture to Kelly and she studied it too. But since then we have never been able to find where Mom hides it.

I know there's a tack hole in the top border and yellow-brown tape marks in two corners, so it might have once hung from the knickknack shelf above the TV or been stuck to a wall somewhere, but I can't remember it ever hanging anywhere. Each time Mom brings the thing out she gets weepy and tells me I am the spitting image of the man, although the photo shows no evidence to support that claim. The face measures no more than a quarter inch, and even under a magnifying glass shows no distinct features other than a short haircut, side parted and slicked back, and a pair of whitish gray eyes—eyes that could be matched up with just about any pair on the planet, human or otherwise.

– 31 –

The same week Martin Luther King was shot dead in Memphis, Patrick McHale, a troublemaker from my school, was found face-down in a shower stall at the Sockanosset Training School for Boys with the back of his skull cracked open. The story was in the newspaper, though not on the front page. Patrick had been my sister's boyfriend—her only ever official boyfriend—the summer she grew breasts, but he was nothing to me. But back in 1967, when Patrick was repeating the ninth grade for the second or third time, he beat up a teacher, Mr. White, for mispronouncing Patrick's last name as McHell. It wasn't the first time some teacher had referred to Patrick as "Mister McHell" so there was probably more to it, but as usual, I didn't get the whole story.

What I do know is Patrick hung around the teacher's parking lot all afternoon and when Mr. White finally came out, Patrick was sitting on the hood of the teacher's Ford Mustang. It wasn't a fair fight. Mr. White was a small man in a baggy suit. Patrick, though just a kid, had the advantage: big for his age, and solid, thick everywhere but not fat. And if size wasn't enough, he had a roll of quarters concealed in each fist, and he smacked Mr. White around pretty good, broke the man's glasses, chipped a front tooth, cracked a rib or two, then fished Mr. White's keys out of his pocket and drove off in the Mustang.

The next day the police found Mr. White's car down by the beach, stuck in the sand, with the boy still in it. Patrick was asleep but the cops woke him up. He was arrested for malicious assault and grand theft auto, taken to jail, and according to Kelly, beaten up at least twice. He got his name in the newspaper three times, once on the front page, and a short while later he was sent to the Sockanosset Training School for Boys and never seen nor heard from again. At least not by me.

Kelly may have written to him a couple of times, or sent him a birthday card, but I'm not sure about that either. I am only including Patrick's story to explain how I learned the trick with the fists full of quarters, and why in the spring of 1968, my sister fell into a deep depression, mourning the deaths of both Patrick McHale and Martin Luther King, wearing nothing but black, refusing to eat, and how during that time she convinced me that it was only a matter of time before our mother got sick of my shenanigans and shipped me off to Sockanosset. "Time to smarten up, little brother. Your days of being her precious baby boy are over."

– 32 –

Things I Used to Get Hit For:
Talking back. Being smart. Acting stupid. Not listening. Not answering the first time. Not doing what I'm told. Not doing it the second time I'm told. Running, jumping, yelling, laughing, falling down, skipping stairs, lying in the snow, rolling in the grass, playing in the dirt, walking in mud, not wiping my feet, not taking my shoes off. Sliding down the banister, acting like a wild Indian in the hallway. Making a mess and leaving it. Pissing my pants, just a little. Peeing the bed, hardly at all. Sleeping with a butter knife under my pillow.

Shitting the bed because I was sick and it just ran out of me, but still my fault because I'm old enough to know better. Saying shit instead of crap or poop or number two. Not knowing better. Knowing something and doing it wrong anyway. Lying. Not confessing the truth even when I don't know it. Telling white lies, even little ones, because fibbing isn't fooling and not the least bit funny. Laughing at anything that's not funny, especially cripples and retards. Covering up my white lies with more lies, black lies. Not coming the exact second I'm called. Getting out of bed too early, sometimes before the birds, and turning on the TV, which is one reason the picture tube died. Wearing out the cheap plastic hole on the channel selector by turning it so fast it sounds like a machine gun. Playing flip-and-catch with the TV's volume button then losing it down the hole next to the radiator pipe. Vomiting. Gagging like I'm going to vomit. Saying puke instead of vomit. Throwing up anyplace but in the toilet or in a designated throw-up bucket. Using scissors on my hair. Cutting Kelly's doll's hair really short. Pinching Kelly. Punching Kelly even though she kicked me first. Tickling her too hard. Taking food without asking. Eating sugar from the sugar bowl. Not sharing. Not remembering to say please and thank you. Mumbling like an idiot. Using the emergency flashlight to read a comic book in bed because batteries don't grow on trees. Splashing in puddles, even the puddles I don't see until it's too late. Giving my mother's good rhinestone earrings to the teacher for Valentine's Day. Splashing in the bathtub and getting the floor wet. Using the good towels. Leaving the good towels on the floor, though sometimes they fall all by themselves. Eating crackers in bed. Staining my shirt, tearing the knee in my pants, ruining my good clothes. Not changing into old clothes that don't fit the minute I get home. Wasting food. Not eating everything on my plate. Hiding lumpy mashed potatoes and butternut squash and rubbery string beans or any food I don't like under the vinyl seat cushions Mom bought for the wooden kitchen chairs. Leaving the butter dish out in summer and ruining the tablecloth. Making bubbles in my milk. Using a straw like a pee shooter. Throwing tooth picks at my sister. Wasting toothpicks and glue making junky little things that no one wants. School papers. Notes from the teacher. Report cards. Whispering in church. Sleeping in church. Notes from the assistant principal. Being late for anything. Walking out of Woolworth's eating a candy bar I didn't pay for. Riding my bike in the street. Leaving my bike out in the rain. Getting my bike stolen while visiting Grandpa Rudy at the hospital because I didn't put a lock on it. Not washing my feet. Spitting. Getting a nosebleed in church. Embarrassing my mother in any way, anywhere, anytime, especially in public. Being a jerk. Acting shy. Being impolite. Forgetting what good manners are for. Being alive in all the wrong places with all the wrong people at all the wrong times.

– 33 –

When we were really young and really stupid, my sister and I used to spend a lot of time digging holes beneath the grape trellis in the side yard. The trellis was just a box frame of gray wood full of rusty nails, and the grapes that grew on it didn't look anything like the grapes in the supermarket. These were much too sour to eat. But the landlady, Mrs. K, used to pluck the leaves, then wrap them around rice and meat and other crazy things, making little cigar shapes. No grass or weeds grew beneath the trellis because no sun ever got through the thick overhanging vines, but there were patches of moss soft as a carpet that we could sit on.

One morning we were on our knees, digging in the cool, black soil. It was raining pretty hard but we weren't getting wet because the vines above us where so thick and snarled, so tightly matted, that nothing could get through. We were using our mother's good spoons, but for once we weren't preparing a grave. No goldfish or dime turtles or dolls had died. We hadn't found a run-over cat in the gutter or stumbled upon another stiff, maggot-filled bird. And we weren't digging a useless hole just to fill it in before the landlady yelled at us and told our mother.

No, on this particular day, my sister and I were tunneling to the other side of the world. Kelly said we'd eventually pop out of the ground in China, where a nice Chinaman and his family would adopt us, but I didn't believe that because I had looked at a globe in school so my guess was we would end up at the bottom of the China Sea.

I can hold my breath better than Kelly, nearly twice as long because she smokes a lot, though I don't think she smoked then. It's possible she had already started stealing my mother's cigarettes. I don't know. But the point is, neither of us had learned how to swim so I knew we were both going to drown, end up eaten by sharks or swallowed by whales, but I kept digging anyhow.

– 34 –

Over the years our mother has beaten us with belts, shoes, rulers, extension cords, hair brushes, a wooden spoon, a fly swatter, a toilet brush, wire coat hangers, wooden coat hangers and sometimes one of our own toys. When you get whacked by your own paddleball paddle or you have to watch your sister getting spanked with a badminton racquet that she asked Santa Claus (AKA Grandma) to bring, you don't feel much like playing with those things ever again.

When I was eight and a half my mother hit me so many times with her sandal that she broke my collarbone. The sandal was just a thin strip of leather, but it had a thick wooden heel and she kept whacking me in the same spot over and over and I guess the bone just gave way. By morning my neck and shoulder had swelled up like the hunchback of Notre Dame and my arm was all bent out of shape. I was running a high fever, so she took me to the hospital. I spent two full days there, and that wasn't bad. I had a real bed all to myself and I got to pick the food I wanted to eat. And I liked the nurses.

My mother told the doctor I had fallen off her bed, that the injury was my fault. She said I had been jumping on the mattress like it was a trampoline, that I had jumped too high and smacked my head on the ceiling, then smashed my shoulder into a table. But such wild behavior was never allowed in our house and I couldn't understand how the doctor could believe her.

– 35 –

First week of September 1967, I needed a bath very badly because I hadn't had an actual bath in months, just washups and wipe-downs with a soapy washcloth or a kitchen sponge. I'd fallen off my bike in July and cracked the bone between my wrist and elbow. I'd been in a cast all summer and my arm smelled like bad cheese. In the morning I would start seventh grade at Jenks Junior High. I didn't want to go but my mother said a busted arm was no excuse to miss the first day of school. She ordered me into the tub. "No more bullshit," she said.

I had to sit awkwardly with the heavy cast held out over the side of the tub, and I had to keep my shoulder stiff, supporting the weight, so that the tub's cold, curved edge didn't press into my armpit. My mother rubbed lots of soap on the cloth and washed my back and chest and across my shoulders then down my good arm. "Give me your hand," she said, and I showed her my hand and she washed it.

She put more soap on the cloth and rubbed it over my knee and down my shin then along the inside of my thigh. I thought she would move on to the other knee which still had a tiny scab on it, but her hand went straight down into the water. She washed between my legs very quickly. I didn't move or say anything. She pulled her hand out and rubbed more soap on the cloth.

She talked about the heat, the late summer weather, while she built up a sudsy white foam on the wash cloth. I waited for her to do the other knee, the one with the scab, so that I would be finished and she would leave. Then she was back in the water and I felt her hand through the fabric. I had an erection and I was embarrassed. She gripped it loosely in her fist for a moment, twisting with the cloth, then she worked at the tip. All around me the water had turned gray with my dirt and it reflected the room and my mother sort of like a mud puddle reflecting the houses around it.

The stab came frighteningly quick. I thumped my cast once against the outside of the tub and splashed water with a jerk of my knee. She immediately withdrew her hand and stood up. "You got water on my blouse," she said very calmly.

I looked straight ahead, my insides twitching.

She folded the washcloth and draped it over the side of the tub. "You can get out now," she said. "You're done."

– 36 –

Mom hates her waitress uniform. It looks like three pieces, but the apron is sewed to the skirt, which is sewed to the blouse like a dress. You can't wash the apron without washing the whole outfit. She calls it her "Halloween costume," says it makes her look dumpy, like Hazel, the TV maid played by Shirley Booth. My grandmother looked a lot like Shirley Booth and cleaned people's houses though she never wore a uniform, just her regular clothes. If anything, Mom looks more like Hazel's boss, Mrs. B, played by Whitney Blake who also starred in the first ever *Perry Mason* episode, though Mrs. B has blonde hair and Mom's hair is dark brown like Kelly's.

Before she leaves for her shift, Mom recites her list of rules: "No one in the house, stay off the phone, don't make a mess, no loud music, stay out of the fridge and the cupboards. Don't touch any of the food. I know what's in there. And don't call me at the diner unless somebody drops dead."

Kelly lies on the couch with her hands folded over her stomach. Her eyes are closed. I think she's pretending she's dead.

"I'm going now," Mom says. "No trouble. I mean it."

Five seconds after the door closes, Kelly pops up and lunges at me. She locks me in a tight embrace, a total clinch. She squeezes like she's trying to lift me. I push up on my toes, making myself taller. Our foreheads touch as we listen for the bang of the downstairs door, then we kiss, a short, gentle kiss, lips closed, eyes open.

"Miss me?" she says. Her eyes seem bigger, the edges darker, the whites brighter, the lashes longer.

I nod and say, "How was it? Was it really bad?"

"First week was hell. They treated me like shit. But a lot of that was my fault. Once I learned the rules and started acting like a human being it was no worse than living here. Put your arms around me."

My elbows are trapped by her arms but she moves them up enough so that I can slide my hands up along her sides. I feel her bones through her shirt but she seems thicker in spots. I line my fingers up with her curves.

"They have a working TV," Kelly says. "A big color set. Reception wasn't bad, but they wouldn't let us watch *The Mod Squad* even though a dozen of us begged."

"What model? Was it an Admiral? You can buy an Admiral now for $250. Three-year warranty on the picture tube."

"I don't know what kind of TV it was."

"Did they have it hooked to a roof antenna or a set of rabbit ears?"

"I didn't see any rabbit ears, so I don't know. But they fed us three meals a day. Real food. Pizza on Saturdays. And I had my own bed. The rooms are smaller than these, but they're nice, and a janitor keeps everything pretty clean, especially the bathrooms. There are a million rules you have to follow. They're pretty serious about their rules. You can't go around acting like a jerk."

"Did you make any friends?"

"A couple, but not really. Most of the kids were creepy, but a few were cool."

"Creepy how?"

"I don't know. Sad. Angry. Dumb. They either talked too much or not at all. I met a girl named Angel. She was scary. She definitely belonged there. Some of the kids really didn't belong there."

"Like you."

"The people are all right. The doctors talk and act nicer than the nurses, but they aren't really. The nurses were nice, all except the head nurse. She was a royal bitch, a regular queen bee. But she didn't work all the time."

"Did anyone do anything?"

"Like what?"

"You know."

"What? Touch my privates?"

I don't say anything.

"The boys don't live in the same ward as the girls. So no. No one came near me."

"Are you sure?"

"I think I'd know."

"Did anybody try?"

She smiles, shows her teeth. "Yeah. Three people. Me, myself, and I." Her smile glows.

"Did you think about me?"

Another smile, a roll of eyes. Then she jabs her knuckle into my ribs.

I fake-punch her shoulder. "Think of me while you played with yourself?"

She pinches my arm and twists the skin. "Don't be a pig."

I shush her because I hear a noise in the hall. We slide-step towards the door, advancing like Tango dancers, the sides of our faces touching.

"It's just Dean," she whispers.

We make certain of the surrounding silence, then exchange a dozen small, tender kisses before our jaw muscles harden and our mouths smother one another, slurping and sucking at each other's breath. "Miss me?" Kelly whispers.

I don't want to stop kissing her. "Say it," she says, pulling my hair.

"Okay. Let go. I missed you."

Our teeth clash as we nibble one another's lips. She tugs the back of my shirt out. "Don't," I say. "She might come back."

"She won't." Her fingers work quickly at my belt.

"No, really. Sometimes she does that."

"She won't," Kelly says, and unzips me.

"I've got my route. I'm already late."

She presses her hand against my underwear. "So you'll be a little later," she says.

We leave a trail of clothes, bump into the doorframe, the door, the dresser. We throw ourselves onto our mother's bed in a hurtling embrace. The springs clang and give out a grating metallic sigh. I've seen them from underneath with the emergency flashlight. They're orange with rust and squeak like hell.

– 37 –

Kelly prefers to be on top, like a cowgirl riding a pony, so she shifts her weight and we roll, but we're stretched horizontally across the mattress and the headboard bangs my back, freezing us in midflip. She nudges me the other way, her pointy breasts squashed against my chest, arms locked around my waist. She's squeezing the air out of me. None of it feels good. Then she snakes her arm between us and her eyes watch mine while her fingers explore my erection.

After some awkward maneuvering I end up centered, her legs over my shoulders. She directs my hips and I slide in easily. As usual, I'm terrified and trembling—scared I'm doing something wrong, afraid I might injure myself or damage something inside her. I make tiny, careful movements. Her eyes are closed but the look on her face builds in intensity until it becomes an expression of pain.

She contorts, arching her back. She grinds slow and it feels nice, but sort of weird, almost creepy. I close my eyes and wait for the sensation to pass. Each time it's the same hollow feeling and I think I shouldn't be doing this because what if she is crazy, what if I'm a little crazy, too? I feel like Pinocchio. A boy made of wood. A stringless puppet. She controls everything—our rhythm, our speed, our position, rocking me until my fear becomes a small, distant thing, displacing flashes of my mother, Huey, Sam, my route, my life, transforming everything into a warmth and a joy I think isn't so bad.

Then it gets easier. I feel her gush, become all slippery inside. She bucks her hips like she's trying to throw me, all the while clutching my ass, digging her nails in. I'm not so much pumping as twisting, grinding, trying to stay balanced.

She's louder than me. Her mouth remains closed but all sorts of noises filter out. Her lips don't move. The sounds just float up from her. There's a rhythm and a resonance that seems more contrived than impulsive, more deliberate and purposeful than reckless and wild, like she's rehearsed the entire performance.

Her hands fall away. She flails her arms; an act of surrender. I take over from there. Our bellies slap as I pound into her, performing pushups at supersonic speed, driving a jackhammer. She clutches at her skull, pulling at her hair, swishing it around like it's all too much for her. She whimpers and moans; heaving her hips upward at the exact moment I squirt inside her. All my muscles lock up, no part of me moves, my head bursts with white light. And then it's over, and she's on her feet, quickly getting dressed.

I can't move. After each episode—this is the eighth time she's let me—it's worse. I'm unable to move for several minutes. I'm usually on my back, gulping for air. This time I'm belly down, barely breathing, certain that I've broken my spine and will remain a cripple for the rest of my life. I lie there and imagine myself trying to do my route from a wheelchair.

While Kelly puts on her clothes, I keep my eyes shut; my mind drifts, almost finding sleep. I imagine myself walking out the door wobbly kneed, then tumbling headfirst down three flights of stairs. When I finally do sit up, she is standing beside the bed fully dressed, grinning down at me. "I'm hungry," she says. "You?"

I blink at her and decide she's crazy. Mom hasn't gone grocery shopping in a month and the cupboards are bare.

"I'm going to eat something," she says, but she doesn't move. She poses, hands on hips: a thin, pretty girl, long straight hair parted perfectly down the middle, a few freckles, no makeup, nice lips, shining eyes. She's wearing scruffy jeans with a wide black belt beneath a puffy peasant blouse that looks like it's made of soft burlap. If you saw her on the street you wouldn't think there was a thing wrong with her.

— 38 —

I find my sister in the bathroom sitting on the toilet, but she's not doing anything because her jeans aren't down and there's a shoebox on her lap. It looks like a dozen other shoeboxes from the high shelf in the closet. One side of it says "Thom McAn," which is where Mom buys all her shoes. Kelly lifts the lid off and takes out not shoes, but a sandwich bag containing dirt and crumbled leaves. I lean in to see what kind of bug she trapped. One Christmas, Aunt Sally gave her an ant farm. It didn't come with any ants, just pictures, but there was a coupon you filled out and mailed to have somebody send live ants to you. Mom wouldn't let us keep it in the house.

"It's grass," Kelly says. "You smoke it."

"I know what grass is."

"You know about pot?"

I nod, though I don't know much.

"You ever get high?"

I don't say anything. I just smile and wonder if drugs are what made her crazy, if she's a dope fiend now, which Grandpa Rudy says is worse than being a drunk.

"Smoke it how? In a funny pipe like that caterpillar?"

"This isn't hash. I wish it was hash." She looks at the bag like she's trying to change it with her mind. "But yeah, you could. In a pipe if you had a pipe. I don't like pipes. I roll joints."

I nod again.

"A joint is a cigarette you make yourself. I'd show you, but I don't have any papers."

"Grandpa Rudy has papers. He uses them when he runs out of real cigarettes."

"I know. I've used those. They're okay if you stick two together."

"Grandpa Rudy's friend Slim only smokes cigarettes he makes himself."

"Don't even talk to me about that asshole," Kelly says.

"Slim or Rudy?"

"He squeezed my breast one Easter."

"Who?"

"Slim. Said he wanted to see if I was wearing a bra."

"Were you?"

"He's a sleaze. See with your eyes not your hands."

"You told him that?"

"And twice he tried to kiss me with his filthy tongue."

"Slim did all that?"

She tilts the cellophane bag and shakes the contents down to one corner. "This is ten bucks worth. Around ten."

"Ten dollars for that."

"I've used some, but yeah."

"Where'd you get ten dollars?"

"Oh, I didn't pay for this."

"You stole?"

"No, I didn't steal. It was a present. A gift."

"From who?"

She sticks her nose in and sniffs with her eyes closed. "It's a dime bag that didn't cost me a dime."

"You said it was ten bucks."

"A dime is ten."

"Ten cents, you mean."

"Don't be dumb. You get nothing for ten cents."

"Who gave it to you?"

"A friend who isn't my friend anymore."

"Who?"

"None of your business."

"Can I hold it?"

"Why?"

I shrug because I don't have a reason.

"Okay," she says. "But don't spill any." Then she says, "No. Forget it. Mom would kill me just for showing it to you."

She rolls the bag tight, drops it in the box, fixes the lid. I'm wondering if I should tell my mother. I decide I should at least watch where Kelly hides the box. She catches me staring. "What? That's it. Shows over."

I don't want her to go, so I say, "Slim rolls his cigarettes with one hand."

"I know. I've seen that trick. Do you have any money?"

"No."

"I need to buy some papers. You must have some change."

I shake my head no.

"You're a paperboy."

"So?"

She looks at me like I'm lying. "Did you ever snort coke?"

"You mean when soda goes up your nose because you're laughing?"

"Yeah, I mean soda," Kelly says.

She carries the box out into the kitchen and I follow her. "Stay here," she says. "Don't look."

"Slim taught himself in the army when his arm was busted."

She stops in the bedroom doorway, turns, and wrinkles her nose. "He was never in the army."

"Mom says he was in the Southern army."

"No such thing. And if there was, that would make him an even bigger creep."

She ducks out of my view. I don't peek. I don't want to know where she hides the box. I open up the refrigerator to see if there's anything to drink. "So how did he touch you?"

"Stay there," she says. "I'll show you."

— 39 —

My grandmother in her last days spent most of her time sitting by a window that overlooked the intersection of Central Avenue and Broadway. There was nothing to see except people going in and out of the delicatessen or the drug store or the pawnshop. One day she grabbed my arm and yanked me onto her lap. Her mind was gone, she had begun to talk mostly in German, and she'd lost a lot of weight in her face, but she still had plenty of strength in her hands and shoulders. She held me to her chest and squeezed as though trying to squash the life out of me. If anyone else ever held me that way, I think I'd scream my lungs out. But this was my grandmother, and she'd never been anything but kind to me, even in her sternest moments. So I just sat there, on her lap, struggling to breathe, and looking out the window. Before she let go, she made me promise to take care of my mother and sister. "Love them, Jack. Always, always. *Liebe wird dich retten.*"*

I said okay.

"You need to promise me, Jack."

So I promised. I crossed my heart and hoped to die, but that wasn't enough. She held on until I actually swore an oath, my right hand to God, which I always feel creepy about doing. "Because I'll be watching," she said. Sometimes I picture her looking down from the edge of a cloud, frowning, or frantically tapping the right shoulder of God, trying to direct his attention. Lucky for me, his eyes are always focused elsewhere.

*Love will save you.

– 40 –

I'm on Exchange Street when I see Crazy Carl, who is almost fifty but still climbs trees, spits into the river, and supposedly still lives with his mother. He's on the opposite sidewalk, jabbering while he duck walks. I need to cross over to make my delivery to Jack & Harry's Hardware, but I can't decide whether to slow down or speed up in order to avoid bumping into Crazy Carl. I make the wrong choice.

When I step onto the curb, Crazy Carl says to the lamppost: "I had a thing with a guy on his mind come back to me twice. Twice! Both times not enough postage. Who was the winner? Not me." Then he notices I'm staring and his face switches gear. "I know you. Don't I know you?"

I nod.

Crazy Carl's eyes flutter. He has the same cleft chin and wide mouth as JFK. He wears a dirty suit jacket with baggy trousers and a loosely knotted tie. With a proper haircut he could pass for a Kennedy, another brother. "You're late," Carl says. "You got my paper?"

I shake my head because Carl's not a real customer and today I don't have any extras, but Carl is already digging in his pocket, rattling change, jingling keys. "I'm on the front page. You see my picture?"

Before I can answer, he makes a clicking sound with his tongue and moves off, speeding up his duck walk until it's a trot. Maybe his mother is calling him home and only he can hear, or maybe her voice is just inside his head. He takes the corner, wobbling like Charlie Chaplin making his exit at the end of a movie. I'm not supposed to talk to Crazy Carl, because my mother says he's queer, though sometimes I talk to him a lot. Today I'm just not in the mood to talk to anybody.

– 41 –

I'll tell you what I think it was, why Mom locked her up: Kelly not knowing when to bite her tongue or how to shut her mouth, always sticking her pretty nose where a kid's nose doesn't belong.

After Grandma died and Aunt Sally moved to Sacramento, my sister got weird. She started acting like Peggy Lipton on *The Mod Squad,* conducting some secret investigation into our mother's past. Questions about our father were delivered in an unfamiliar and eerie tone that noticeably rattled my mother. "Where are your wedding pictures? You had a wedding, right?"

"Of course I had a wedding. A very nice wedding."

"Who went?"

"Lots of people."

"Name two."

"It was a small ceremony. Not like that hullabaloo your aunt and uncle threw. Nobody was paying for my wedding."

Kelly paced like Perry Mason. "So where's your wedding album?"

"Why?"

"I want to see it."

"What the hell for?"

"Jack wants to see it too. Don't you, Jack?"

I put my arms out, palms up, and shrugged.

My mother said, "Your father might have it. I think he packed it with the rest of his junk when I threw the drunken son of a bitch out of here."

"But you've got other pictures, right. Snapshots? People must have brought cameras."

"No."

"You don't have a single picture?"

"No. No one took any."

"Not one person had a camera?"

"Whatever pictures I had I threw away. I tore them up a long time ago."

"Why would you do that?"

"Because they were bad memories and I didn't want them. Okay? Why the hell do you care? What, are you writing a book?"

"Yeah, I am. I'm writing a book about my life."

"Well, leave me the hell out of it," my mother said.

The battle continued for days. Each round became more intense, more probing, my sister's questions more daring. She asked about dates and places, jobs our father worked, people he knew.

I watched the color drain from Mom's face, and the light blue veins on her neck darken as her irritation increased. For every stuttering answer Mom offered, Kelly snapped back with another question. Finally Mom warned Kelly not to forget that curiosity killed the cat.

"What does that mean?" Kelly said.

"It means don't bite off more than you can chew. You don't know everything, you know. There are lots of things you wouldn't understand."

To which my sister responded in a singsong voice as though completing a nursery rhyme: "I know all liars go to hell."

To which my mother replied, "Watch your mouth!" and struck Kelly hard across the face.

Kelly recoiled from the slap then froze as though she'd been struck by a paralyzing ray. One side of her face swelled red, but she didn't raise a finger to touch it. She held her ground and stared defiantly at my mother. "Hitting me doesn't change anything. Why aren't there any pictures of me and my father. Or with Jack and him? With all of us together?"

Kelly's argument was that if our father had lived with us until she was four and I was almost three, she would have retained some memory of the man, something besides the stories Mom had fed us. "I would remember something," she insisted.

"You were just a baby. How would you remember?"

"Four is not a baby. I would remember something. His face. His voice. Something."

"Why?" Mom said. "Why would you remember anything? Why would you want to? He wasn't a very nice man."

– 42 –

Unlike Mom or me, my sister speaks the new language. She calls it her lingo. Mom calls it garbage. She says Kelly is full of baloney, chumming around with the wrong kind of people, trying to be something she's not. I'm not sure what to believe. Kelly says Mom is uptight and out of style and doesn't understand what's mod (modern?) and what's not because she's stuck on the wrong side of the generation gap. My sister, I guess, is on the other side where life is usually a bummer or a downer. When she's in a good mood life is a gas or a mind blower. Then everything is cool, hip, or groovy.

Everything except me. I'm a square who doesn't know when to chill out or how to get his kicks. My hair is too short and my jeans are too straight. When she's in a really pissy mood, she tells me to get lost or go jump off a cliff. When I don't, she says I'm "a walking joke so fucking out of it that it's not even funny, man." Though she never tells me what the joke is or how I can get inside it.

Cops are the fuzz. Sunglasses are shades. Cigarettes are smokes. She calls money bread, and says Grandpa Rudy is probably going to croak any day now. When she speaks I have to pay really close attention and even then I don't always understand. So usually I'll just nod, smiling when she smiles, frowning when she frowns. When I do that, she says, "See. Now you're getting it, little brother."

— 43 —

Four perfectly boring days in a row I go to school, Mom goes to work, Kelly sleeps on the couch. Mom says Kelly's not going to get promoted anyway, so what difference does it make? When I grumble, Kelly says I'm jealous, but that's not it. I just think it's wrong. Who knows when she gets up, what she eats, where she goes, who she has over, or what they do to one another. The only rule Mom gives us is to be home for supper. "It's important we eat together and try to act like a family."

I don't have a problem with that. What bothers me is that there's no food in the fridge and Mom blows through half the grocery money in two days. We eat Chinese one night, pizza the next, then leftover Chinese and pizza the third night. We play Crazy Eight and Monopoly. Nobody fights, nobody yells.

Then I don't know what happens or where it takes place, what Kelly said or did, or how Mom finds out, but it is some seriously deep shit. When I get back from my route, Kelly's on the couch like a zombie and Mom's in the kitchen wearing a pained expression, her eyes glazed. She screams at me: "Your sister never learns. She's thickheaded, worse than your father."

So from now on, I'm Mom's eyes and ears when she's not around. I'm to report everything Kelly does. Everything. "I want to know when that girl shits and when she sneezes."

I'm confused about what Kelly did, though sort of excited about being Mom's spy. I'm thinking she might buy me a pair of binoculars or a telescope that isn't a cheap, plastic toy. When I ask what the hell happened, Mom says, "Watch your mouth, mister! You're not too old for a mouthful of pepper."

When I rephrase the question, she says, "Drop it. It doesn't concern you."

I'm looking through the cupboards wondering what we're going to eat when she sends me into the parlor to peek on Kelly and make sure she isn't on the phone. I find my sister sitting on the couch holding a throw pillow against each ear like giant earmuffs. Her knees are together and she's squeezing her eyes shut. While I'm in there, Mom says, "I'm all done playing games, missy." She says it loud enough for anyone to hear, even someone with throw pillows over their ears.

Later, when things have calmed down and Mom's heating water for macaroni, I ask again. "Jesus," she says, "are you writing a goddamned book?"

I'm not, but I do get my green book and tear out a blank page then sit down to make a list—a list based on nothing.

- Spray-painted Mr. Cooper's little white dog and made it look like a zebra.
- Pierced some part of her body besides her ears with a safety pin.
- Got caught leaning over the bridge rail and spitting into the Blackstone then told another cop to mind his own fucking business.
- Called Miss Oates, the lady who lives on the corner and dresses like a man, a dyke, which everyone knows, but Kelly said it out loud and to the woman's face.
- Got caught doing yoga exercises in the nude, but this time not by me.
- Called Aunt Sally in Sacramento, long-distance, and talked for an hour.
- Threatened Mom with a can of bug spray that she didn't know was empty.
- Used Mrs. K's spare set of keys to let herself into Dean's apartment to watch his TV and eat his food which she has done before when Dean worked double shifts or got so drunk he couldn't drive home.

When I show the list to Kelly, she reads it really fast, then hands it back. "Nope. Guess again."

— 44 —

Huey's eyes look raw and pink, a deeper, darker pink than the wrinkly burned flesh on his face and neck. When I ask him if he has a cold, he tells me that Larry White is dead. "I just found out," he says. "Not five minutes ago." He daps at his eyes with his dirty handkerchief. "Terrible, terrible. Another good kid wasted in Vietnam." I don't know who Larry White is and I don't ask, but Huey looks upset. His elbows tremble when he blows his nose.

A man in a suit stoops to pick up a copy of *The Record American* and leaves a quarter on the pile. Huey says, "God bless you, sir."

The man keeps walking.

I wait for Huey to pick up the quarter and put it in his change pouch, but he just stands there looking down at it. "Larry used to have your route. Long, long time ago. I knew Larry when he was no older than you. Back then he must have had over a hundred customers. If I remember right, he may have built it up to a hundred and fifty before he quit. Sam would know." He finally picks up the quarter and drops it in his pouch. "That was four, five years ago. The city has changed."

He lifts one of the bricks that keep the papers from blowing away and centers it on the pile though there isn't any wind today. "Don't ever go to war," Huey says very softly. "If they try and draft you, run the other way."

I nod even though I would like to know how to fire a machine gun. While Huey counts my papers, I make a V with my fingers and aim at people and cars. Then I load my sack and head out dragging my feet, thinking about Kelly's war with my mother and how I've been drafted into fighting on my sister's side even though it's a war we can't win.

— 45 —

Wednesday, May 8, 1969—For supper I'm heating up a can of Chef Boyardee spaghetti in Grandma's skillet thinking about bloody worms and remembering the dead bird I found with maggots crawling out of its belly. I'm wondering where Mom hid the peanut butter. She's down at Mrs. K's, probably talking about her money troubles again, and my sister's banging things around in the closet. I don't know what Kelly is looking for, but I remember I once found a jar of Skippy in there. When she comes into the kitchen empty-handed, clip-clopping across the linoleum, I say, "Those are Mom's."

"So?"

"So you better take 'em off before you get us both in trouble."

"She won't know if you don't blab."

I think about running downstairs and telling my mother but I'd probably get in trouble for being a tattletale and a snitch. While I stir the spaghetti, Kelly walks from the sink to the bathroom doorway to the refrigerator like she's doing something in a hurry. The shoes shine like they're wet or oily and the heels look too thin to support anything. When Kelly stands still, her ankles tremble.

"Why do you want to wear those? You can't run in them."

She frowns at me like I'm stupid. "They make me three inches taller. And they make me look older."

"No, they don't."

"And they give me power."

"What power?" I think about Catwoman played by Julie Newmar and try to remember if her shoes did anything special.

"Different kinds," Kelly says.

"Like what?"

"Like if I got in a fight, I could take somebody's eye out."

"You better not wear those outside."

"I will if I want. I've done it before. Mom never wears them."

I shut off the gas and grab a plate from the dish rack. "Did you ever take someone's eye out?"

"Nope, but I bet I could. I kicked a boy in his knee and made him bleed."

"Was he wearing pants or shorts?"

"Underwear," she says presenting a smile too innocent to be real. "The jerk wanted me to do something I didn't want to do. Claimed I owed him."

I nod like I understand.

"And two times," she says, "I've practiced throwing them like Batgirl does her batarang."

"What did you aim at?"

"Pear tree."

"How'd you do?"

"Pretty good. I stuck one heel right through the middle of a pear. Sent it flying."

"Liar."

She kicks the shoes off, picks them up, and hurries into the bedroom. "The pear landed near the hedges with the shoe still in it."

I hear footsteps on the stairs. Mom. Her thumps don't sound happy.

"I could do that," I tell my sister.

"Good luck trying."

— 46 —

Saturday, May 10, 1969—I dump everything out onto a pile of Life magazines and separate the quarters into stacks of four and the dimes into stacks of ten. I put the nickels in short stacks of five, keeping them in groups of four. I'm working on the pennies when Sam comes over. He adds it all up in a glance. "I hope you've got more than that," he says.

I hand him the four one-dollar bills, folded over so they look like more. He tugs and stretches each bill as he counts. The flesh beneath his jaw shakes. Sam has the face of an old dog. "What else? Fives, tens?"

"That's all of it," I say.

"You're kidding me." He drops the four dollars on top of the pennies. "You've got to have more than this."

I don't say anything. What am I going to say? Sam is waiting, so I check my side pockets, then my back pockets, then I shrug.

"This is no good," he says. "You're telling me this is all of it, every nickel you collected? All week?"

I nod yes.

"No, no. I can't believe that. I won't believe it."

I rock on my sneakers because I don't know what to say.

Sam fingers a spot above his eyes. "Where's your book? Are you marking your book?"

I take out the green book and hold it open but he doesn't take it, doesn't look at it.

"Don't give me a cock-and-bull story, now," Sam says. "You must have collected more than this."

I tell him a lot of customers owe, I tell him a couple more moved. "How many and how much?" he says. His voice is fierce, hard. "Because this doesn't hold water, you know, week after week. It makes no sense."

I'm holding the book, ready to burst into tears. I start flipping the pages.

"You go through that book and count up all the customers that owe. Get me dates and amounts and give me a grand total. You've got twelve dollars here.

Maybe thirteen with the pennies. Get a piece of paper and copy down all the names and addresses of anyone who owes you. And I'm telling you right now, it all better add up."

I go through the book one name at a time. I rip out a page from the back and use it to make my notes. Ten minutes later Sam is back and I hand him the paper. "What's this? A bunch of scribbles. I can't read this."

"You made me nervous," I say. "I can't write when I'm nervous."

He closes his eyes like he just fell dead asleep on his feet. He keeps them closed and crumbles the paper in his fist. He hands me the four bucks. "Take this and get the hell out of here."

— 47 —

Mom is frying frozen hamburger patties in Grandma's cast-iron skillet. We're going to eat them on Sunbeam bread, which means they'll be soggy. I'm wondering if toast would work better when Kelly extends an arm across the table. She curls one finger, gesturing for me to come closer, so I lean toward her, supporting my face on my elbows. She bends forward, arching her back until her breasts are almost touching the table. "I'm thinking about bleaching my hair," she whispers. "Going blonde. But I don't know. I really hate the way I look. What do you think?"

Before I can answer, Mom says, "I think you should leave your head alone. It's fine just the way it is."

"Nobody is asking you."

Mom flips the burgers. "Bleaching makes you look cheap, not to mention it ruins your hair."

"I'm talking to Jack," Kelly says.

"He doesn't know anything about hair, but I do." She points her spatula at us. "Bleach is the last thing you want to use. You'll end up bald, wearing a wig the rest of your life."

Kelly's fists are behind her ears and her eyes are closed. She starts breathing out the side of her mouth like she's puffing a cigar, squeezing her face so tight, she's making tiny wrinkles. Mom twists the knob on the burner, killing the flame. The skillet keeps sizzling, spitting grease. "Hey, that's just my two cents, missy. I know it's not much. And if you don't like it, go find three pennies in the street and make a nickel."

– 48 –

This is important. The day before my fourteenth birthday when my sister was still in Emerson, I dragged my ass back to the newsstand to settle my weekly bill. I hadn't even added up my collections because I knew I'd be short. Every week I was short.

Huey was working the corner. Sam was talking to him and another man. I dumped all the money out and started to stack the quarters in piles of four. There were three crumpled dollar bills. Sam came over and picked them up. He smoothed them flat and put the bills in his pocket. I was stacking dimes when he told me to stop. He took the pencil off his ear. He already had his book out. I think he was counting with his eyes. Then he swept all the change into his apron pouch. I don't know what he wrote in his book.

"Huey tells me it's your birthday tomorrow. That right?"

I nodded.

"How old?"

"Fourteen," I said.

Sam nodded. He told me not to go anywhere. I figured he was going to fire me. I didn't care. My stomach felt like I was running really fast. I didn't want Sam to yell at me the way he sometimes yelled at Huey. A few minutes later he pointed at his car. "Get in," he said. I opened the door and sat with my feet out. I thought about what I would tell my mother. She wouldn't like losing her ten dollars a week.

When Sam got behind the wheel, he told me to shut my door. He started the engine, but I didn't ask where we were going. Halfway up the hill he turned the radio on. The Red Sox were playing. "You play baseball," Sam asked.

"No," I said.

"But you like the Red Sox, right?"

"I used to watch with Grandpa Rudy," I said.

"Your grandpa a fan, is he?"

"I guess."

"What's his name again?"

"Rudy," I said.

Sam nodded. He drove us across town past the mills and up Armistice Boulevard. "There's a Joe Rudy, first baseman for the Oakland Athletics." I didn't know what to say about that so I said nothing. When we crossed over Newport Avenue, he asked if I knew were we were going, but he didn't give me any time to guess. "My house," he said. "For dinner. So I hope you're hungry."

I looked at the houses and the cars we were passing. "Do you have a phone," I said.

"Sure do. Why?"

"I'll need to call my mother," I said.

"Understandable," Sam said.

"Soon as we get there."

"Not a problem," Sam said.

"She likes to know where I am."

He nodded.

"She'll probably want me to come right home."

"You tell her it's a birthday celebration. Say we're having a little party."

"But it's not my birthday."

"Close enough, don't you think?"

"She might say it's not."

"You tell her it's a gift," Sam said. "A gift of a meal. You could use a meal, am I right?"

I looked at the houses again. Small, single-family homes. I said, "She's going to yell. I might get in trouble."

"What kind of trouble could you possibly get in for sitting down to a nice dinner?"

"My mother doesn't like me to eat at strangers' houses."

"Why not?"

"I don't know."

"Well, I'm hardly a stranger. I'm sure she won't mind."

I shrugged.

Sam drove without talking. He steered the car with one hand for a while, then with both hands. "How about this," he said. "How about you eat first then call."

"What are you cooking?"

"I don't know, but I'm sure it's good."

"That might make it worse," I said.

"Okay, all right. What do you want to do, then? You decide. What's your say in all this?"

I wrinkled my nose like I was thinking.

"You want to eat a nice, home-cooked meal, or would you rather I just drive you home and we forget the whole thing." He turned the wheel, steering us onto a street with trees along the sidewalk. Sunlight moved across his face and I could see the white hairs in his eyebrows.

84

I nodded my head yes.

"Dumb idea in the first place," Sam said.

– 49 –

Sunday, May 21, 1969—Mom and Kelly start Mother's Day by screaming at each other. They're in the kitchen, but their voices pull me from a dream where I'm trying to deliver a paper to the Apollo 10 astronauts who won't take off until next week, but in my dream are already strapped into their seats, sealed inside the Saturn rocket, which is taller than the Times building. The fight concerns shoes, but I'm not really sure what the problem is. Kelly says, "Then I'll wear my flip-flops."

"Don't be ridiculous."

"Then I'll go barefoot."

"You're not going to church barefoot. Don't be ridiculous. You'll step on a piece of glass and rip your foot open."

"I hope I do," Kelly says.

"Well, I'm not carting you to the emergency room. And forget about riding in an ambulance because I don't have money for that."

I squeeze my pillow around my head like giant earmuffs. I need to pee but I stay on my rollaway cart until the screaming stops. The wire frame squeaks when I get up. No one says anything when I come in. Mom is by the sink, Kelly by the stove. They both turn their faces toward me. "She hit me again," Kelly says.

"Nobody hit you," my mother says.

"Jack, look at me. Is there a mark on my face?"

"I didn't touch your face."

Kelly takes a giant step toward me with her head tilted to one side like her neck is broken. I shrug because I don't see any mark.

"Well, it hurts."

"Believe me, you'd know if I hit you."

"Somebody hit me. I felt it."

I look from one to the other. "I have to use the bathroom," I say, walking between them.

"Go ahead," my mother says. "Who's stopping you?"

I close the door halfway, then stick my head out. Kelly's back is turned. When

Grandma died, Mom officially put an end to Mother's Day. She told us no more gifts, no more cards, that it was just another day now. But I smile and say, "Happy Mother's Day."

She just rolls her eyes toward heaven.

— 50 —

Monday, May 12, 1969—I'm not even halfway through my deliveries when it really starts pouring. I sprint along the sidewalk on Saint Mary's way and duck beneath the canopy of an abandoned house. My hair and clothes are soaked. My sack is slick and heavy, but my papers are dry except for the edges of a few. I'm all out of breath from running. I wiggle my toes inside the sneaker with the hole in it. My sock feels like a sponge.

A car goes by and honks. It slows and pulls up to the curb a couple of houses away. I can't see the driver. It honks again and I raise an arm and wave just in case it is someone who knows me—one of my customers, or someone who knows my mother. The horn honks again and I take that as a reply, a signal, though I don't recognize the car. The brake lights go off and the reverse lights come on. It's a white Ford with a dented door. The driver slowly backs up, then stops in front of the gate of the house right next to where I'm standing. The horn sounds again.

I can't see into the car and don't think I know anyone who owns a white Ford, but it might still be for me, a messenger sent to track me down, a neighbor trying to find me because my mother has been murdered, or Grandpa Rudy dropped dead, or my sister leaned too far over the bridge rail and fell into the Blackstone River.

A man comes out of the house where the car is parked. He stands on the stoop and waves at the street. He's wearing a white shirt and black trousers. The Ford honks again and the man stops waving. He runs down the walkway, through the gate, and opens the passenger door. He's already wetter than I am. He kneels awkwardly on the seat and leans half his body in, then he pulls back and stands in the gutter, the rain streaming off of him. His hair is flat, like a black swim cap. He moves his head and shakes his fist and says something that the roar of rain rattling the canopy drowns out. Then he slams the door and kicks at the dent. The Ford drives off spraying water.

The man runs back into the house, and three seconds later, the rain slows to barely a drizzle. Across the street there's a gap between the houses and I can see above the long, low roof of the Carol Cable Company. The sky has a band of light, like the sun is trying to push through. I feel I've missed my chance, a once-in-a-lifetime opportunity, that I could have gotten in that car and driven away, gone anyplace, become someone else.

— 51 —

Birds are screeching, but that's not what wakes me. When I blink my eyes, my mother is standing over me. Her hair is in curlers. She's wearing her pink robe.

"What time is it?"

"Never mind." She reaches down by her feet and brings up a shoebox. "This belong to you?" She sets it on the cart and lifts the lid.

I lean on one arm. The squeaky frame sounds just like a morning bird. I don't know where Kelly is, but I know she's screwed. Inside the box is a pack of rolling papers. Her bag of dope isn't there, but still, my mother isn't stupid.

I play dumb. I stare into the box for a long time, then look at my mother like I'm retarded. She shakes the box and the papers shift around. "Is it yours?"

"No," I say.

"Is it your sister's?" I shrug and avoid her eyes. She shakes the box so hard the rolling papers jump out. "Don't lie to me."

I nod, and I keep nodding. I can't stop. My mouth falls open. I don't know why I'm nodding so much. Mom rests the box on the edge of the couch. She holds the top of her robe as she stoops to pick up the papers. "Okay," she says, dropping them in the box. She fits the lid on. "Go back to sleep."

She holds the box in both hands and presses it against her chest like she's holding a doll or a baby. I remember the time Kelly and I buried a pet turtle named Speedy in a shoebox. We dug a huge hole beneath the grape trellis even though Mrs. K's car was in the driveway. Right before placing the box in the ground, Kelly said the Lord's Prayer, then kissed the lid. I wait for my mother to kiss this box and make it go away. It's hurting my head just to look at.

"What are you going to do?" I say.

She blinks as though snapping out of a trance. "I don't know. I'll figure it out in the morning."

"What time is it?"

"Don't worry about it," she says and kills the light.

I stare at nothing for a while, waiting for my eyes to adjust. After a minute, the

windows look lighter than they did. "Where's Kelly," I say.
"Ha. That's the sixty-four-thousand-dollar question."

– 52 –

Thursday, May 15, 1969—Kelly wants to buy a bus ticket to Sacramento. She is trying to raise money by selling watered-down juice she made by mixing a bunch of stuff: one can of our mother's ginger ale, some flat Coca-Cola, the last of the Welch's grape juice and a packet of orange Kool-Aid powder. She stirred everything in a bowl with ice cubes, then poured it into a half-gallon milk bottle without spilling a drop. She served me a sample in a Dixie cup and told me to taste it, so I dipped my tongue. "It's bitter."

"It's supposed to be. It's vampire lemonade. One sip will change your life forever."

I swallowed the whole cup. It didn't taste bad, but there wasn't enough in the bottle to sell more than six or eight cups, so she filled the milk bottle almost halfway with water. Then it tasted flat, so she added four heaping spoonfuls of sugar, and now it tastes better than before, but it looks like watery puke and all the ice cubes have melted.

She tells me to make a sign. I ask her what she's going to call it, and she says, "Kelly's Homemade Lemon Aid."

I tell her that's dumb because she didn't use lemons and there's no lemon taste. "And the color is all wrong."

She says that it is not her fault we don't have any lemons. I tell her I'm pretty sure it's against the law to sell lemon aid that doesn't contain lemons. I shake my head at her. "They'll throw you in jail for false advertising."

She says, "Who's going to know."

I tell her everybody.

"Okay. We'll call it Kelly's Homemade Sweet Juice. That's legal. It is sweet," she says, and I can't argue with that. "Okay. Now you just have to make the stand." The deal is I get half the money she makes if I build a box or a table, something we can set up on the sidewalk.

"Where am I supposed to find wood?"

"Look for some."

"Where?"

"I don't know. Chop down a tree," she says.

"With what?"

"You're the boy, figure it out."

To make fake wood I use a steak knife to cut wide strips from a couple of cardboard boxes I find in the back hall. Kelly doesn't help. She just sips her juice and watches from the doorway. When I try Scotch-taping the strips together, the sides won't stand straight. Kelly says, "Scotch tape won't support any weight. You need nails."

While she goes to the bathroom I gulp down a couple of mouthfuls from the bottle then add more water so she won't notice. When she comes out we carry two kitchen chairs down the stairs and onto the porch, then we go back up to the apartment and get our mother's ironing board. We bring everything out to the curb and set the ironing board across the two chairs. Kelly sets the bottle and four Dixie cups on top, then sits down on the sidewalk, her legs folded like a guru. She's blocking the way if anyone wants to walk by, which I think is another law she's breaking. She tells me to go in the house and make the sign. I tell her she should do it because I'm no good at making signs.

"I can't go," she says. "I have to mind the store."

"I'll stay. You print better than I do."

She doesn't argue. She doesn't say anything. She squeezes all the muscles in her face, making tiny wrinkles. I get down on the ground and watch the sun through the milk bottle while Kelly holds her hand against her chin like Jack Benny pretending to think.

After a while, I tell her: "If I write the sign no one will be able to read it."

She says, "That's true," then slowly gets to her feet. She pours herself a Dixie cup of juice and swigs it down in one gulp. "Go get the crayons and bring them outside. We'll make the sign together. I'll show you how to print block letters in 3D."

— 53 —

Friday, May 16, 1969—First yellow house on Roosevelt owes me eight weeks, so I ring the doorbell and wait. I slide my bag off my shoulder because I'm going to be here a while. No one answers, no one ever answers. Last few days I've been ringing five or six times, sometimes ten. All short polite rings. Today I press on the bell for a minute straight, then step back on the stoop and wait. I think about shutting them off, holding back delivery until they pay up. I think about this every day while I wait. Then I leave the paper inside the screen door.

Today's paper is unusually thin with very little news and no ad inserts. My sack is as light as a Saturday run. I blow through my route then swing back down to Roosevelt for a second try at the yellow house. Bingo! There is a car in the driveway, so I go through the gate and up onto the stoop. The shades are down but I can hear the sound of a TV, or maybe it's a radio. I hold the screen door open with my shoulder and ring the doorbell. I lean on the button a long time, then take out a quarter and rap on the window.

First the TV sound goes away, then a man opens the door. He's around my mother's age, wearing dark trousers and an open white shirt with a T-shirt underneath. His belly spills over his belt. "What?" he says. "What is it?"

I tell him who I am and why I'm here. He fights through a yawn and tells me his wife takes care of the bill. Then he inches the door forward. "You owe eight weeks," I say.

"Eight?" he says. "No way. Can't be." He takes his hand off the door and rubs above his eyes. "Can't be eight. Hasn't my wife been paying you?"

I tell him no one has paid me since I started the route. "Not possible," he says. "Doesn't she leave the money for you every week?"

I say no.

"In a little envelope," he says.

I shake my head and the man shakes his. "I don't know what to tell you," he says and works two fingers into the flesh beneath his chin. After an awkward silence, he says, "You're new, you said—is that right?"

I nod.

He leans a little bit forward, then rocks back. "I think you've got us mixed up with another house. My wife pays by the week. Always has."

I explain to him no one has paid me anything.

"Yeah, well you might want to double-check that."

I explain that I have double-checked and I'm sure it's eight weeks.

"Maybe she paid the other kid. You check with him?"

I tell him I've been doing the route alone now for over two months.

"Two months, huh? I don't get it," he says. "And nobody's been paying you?"

"Not yet."

"That doesn't make sense. That makes no sense at all," the man says. "Show me what I owe. Show me something in writing."

I reach into my sack and find my green book. My hand is shaking as I flip though the pages. I find the number of the yellow house and show him the row of empty checkboxes.

"Can I see that?" he says. He grabs the book from me and studies the page, then he flips a couple of pages forward. "This doesn't make any sense," he says. "None of it. You've got scribbles all over this thing."

He jumps to the back of the book where the pages are still blank, then he closes it and hands it back. "That don't mean a thing. What does that prove?"

I open the book and find the right page. I count the empty boxes, saying the numbers out loud. When I say "eight," the man shakes his head.

"I know what it says there," he tells me. "What I'm saying is that doesn't mean anything." His voice sounds tired. I close the book, drop it in my sack. "I don't like this," the man says. "We never had this problem with the other kid. What's your name again?"

"Jack."

He looks me over like I've just shown up. "Look, Jack. For all I know, my wife could have paid you ten times and you never wrote a thing down. She works, I work. We're not here to see you write in that book. I'm not saying you're a crook. You might have forgotten to write it down. What I'm saying is I've never seen you or that book before in my life." He steps back, his hand on the door. "You'll have to talk to her, okay? I'm sorry. Empty boxes in a green book mean nothing to me. You work it out with her." The door starts to come around again. "You come back when she's here. She'll straighten it all out." He closes the door so that only his face shows. "I can't help you."

I pull at the strap, hitch my bag higher. "Okay. When?"

His mouth opens and closes as he swings the door back just enough to fit his shoulders through. "Look, I'm busy right now. Really busy. Come back Sunday. Okay? Any time Sunday. She's off all day."

"I can't," I say.

He stares.

"I don't work Sunday. There's no paper."

He rolls his eyes, drops his hand from the door. "Jesus," he says. "Hold on a minute, for God's sake," he says.

He lets go of the door and it swings all the way open by itself. He mumbles something with his back to me, then disappears through an archway. I lean to the left until I can see half of a TV. The picture is in color. I try to guess what show he's watching.

He comes right back. "Eight weeks you said? Here." He hands me a five-dollar bill. "That takes care of it. Okay? We're square, according to your little book there. Now you don't have to bother anybody Sunday or any other day. But I'm checking with my wife on this, you bet I am. I'm asking her when and what she's paid you. I'm doing a full investigation, you hear? And from now on, I want a receipt, you understand? I'm telling her we're all paid up and not to give you another dime unless she gets a receipt."

I clear my throat and tell the man that eight weeks is five twenty.

"Five twenty? Why five twenty?"

I hold up the five-dollar bill in case he wants it back.

He puffs his chest up. "Where you getting that number from? The paper is a dime, right? Six papers a week is sixty cents. Eight weeks is four eighty. I'm including a twenty cent tip in there."

"It's sixty-five a week. They charge extra for home delivery," I say.

"Who does?"

"The newspaper, the people at *The Times*."

He makes a sour face and reaches into his trousers. He hands me another dollar. It's crumpled and dirty, like a piece of old cloth. I put it in my pocket and step away from the screen door, but he moves forward and catches it before it closes. "So you're telling me it's cheaper for me to walk down to the corner any day of the week and I can buy the same paper for less money?"

I shrug, walking backwards. He's smiling but I can't figure why.

When I'm out the gate and a few steps down Roosevelt, he says, "If you ask me, somebody's making a nickel."

— 54 —

Monday, May 19, 1969—Mom brings home the stink of the river mixed with the greasy smell of the diner. She carries a brown paper bag dotted with grease stains. She's not smiling, but she doesn't seem in a bad mood. She drops the bag on the table between Kelly and me. "Help yourselves," she says.

"What is it?" Kelly says.

"French fries. Rocky was throwing them out."

"What's wrong with them?" I say.

"Nothing."

Kelly snatches the bag and unravels the top. She looks inside, shakes the bag, then reaches in and pulls out a single fry. She wiggles it beneath her nose, then licks it with her tongue. "They're cold," she says.

"So stick 'em in the oven and heat 'em up," Mom says. "Four hundred degrees for ten minutes." She goes into the bathroom and opens both faucets in the tub.

Kelly pops the fry into her mouth. I watch her face, waiting for her to spit it out, but she chews and swallows. "Yuk! They're old and stale."

The bathroom faucets squeak and the pipes rumble. The echo sounds like a waterfall.

"Garbage," Kelly says. "Ice-cold."

"Let me have some," I say, and Kelly tosses the bag across the table. It lands on its side and a few fries spill out. I reach for one as my mother returns to the table.

"Frank is buying me dinner," she says as I slip a fry into my mouth.

"Don't eat those," Kelly says. "You'll get sick and die."

"Who's Frank?" I say to my mother.

"Don't tell him what to eat," Mom says. "What the hell do you know about anything?"

"I'm not eating somebody's leftover garbage," Kelly says.

My mother's face twitches and she closes her eyes a second. She's making an effort not to get mad. In a cool voice, she says, "Then starve you ungrateful little shit."

"Okay," Kelly says. "I will."

They're eyeing one another like two wrestlers who just stepped into the ring. "Do we have any ketchup," I say, though I already know we don't. All I'm trying to do is keep the peace, prevent the situation from escalating into violence.

After my mother leaves, Kelly will stomp around, shouting curse words and calling my mother filthy names. Her mood will swing from rage to giddiness then back to rage. She'll fish a half cigarette from the ashtray and smoke it by the window, gazing out, fuming, plotting. Then she'll come to me like she often does and with a glazed look in her eyes tell me to pull my pants down.

– 55 –

Sometimes I think we're better off without a working TV. All we ever did was fight over who wanted to watch what. I remember one battle that broke out a few weeks after we buried our grandmother. I wanted to watch "Hercules vs. the Hydra" starring Jayne Mansfield. I loved Jayne Mansfield even though I knew she was dead. I had already seen the movie a couple of times, and though the story was dumber than a cartoon, I wanted to see the part where Hercules lifts Jayne like she has no weight at all, then kisses her on the mouth and makes her swoon. Kelly had "The Outer Limits" on, the one where Robert Culp plays a man with no memory who is being hunted by alien invaders. One of Culp's hands is a talking computer made of glass, but it's missing three fingers. The hand gives him instructions, but it can't tell him who he is or anything about his secret mission until the missing fingers are restored, and the creepy aliens have those.

Kelly wasn't even watching. She had a library book with a Mylar jacket open on her lap. She jumped off the couch and pinched my arm when I tried to change the channel. I knocked the book out of her hand. She punched me hard in the chest and screamed: "That's a library book, you jerk!"

After more slaps and punches, we wrestled on the carpet, pulling each other's hair. I got her down. I had her pinned, both arms above her head. I was winning, using all my weight against her, when she started to bump her groin into mine. Not hard. She looked right at me as she arched up, grinding her hips, her eyes flat as winter blue.

When your crazy sister is dry humping you, there are a number of things you can do. I didn't do any of them. I closed my eyes and let her grind away. Before I knew it, it was over. My orgasm ripped through me. She pushed me onto my side and I flopped onto my back. I felt only exhaustion.

Kelly stood over me, looking down, shaking her head. "What a little pervert," she said.

On the TV, the Glass Hand was saying: "Stay alive. Above all, stay alive. Destiny is in your whole hand."

99

— 56 —

Wednesday, May 21, 1969—On the couch, a forearm covering her eyes, my sister says, "I'm not crazy, you know."

I say "I know" very softly because I'm guessing she has a headache. Then I try and think of something else to say to her, something funny, because the part of her face that I can see looks terribly hard and I'm sure it hurts.

"Sometimes I just get angry, you know? I get so fucking pissed at everybody." Her pink tongue darts out, just for a second, sweeping across her bottom lip. "Dr. Rob says that's more normal than crazy. He says it's perfectly all right to feel angry and to release that anger, but he says I have a problem with escalating rage." She drags her arm across her face until her hand drops over the side of the couch. She rolls her eyes like she's fainted, then tilts her face toward me. "So I'm working on that. My rage. Or at least I'm supposed to be working on it. How I act on my feelings."

I shrug and stare at the carpet beneath my sneakers. I don't like it when she talks about Dr. Rob.

"And at other times," she says, "I just get so sad, and I feel...I don't know. I just feel so alone. And cold. Like I'm wrapped in ice, you know? Like I've been dropped beneath the South Pole. You ever get cold like that?"

I shake my head no.

"And then all I want to do is cry or scream very loud, so then I do, I cry or I start screaming, but all I ever do is scare other people and myself. Then I become more frightened by the sadness and the ache, the ache that never quits, and I end up confused. Because why am I always so fucking sad? Like all the time. And so pissed off at everything and everybody. But those are my feelings, just feelings. I don't think that matters. I mean, Dr. Rob says they're real, those feelings, and I need to deal with actual, genuine feelings, and not just shit that I'm thinking about. Do you think he's right?"

I don't say anything.

"Do you think you go crazy if you have too many feelings at one time?"

I shrug and shake my head because I don't understand the question.

"Sometimes I pray," she says.

"You pray?"

"Not a lot, but sometimes. Whenever I feel it's no use and I should just give up. I prayed the first night they locked me up. I kicked and banged the door for about an hour, but after I got tired of that, I prayed all night. But I've prayed before."

"What do you pray for?"

"Another life."

After a silence and an exchange of grins, I say, "Good luck with that."

"Thanks."

"Do you pray for anything else?"

She thinks about it, then shakes her head so slowly her hair hardly moves. "Sometimes I pray to understand what is happening inside of me. I mean, I don't ever expect to understand all of it because I don't believe that's possible, but I do think maybe it would help to know where these feelings come from. And how they got there; inside me, I mean. I wish I knew that. I think it would help a lot to know. Though Dr. Roy says it might not make any difference at all. So I don't know. I'm not an expert. I just wish someone cared enough to go inside me and find out. Someone besides Dr. Rob, who is just getting paid to do it. All I want, really, is for the ache to go away."

"Where's the ache?"

"Everywhere. Head, stomach, chest, heart. You name it, the ache's been there." She hugs herself and rubs her arms like she's cold, and I guess I'm looking at her with baby-brother puppy-dog eyes, because she says, "Knock it off. I'm not the kind of girl they find dead with an empty bottle of sleeping pills in her hand. That's not me at all."

– 57 –

At first I don't like it. Her hands are in my hair and she pulls all the air from my mouth and it feels like she's trying to swallow my tongue. She's got a firm grip on my skull, like when my mother washes my hair, but I manage to turn my head away. All around my mouth feels wet, sloppy, like I've been drinking from a bubbler with my lips together. I tell her that's not how you kiss.
 She says, "What do you know about kissing?"
 I'm still trying to think of an answer, some small lie, while she recites instructions. Her tone is strict, like an old teacher, and I don't like it.
 "Don't boss me," I say.
 "Do you want to learn or not?"
 I pull in a deep breath, then follow her commands. I stand there limp, slightly slumped, with my mouth open, my jaw relaxed. My eyes are closed, but I feel her breath on my chin when she leans toward me. Her breasts are pressing into me, but her lips are barely touching mine as she uses her tongue to trace the underside of my teeth. She snakes her tongue around. I stab back at hers and our tongues have a brief sword fight, then her mouth is covering mine again and her lips create a vacuum seal. She tilts her head down and my knees buckle as our noses bump then slide past one another, but it doesn't hurt. Nothing about it hurts, though my heart is pounding like a jackhammer.
 When we break for breath she looks at me cross-eyed, her hands still on my back. "That's how you kiss," she says.

— 58 —

After completing my route, I race all the way home, then up the stairs. I'm six steps from the top when I see Dean's door is wide open. I stop and listen in case he's watching TV. Sometimes I stand by his door and try to hear what he's watching.

Dean is in his chair, bent over, lacing up heavy work boots. He's sweating in the heat, his long-sleeved shirt rolled up to his elbows. He tilts his head up, doesn't seem surprised to see me. "Too fucking hot," he says, and I nod. His forehead shines beneath his oily hair. "Too hot to work," he says, and I nod again. He puts his hands on his knees and pushes himself up. His mouth is open, his nostrils are flared, and his eyes look like he might be drunk. "Do me a favor," he says. "Say hello to your sister for me."

And I nod again.

"Don't forget," he says.

— 59 —

The window fan is roaring on high, rumbling like a jet engine, but it's not doing any good, just wasting electricity. Our parlor feels hotter than the hallway. The air is steamy and smells like Breck Shampoo. Kelly raises her hand and waves for me to come closer. She's on the phone, on the couch, a bath towel knotted around her torso, her legs curled beneath her. Her hair is damp and straggly and there's a shine to her forehead like she scrubbed it with a Brillo pad. "Wait. Don't hang up. He just came in," she says into the phone. "Hold on a second."

When I move in front of the fan she holds the phone above her head. "Take it," she says.

"Who is it?"

She holds the curled cord away from her face. "Say hello."

"Who is it?"

"Aunt Sally."

I move back a step and shake my head.

"Take the phone. She wants to talk to you."

I shake my head again and back up another step. The fan is blowing hot air like a furnace.

"Hurry up. She's calling long-distance."

"I don't care. I don't feel like talking."

Kelly makes a sour face, then puts the phone to her ear. "Auntie? Jack can't talk now. He just ran into the bathroom. I think he's got diarrhea." She bats her eyelids, listening. "Yeah, well, he's been living on Froot Loops, Twinkies, and root beer. Mom never cooks when it's hot outside. But I'll tell him you called and I'll talk to you soon."

She leaves the phone on her ear but presses the button on the cradle. "Why wouldn't you say hello? What's wrong with you? She's your aunt."

"I don't like her," I say.

"Since when?"

"Since forever," I say. "She always treated Grandma like shit."

"So what? Everybody did, including Mom."

104

I plop myself in Mom's chair and put my head back. "I know. I remember." Sweat streams off my brow, stinging my eyes, making them burn.

"Everybody took Grandma for granted," Kelly says. "Including you."

"Yeah, but I was just a little kid. I didn't know any better."

redundant

– 60 –

When I go outside there's a black man sitting in a car in front of the house. It's an old car, gray, a four-door sedan with rust spots along the bottom of the doors. No black people live on our street, so instead of stomping ants, I sit and stare at the car. The windows are down but the sun is too bright and I can't see the driver very well. All I can tell is that he's dark-skinned with high fuzzy hair like Linc from *The Mod Squad*. He lights a cigarette with a match and for a second I see his eyes and his teeth and his pink tongue. After a couple of puffs the man ducks down looking at me or at our house, then he starts the engine and drives off.

Two minutes later my sister comes around the side of the house. She's holding her hair back in a fist though there isn't any wind. She stops four feet away and looks at the street but not at me. She's wearing too much makeup and the pricey jeans Aunt Sally bought her and a shirt I've never seen before. "What are you doing?" she says.

"Nothing. Why?"

There are ants crawling across her shadow but she ignores them. She walks down to the street and stands at the curb like she's waiting to cross. She rests one hand on the parking meter, sort of posing on one foot, turning her head one way, then the other. After a minute she turns around and looks at me. Then she comes back into the yard, but not very far. "Did you see anybody?" she says. "A guy in a gray car?"

I don't look at her so she can't see my eyes. "Nope," I say.

"Are you sure?"

"Yup."

– 61 –

The first time my sister put my penis in her mouth, I thought I was dying. I worried about her teeth though it really felt like she had no teeth. I liked the wild mix of feelings and the warmth, but still thought it might be a trick and any second she'd bite down hard. I worried about our mother walking in. I'd catch the beating of my life, then wake up in the Sockanosset Training School for Boys. Did they even have a hospital there? Then my mind began to swirl and I didn't care about any of those things. I looked at the ceiling. My head went so far back, I thought the bone in my neck would snap like a No. 2 pencil.

A couple of minutes later, when my brain started working again, I sort of wished I had died. My heart was beating normally but I felt too good, too relieved to be alive. I can't say how Kelly felt. She hadn't said a word though I think she was pissed that I made a mess on her blouse. I shut myself in the bathroom and looked at my penis for ten or twenty minutes. I tried to pee but couldn't, so I sat on the toilet like a girl and flipped through a comic book that I had read a dozen times before. I read the ads for life-size monsters and X-ray specs and a mini-camera that you could hide in one hand. I felt like taking a bath, but I was afraid I'd fall asleep and drown or that some great force would pull me down the drain and I'd wake up in the sewer with rats crawling over me.

An hour later, when I asked Kelly if she would do it again, she looked at me cockeyed. She bit her thumbnail in silence for ten or twenty seconds. Then she said I should throw away my sneakers, burn them in the rubbish barrel, because my footprints were everywhere.

"You've seen *The Fugitive*, right?"

I nodded.

"So you know what happened to Richard Kimble when he returned to the scene of the crime."

I didn't know what she was talking about and I didn't care. I asked if she wanted to do it or not. I said I didn't care either way, which was a great, big lie and I think she knew that, because then she made me beg.

"Only if you say pretty please with sugar on top."

I told her I wasn't saying that, no way, and then I went ahead and said it.

"Tell me you love me," Kelly said.

"I love you," I said.

"Tell me I'm the prettiest girl you know."

So I said that, too.

"Swear you're not lying."

So I swore.

Then she pointed her finger at me like a teacher catching me carving my name into the desk alongside all the other names. "You have to follow my rules."

"What rules?"

She patted the couch cushion beside her. "Relax. There are only two. Sit."

So I sat.

"Okay. Rule number one: I don't want any of your goo on me. You squirt it in my mouth. No pulling it out."

I nodded.

"And rule number two is you don't tell anyone."

"Who would I tell?"

"Swear on Grandma's grave."

And that's something I don't like to do, not ever, but I said, "Okay. I swear."

"Nobody can find out. Not your friends. Nobody. Not ever."

I didn't tell her I had no friends. The TV was on, but the sound was off. We were in the parlor, but I could hear the hum of the refrigerator. The windows were closed, but I could hear the trucks moving on the highway. I couldn't stop my legs from trembling. "Anything else?" I said.

She folded her arms across her chest and looked at me with her head tilted to one side. "Okay. Hands behind your back and keep them there. No touching. I mean it. You lay a finger on me, I'll never do this again."

Despite the no touching rule, at her request, I ended up holding her hair back with my fist in a sort of ponytail. Afterwards, when I caught my breath, I asked what she thought about when she was doing it and she made a sour face, meaning, I guess, she didn't want to talk about it. But I kept asking, posing the question a few different ways, until she told me to shut up and pull up my pants before our mother walked in.

− 62 −

It's too hot to be outside. There's no shade, no clouds. The sun is too bright and really hard to look at. White light is reflecting off of everything. Huey is wearing sunglasses that Sam bought him. They make him look like a cop. He's not in a talking mood and the pink and yellow scars on his face shine when he sweats. While waiting for him to count my papers, I burn my stupid elbow just by leaning against a parked car. When Huey catches me looking and rubbing the spot, he says, "That's what you get." I can see myself, two of me, reflected in his dark glasses.

All during my route my shadow moves slantwise across the sidewalk or slides along the sides of buildings. When I go onto a porch or inside a house to drop off a paper, my shadow waits outside. Sometimes it's behind me, hooked to my heels; other times the whole thing stretches out in front, a larger-than-life silhouette. Every so often, I attempt to ambush it. I run up quick to stomp on its legs, trying to trap it beneath my feet and stop it from going any further. But each time I do that, I fail. The sun isn't like the moon. Sunlight is unforgiving in the way it sharpens the edges of everything real.

– 63 –

Three and a half hours later, I'm done, walking past the Parker house dragging my empty sack like it's a dead animal, when a car horn honks, but I'm too tired to even bother looking up. I just keep walking.

Mrs. K's car isn't in the driveway. The patch of weeds she calls a garden looks wet though it hasn't rained in a week. Kelly is sitting on the front steps. Her head is down, so I think she's watching ants. She's wearing a man's hat, a gray Fedora pulled down low, and there's an unlit cigarette dangling from one corner of her mouth. When I ask her where she got the hat, she says, "Dean," then squints at me like a gangster. Her eyes look raw, like she's been rubbing them too much. "You got any money?" she says. "I need some."

"How much?"

She tilts the hat back. "How much have you got?"

– 64 –

The Thursday night that our mother goes to meet some Puerto Rican accordion player at the VFW, my sister spreads her legs beneath me and my penis slides into her so fast, so easily, I don't realize what I've done. When I try to pull back, her muscles tighten around me like a fist. When I move again, trying to center myself, my eyes close all by themselves. I think I've died and gone to heaven. My head jerks back all by itself like there's a rope around my neck. The muscles in my legs lock, then my hips start twitching, shuddering all out of control. She presses a forearm against my chest and tells me to stop.

"Don't move," she says, so I freeze in an awkward half-pushup position, my back arched, all my weight supported by stiff arms on top of curved fingers. She whispers something, instructions I think, using words I don't understand. When she removes her forearm from my chest, I look down; she's posing with her limbs spread, forming a star-shaped girl. Her eyes are closed again. She looks like she's waiting, but I don't know what she wants me to do. Meanwhile, my elbows and shoulders are trembling like when I'm in gym class, waiting for the whistle.

"Move up a couple inches," she instructs, so I shift my weight forward. "Oh, shit," she says, but her tone is soft not angry. "Okay. All right. Go slow," she says. "There's no rush. Take your time." All her words tremble like she's singing them.

But I'm still unsure and more than a little afraid I'm going to hurt myself, so I hold my position, semi-paralyzed. I'm Pinocchio before the Blue Fairy shows up and grants his wish, stuck on a shelf, suspended by invisible wires. Kelly keeps shifting beneath me, making tiny adjustments. She poses like an Egyptian hieroglyph, then like a dead woman who fell out a window. Her eyes are open, but only a little. Her lips are parted just enough to show her teeth are together. My toes start to cramp because I've been resting half my weight on them.

"Stop pressing. You don't need to push down so hard. And quit squirming. What are you doing?"

I tell her I'm not breathing right, that my heart is beating too fast and my mouth feels full of spit and I'm having a lot of trouble swallowing. I say all this with my eyes because I can't talk. Maybe she reads my mind, because she shifts her hips, rising up until we're perfectly centered. Her eyes open really wide and her pupils dart around like she's reading. She starts pushing back, slowly grinding. "How's that? Is that better?"

Before I can answer she drops flat, pulling me down with her; our pelvis bones bump and I slide all the way in. She hooks both arms around my neck and swings one leg over my back, then the other leg. I feel trapped, a dumb bug caught by a spider. My nose ends up an inch from her ear and I can feel her breath like warm wind on my shoulder.

The box spring is squeaking and I'm breathing hard, like I'm running uphill, but otherwise I'm not making a sound. Kelly makes enough noise for both of us. After a string of grunts and groans, right in the middle of a long, open-mouthed moan, her ankles lock around my back. Now I'm really trapped, but I no longer care. She's quivering, or maybe we both are. Her hands are on my hips directing my motion, setting the pace, working me in and out. She's pinching and digging her nails in. And I don't care.

I eventually make a noise—a long, hard sound, barely audible, like a growl scratching its way out of my throat. It's loud enough for someone in the hall to hear. If my mother were climbing the stairs, she'd hear it for sure. My nostrils aren't working. Air rushes past my lips. My mouth turns dry and my tongue tastes like metal. I'm thirsty, hot, breathless, sleepy, delighted, thrilled, all at once. Then my heart tears away, popping all the veins and arteries. They become loose wires after my heart shoots up my throat, into my brain, and crashes right behind my eyes. It's pounding like Tarzan just swung into the village with his knife between his teeth. The warning drums are sounding and any second I expect to die. And then I do die. Thank God. And it's a wonderful death. Painfully, joyfully slow. In shuddering waves, one rolling over the other, all my muscles give out and I collapse. I go from moon gravity to earth gravity and become dead weight. It takes me forever to catch my breath.

I'm almost asleep when Kelly taps my forehead. "Get up. Get off me. We've got to make the bed before the wicked witch returns to Oz."

Which strikes me as hysterically funny, though I don't laugh or crack a smile because I'm paralyzed from the nose down. And I don't dare open my eyes, knowing I'll see my sister, the bed, this room, my mother in the doorway, sour-faced, and behind her the ghost of my dead grandmother, wagging her finger like a German sausage.

– 65 –

On rainy days and damp days or when it's cold, Huey limps so bad I feel sorry for him, so on those afternoons I load up fast and get the hell out of there, using the weather as an excuse, but really it's because my grandmother had a crooked foot and used to limp worse than that all the time. She supposedly broke her ankle when she was a little girl and no one took her to the doctor so the bone never healed right. Her left foot was so crooked, she always wore out the side of that shoe before the soles. The bottoms would look brand-new, but she'd have to buy another pair. She hated that the stores wouldn't sell her just one shoe.

I think Sam should buy Huey a wheelchair for bad-weather days. One with a little horn in case passing cars don't see him trying to cross the street.

− 66 −

"It's simple," she says. "No blood, no eggs. No eggs, no problem." She's down on the floor trying to sit cross-legged like the Maharishi Mahesh Yogi, the Indian guru who hangs out with the Beatles. "Until I start bleeding everything's cool."

She might be telling the truth because I don't know anything, though Dave the crossing guard says both his sisters have been bleeding since they were twelve. I kneel so I can stare at her eyes which are ringed with mascara. I look at her pupils, but I can't tell if she's lying. She might be. Her eyelashes look too long to be real.

"At Emerson, when they found out, they didn't blink. Nobody ever panicked there. A nurse brought me downstairs to see a lady doctor, who turned out to be a very nice person. She talked to me, asked a few questions, then she gave me a pelvic exam."

"What's that?"

"No big deal. It took, like, three minutes. She put on rubber gloves and stuck two fingers into me. She pressed against my stomach with her other hand. Then she stuck a finger in my butt to feel inside there."

"Why?"

Kelly shrugs. "I don't know, but she kept apologizing. She had a nice voice. Soft like Grandma's, though she wasn't that old. I told her it was cool because she obviously wasn't trying to hurt me, and she could have. She said it's not uncommon, especially for girls who don't eat right, to not start their period on time. So it's Mom's fault, really. Years of shitty nutrition put me behind schedule. The doctor talked to me about my diet. She said I need to eat better and gain more weight and then I'll catch up with girls my age, and my breasts will get bigger too, though she didn't say when or how big. I could start bleeding any day, or maybe not for another year. It's not up to me, but I hope I never get it. Just don't tell Mom."

"Doesn't she know?"

"Nope. And if you say anything she'll freak."

"How can she not know?"

"You didn't know," my sister says. "Mom thinks I get my period every month like clockwork. She thinks I'm a heavy bleeder because I go through so many tampons."

"What do you need those for?"

"I don't buy them. I use the money for other stuff."

"How much money are we talking about?"

"A couple of bucks. Why?"

"Never mind. That's not enough."

"Enough for what?"

"A couple of bucks is nothing."

"But it's every month," my sister says. "Like allowance."

– 67 –

Kelly and I play Crazy Eights with a deck of cards Aunt Sally sent her in the mail. All the cards show the Sacramento skyline but it doesn't look like anything special, just buildings by a river. The boats look too big compared to the buildings and there aren't any bridges. It's not a very good picture. It doesn't look like anyplace I'd want to live. The Queen of Hearts is missing, so we use one of the Jokers in her place.

My sister is smiling in a funny, crooked, weird sort of way. She keeps rolling her eyes like a magazine model trying to peek at the pages stacked behind her.

I usually like it when anybody smiles at me but this smile is almost creepy. She might simply be out of practice. I know my mother doesn't smile enough. And I know Kelly's back teeth are bad, three missing adult teeth, which the dentist pulled, so she can't chew very good on one side, but her smile is still pretty. Her front teeth line up straighter than mine. She brushes more than I do. It's only when she yawns or laughs really hard that her mouth looks bad. I've never sat in a dentists chair. Kelly said it wasn't fun. Mom says they charge an arm and a leg. I remember a lady from the dentist's office called every day for two weeks until the bill was paid.

– 68 –

Thursday, May 22, 1969—I'm on my back on the first-floor landing, lying motionless at the bottom of the stairs. Kelly's going on an afternoon date with someone named Terry, so I'm pretending I'm dead. But I'm cheating, using my rolled-up canvas bag as a pillow. When I hear my sister coming down, I hold my neck crooked and make slits of my eyes. I peek at her through my eyelashes. I can't tell what she's wearing. She's just a blur that runs down the stairs, leaps over my legs, then opens the outside door and walks out of the house. I decide to give her a minute. I hold my position even though my neck is stiff and beginning to hurt my jaw.

I'm still lying there, thinking about my route, wondering if any more customers have moved away, whether Terry is a boy or a girl, if Kelly kisses him, if she puts his thing in her mouth, when I hear the door open. I keep my eyes closed.

After five or six heartbeats, Dean says, "What are you doing?"

I look at him and blink. "Did you fall?" he says.

I straighten my neck and shake my head no. He's carrying a case of Narragansett under one arm like it has no weight at all. He stares at me for a second, then swings the case forward as he steps over. Kelly says Dean can drink a case of beer in one night—twenty-four bottles, though I don't know if that's possible.

"You shouldn't lie there, you know. You're going to cripple someone."

I don't say anything. I close my eyes and go back to being dead for my sister.

– 69 –

Friday, May 23, 1969—Mystery solved. Mom has a new boyfriend, though we haven't met him yet and she won't tell us his name. Apparently, she's been dating him for a while but hasn't once brought him home. Kelly says Mom doesn't tell the men she meets that she has kids because she doesn't want to scare them off. "That's why she meets them downtown," she says. "I bet'cha this guy doesn't even know we exist."

Twice already, Mom spent the weekend at his place. She didn't leave a number. Both times she went to work on Friday and we didn't see her again until Sunday night. The first time she stayed away she called on Saturday and again on Sunday morning, waking me up, drilling us with questions, reminding us of the rules, but the last time she didn't call at all.

Last Sunday Kelly and I cleaned every room, top to bottom. We wiped down all the doors and woodwork. We swept and mopped the kitchen floor and left no dirty dishes in the sink. For breakfast we ate peanut butter sandwiches made with crackers and washed them down with tea, then took a nap on Mom's bed, though neither one of us slept very long. We fooled around for an hour, then we changed the sheets and put on a pink bedspread, tucking the corners tight like they make you do in the army.

"What a nice surprise," Mom said when she strolled in. "Thank you both."

"It was my idea," Kelly said, which was true, though I did half the work.

"Even better," our mother said.

– 70 –

Monday, May 26, 1969—On Blackstone Avenue there's a girl in jean shorts and an orange shirt stretched across the trunk of a white Chevrolet. She's got her back against the rear windshield, arms crossed, face pointed toward the sky. Her hair is light blond, almost as white as the Chevy. I'm two houses away, but I like what I see.

I drop a paper on top of the milk box at the side entrance of 8 Blackstone, then immediately check for the girl. Still there, hasn't moved. I advance slowly, keeping my eyes on the girl who keeps her face pointed toward the sky. The closer I get, the cuter she looks. She has flawless skin. Her hair is straight like Kelly's, but several inches longer. I get close enough to see that her eyes are closed. She has small, round breasts beneath an orange half-shirt that shows off her flat stomach. Her jean shorts are high and frayed, her legs slightly tanned, long and wonderful.

She doesn't flinch when I open the gate. I'm close enough to spit at her. I hitch my bag and think about saying hello, but what would that get me? I go through and shut the gate and decide I'll say something on my way out.

"I hate to be the bearer of more bad news," she says, "but two more houses emptied."

I stop walking and turn around. "What did you say?"

"Down there." She waves toward Saint Mary's Way. "Two more houses. I saw the people carrying their stuff out."

"Which houses?"

"The brown one and the green one."

"Which green?" I look past her, at a pile of black garbage bags beside a doorless refrigerator marking the beginning of Saint Mary's Way.

"I don't know who they were. I'm not allowed down there. They moved out Saturday night and Sunday morning."

"I don't deliver to the brown house."

"I think it was the green house, the double-decker, last from the corner."

"I have two customers there."

"Not anymore, I don't think." She tilts her face toward me and shields her eyes with one hand. "One was a Jewish family because when they rode by with all their stuff my stepfather said, 'Good riddance.'"

"Why good riddance?"

"Because he's a jerk and because he hates Jews."

I slip my bag off my shoulder and nod. "I work for a Jew."

"So does he. Though he might have meant one of the colored families. I don't know. He hates pretty much everybody." She swings her feet over the side of the car and rocks into a sitting position. "Hi, I'm Elizabeth. I live in here." She nods at the house then extends her arm like she means to shake my hand. I step forward, but when I reach out, she slaps her thigh like she's swatting a bug.

"Ha! Got ya," she says and giggles. Her hair moves in a delightful way. "Everybody wants to shake my hand," she says. "Especially boys. Why is that, do you think?"

I shrug my shoulders and lower my chin, trying to make my neck disappear, but she doesn't see. She stares toward Roosevelt and pulls at a couple of strands caught in the corner of her pretty mouth. "My stepfather is pretty much a jerk but he says you're more reliable than the last paperboy. The fat kid before you." She shifts her body and looks toward the white Victorian. "I thought you should know. And about those houses. The people moving and all." She squints and shields her eyes, still looking uphill. "I'm waiting for my boyfriend, so I can't really talk anymore." She scoots backward, lifting on her hands, and drops into her tanning position. "Bye!" Her head goes back. "Nice to meet you, whatever your name is."

I hitch my bag and stand there looking at her for five or ten seconds. A car comes up the street and slows as it passes, but she doesn't look. I reach into my sack for a paper and head toward the house. Over my shoulder I say, "Jack."

She giggles.

The door is wedged open, held by a brick, so I leap over the stoop and into the hallway. Then I take the stairs two at a time. I toss the newspaper up onto the landing without folding it first and it lands all wrong. The inside section falls out and it sits there like a paper hat. I climb up and fix the pages, then hurry back outside. The white car is gone and Elizabeth is nowhere in sight. I look toward Roosevelt, then up at the white Victorian, then I hitch my bag and start down Saint Mary's Way, ready for more bad news.

All along the street are oak trees tall as houses with thick roots that have broken the sidewalk. I hop over the cracks, then rest in a patch of shade for a minute. I watch a swarm of baby ants climbing over one another. It's almost suppertime and the scent of roses and fried onions clings to the warm air.

– 71 –

Friday, May 30, 1969—It's a good day for stomping: bright sun, sharp shadows, lots of big, black ants zigzagging across the cement walkway. I detour a couple with my sneaker, forcing them to walk around my shadow, but I don't crush any. I'm not in a killing mood. I was short seven dollars and thirty cents on my bill, which is better than last week, but Sam didn't think so. He gave me another long speech. He said I was as useless as Huey. Then he apologized, told me to forget what he said. I allow the ants, who I imagine to be soldiers on a mission from the queen, to continue their journey to the patch of overgrowth Mrs. K calls a garden.

Speaking of queens: my sister stands by the chainlink fence gazing past Mrs. K's rosebushes. She looks pale, almost white in the sun, squinting in the crooked shadow of the house. I can't decide what she's gazing at. When I step close, she says, "I hate my name. I think I'm going to change it."

I'm careful around the rosebushes' sharp thorns. When the flowers bloom, the stems lie heavy over the chainlink fence. Any day now, Mrs. K will grind them up and make rose jelly. "You can't just change your name."

"Why not? It's my name."

"Exactly. That's why you can't change it."

Her face is just inches from a leaning rose. I wait for her to get pricked. She says, "People change their names all the time." She touches her thumb to a thorn and I think about giving her a shove.

"Like who? Name one person you know who changed their name."

She jabs, measuring for sharpness. "People do. Movie stars. Musicians. "

"They're adults. You're a kid."

"I can still change it if I want."

"It won't count. You'll still be you."

"I can change it for now, then when I'm all grown up, I can change it for real."

"To what?"

"I don't know," she says. "I need to think about it. Make a list of names. I don't know what I want to call myself."

"What should I call you until you make up your mind."

"Bonnie," Kelly says.

"Why Bonnie? That's nuts."

"Like the movie. I'll be Bonnie and you'll be Clyde."

"I'm not changing my name."

"You have to if I do."

"Not Clyde. That's worse than Jack. No, thank you, I'm keeping my name."

"Bonnie and Jack doesn't work," Kelly says. "You have to be Clyde."

I shake my head at her, but she's not paying attention. Now she's got her nose in the roses. I think about pushing her into the thorns. Instead, I stomp a couple of ants, one, two. "My bonnie lies over the ocean." I stomp another. "My bonnie lies over the sea."

Kelly plucks a rose without pricking herself. She moves the petals beneath her nose and across her lips, then slides it above her ear. "Don't be snide, Clyde. I don't want to shoot you, but if you make me, I will."

– 72 –

I keep my eyes closed tight and pretend it's Elizabeth making me feel so good, and then I feel bad about doing that, because she seemed like such a nice girl. So I picture Mrs. Brown, a woman from our church with crazy-long red nails, all through the rest of it.

When I use my underwear to dab at the drops of semen on my stomach, Kelly takes my penis in her hand and says, "It's a sad little pink bunny now. See the floppy ears."

She lifts and stretches the flesh around my testicles until I put my hand over her hand. I tell her not to yank so hard.

"What's the matter? Too sensitive?"

"It's just not a good idea. You could break something, or tear something inside."

She takes her hand away. "Like what?"

"I don't know. A vein, an artery, some tube."

"A tube? What kind of tube?"

"Something that could ruin me for life."

Patting her hands together like she's wiping away dirt, she says, "Too late. Already done that."

– 73 –

Saturday, May 31, 1969—She's touching up her pink lipstick and I wonder where she's going. She's too absorbed in her reflection to notice me. She stretches her mouth into an O shape, traces it with the tube, then brings her lips together, pressing them into a flat line. She leans toward the mirror, practicing pouts and smiles. Her mouth looks like a piece of candy and her cheeks are rosy, but there is something unsettling about her eyes, a rawness like she's been rubbing them too much.

I clear my throat and she shifts her glare to me in the mirror. "What?"

"Nothing."

She twists the tube and the lipstick winds down. "Stop being a pervert."

I make a face like she's crazy, then lean against my cot, which is folded up and pushed back against the wall.

"I know what you're thinking," she says, and right away I say, "No, you don't."

While she's pinching and straightening her pantyhose, I tell her she better not let Mom catch her dressed like that. "Like what?" she says.

"Like a tease."

She shrieks a short, fake laugh. Today she's wearing her denim miniskirt and a sleeveless blouse. With her hair twisted and pinned on top, she looks old enough to vote. "I like dressing up." She puts on one shoe, then the other. "Men are a lot easier to tease than boys." When she stands, she is several inches taller. "Most boys don't know what they're feeling when they spot a pretty girl in a miniskirt and high heels. It's really pretty pathetic how fast their brains stop working. Most of them freeze. They become dumb statues or act like goofballs. Something wrong?"

She catches me staring at her legs so I step away from the cot and try not to look like a goofball.

"I ignore the boys, most of the boys, especially if I know them. Unless they're with girls that I do know. Then I'll smile at the guys just to make their girlfriends hate me." She angles her face, checking one side, then the other. "The best place is probably the supermarket. I go there and play a game I call Pig Hunt."

She gives me a long, centered look, briefly touches her pinky to the corner of her mouth, smiles. Perfect. "I pay no attention to the poor old guys who come in alone. I can't stop them from looking, but when they talk to me, I don't answer. I only go after couples, the more married the better, because I get this thrill when the guy jerks his head and almost breaks his neck to get a better look. Sometimes I have to bite the inside of my mouth to keep from laughing when the girl catches her man gaping, all goggle-eyed. I like that feeling. I like it a lot. It makes me warm inside.

"Sometimes husbands walk away from their wives and follow me. They think they're being sneaky, pretending to look for disposable diapers or dishwasher detergent, but I catch them peeking. They scoot up one aisle so they can come down the one I'm in. Sometimes one will come up to me and ask if he can help me find something. Or they'll ask me my name, right out of nowhere. I don't answer. I never talk to any of them. I stare into their eyes and give them a look that says, 'Why are you even talking to me, you creep.' You should come with me sometime. It's more fun than Christmas."

– 74 –

Mom's sleeping out again and Kelly says if we play any more records, someone might call the fuzz. Then she sorts through her albums, looking for one more. The speakers in Mom's stereo hum like a hornet's nest if you turn the volume low. I close my eyes for maybe a second and that's a mistake, because when I open them it's almost 1:00 a.m. My sister isn't in the room. I get up off the couch, but she isn't on Mom's bed. I keep walking, but she's not in the kitchen. The bathroom door is closed so I figure she's taking a bath or having a shit, but she isn't in there either. I pee, then go back to the couch.

I sit and guess at all the places Kelly could be. I decide it would be a good idea to make a list, but I don't have a pen and paper. I think about dialing the operator and telling her to send a patrol car to look for my sister. I picture Kelly leaning over the bridge's rail, smoking a cigarette, and spitting into the Blackstone while a cop goes racing by, siren screaming. Then a second police car. Then a third. They'll come here and I'll end up in handcuffs, dragged downtown, slapped around until I confess to killing my sister and burying her body, which they'll never find because my sister will be somewhere between here and Sacramento, hitchhiking from one truck to another. Mom says truck drivers will always give a girl a ride no matter where she's going.

Then the door opens and Kelly walks in.

"What the fuck! Where were you?" I say. "Why didn't you leave a note? Where the hell did you go?"

"Chill out," she says, because I'm shouting and sticking my nose in her face.

I back up and take a breath. She's not even dressed, still wearing Mom's pink bathrobe and fuzzy slippers.

"You passed out, so I went next door to watch TV." She plops on the couch like Mom does after a hard day's work. I go to sit next to her but she swings her feet up.

"Is Dean home?"

She yanks Mrs. K's spare set of keys from her pocket and drops them on her belly. "What do you think?"

– 75 –

Monday, June 2, 1969—It's hot. The river stinks like a sewer. Kelly stops to look over the rail. I keep walking until I'm almost to the end of the bridge, then I go back and stand close enough to grab her in case she leans too far and starts to fall. We're directly above the man-made waterfall, but today the water is low, trickling down instead of rushing. Beneath the flow I can see the hundred-year-old bricks.

"She wanted to die, you know. She prayed for God to take her."

"Who?"

"Who do you think?" my sister says.

I shrug, because I don't know if she's talking about herself or someone she met at the mental hospital. She shifts her gaze toward the Old Slater Mill Museum, the country's first cotton mill, so I look that way too. "I still don't know who you're talking about."

Kelly bulges her eyes and stares at me for two seconds. "Are you retarded? Grandma. Who did you think?"

"Oh," I say. "What about Grandma?"

"She didn't want to live. That's all. She said she was all done living."

"How do you know that?"

"Because I heard her. She talked all night, every night. She never shut up. Sometimes I would get up and ask what she said, and she'd tell me she wasn't talking to me. So mostly I would pretend to be asleep and try to make out what she was mumbling. And then I'd be sorry because it was just one crazy thing after another."

"Like what?"

"Stuff."

"What stuff?"

"Stuff you don't want to know. Things nobody wants to hear about."

"Like what?"

"Can't say. I'm not a snitch. Plus, I promised."

"Promised what?"

"I took an oath, sort of. Though I didn't raise my hand or swear to God or anything."

"Oath to who?"

"Doesn't matter." She puts one foot on the bottom rail and boosts herself up. "Point is, I crossed my heart and promised never to repeat a word. Not a word. Not ever."

"Promised who?"

"Auntie." Kelly says. She drools spit from her lips, then she leans further so she can watch it fall. "But that's all I'm telling you."

I move my tongue around, trying to work up enough saliva to spit. "What does Aunt Sally have to do with anything? She lives in Sacramento now."

Kelly works her jaw, then spits and leans even further, but it's impossible to see anything against the waterfall's spray. "Where she lives doesn't matter. What's important is she was there."

"Where?"

"Here," Kelly says. "Growing up, I mean. With Mom and Grandma and Rudy. She knows everyone's secrets."

"Tell me about Grandma, what Grandma said."

Kelly pushes off the rail and starts hop-skipping ahead of me. "She didn't want to live anymore. That's all. She prayed every night for God to take her. I think she was fed up with all of it."

"I don't believe you."

"Don't. It's still true. She was sixty-three and tired of living. Her exact words were, 'I am worn-out from this life.'"

"She wouldn't say that."

"I heard her."

"Why would she say it to you?"

"Not to me, goofball. I told you, she was praying. Talking to God or whoever. I don't know who she thought she was talking to. She kept asking for forgiveness, saying she was sorry for not doing a better job with things."

"What things?"

"Can't tell," she shrugs. "Lips are sealed."

A man in a suit is walking towards us. He's dressed neat enough to be a spy or an undertaker. Kelly keeps her shoulders up, scrunching her neck, walking with her elbows out, high-stepping like some kind of long-legged bird. "Just things she could have done and didn't. Things she should have stopped. Things Rudy did, mostly."

The man passes without giving us a glance. He looks a little like Sean Connery.

"What's Grandpa Rudy got to do with it?"

"Stop asking me," Kelly says. "If I break my oath I'll go to hell."

"You're going anyway."

She turns, frowns, walks backwards, still watching the man. "Maybe not."

"Mom says we're all going there in a hand basket. Every last one of us."

"Yeah. Aunt Sally talks like that too," Kelly says, stopping long enough for me to catch up with her. When I do, she doesn't move. She's still watching the man. The breeze pushes her hair across her eyes.

I tell her: "You told me you don't believe in hell."

"I don't," she says. "But I suppose I will when I get there."

— 76 —

Tuesday, June 3, 1969—After school I head straight home and come up the back stairs. Kelly and Mom are inside screaming at one another, thumping around like elephants, so I wait in the hall.

Kelly says, "Send me back. I don't care."

Mom says, "Don't think I won't! You're good for nothing. Spoiled rotten. You don't lift a finger!"

"Spoiled? How the fuck can I be spoiled?"

"Ungrateful. Rude."

"Who the hell spoiled me?"

"Foulmouthed. Hurtful."

"You never buy me anything."

"And sick. You're sick in the head. I don't know what's wrong with you but I can't deal with a crazy kid."

Kelly screams: "You're my mother. Do something!"

They talk at the same time, their voices crashing like screeching birds. I can't make out the words.

I think about going back downstairs and waiting outside until they settle down. I should do my route and get it over with. I could hang around and talk to Huey until the papers arrive, but I need my bag and my green book.

I open the door in time to see Mom chase after her waving the red belt. There are no good places to hide in our apartment. Kelly runs into the parlor with Mom a few steps behind, then Kelly comes out of the parlor through the bedroom, back into the kitchen, but instead of escaping out the back door which is the smart thing to do, she dances around the table, keeping my mother on one side, faking left, going right, then running through the bedroom back into the parlor. My mother catches her there. I stay in the kitchen with my hands over my ears, but I can still hear the slaps the belt makes. I can tell which blows find flesh and which strike clothing or miss. Kelly doesn't scream. She doesn't make a sound through any of it. I don't know how she holds it in, but she doesn't cry until the beating is over and our mother has gone downstairs to have coffee with Mrs. K.

Then she wails and screams like a wounded monkey, but only for a minute. When I can no longer hear her sobbing, I dampen a facecloth with cold water and bring it to her. I stand there holding it out, but she only looks at it. She's too busy examining the red marks on her arms and legs. Her eyes are bloodshot and puffy, but I don't see any tears. I wonder if the belt caught her in the face. Mom always aims below the shoulders, but sometimes she misses. Once the belt got away from her and the buckle struck Kelly below the left eye.

I set the wet facecloth down on the coffee table and go back to the kitchen. I sit at the table and flip through the pages of the green book trying to make some sense of it. I use a pencil to X out the customers that have moved away. I circle the number of weeks they owe. I don't bother to add them up because it's money I'll never see. I close the dumb book and try to think about something else. I wonder what the astronauts are doing. I hear a low sound that might be Kelly calling my name, but I don't get up to find out.

− 77 −

Starring at the flame of her Zippo lighter, Kelly says, "My second week there, I met this girl named Angel who wanted to buy a cigarette from me, but I didn't have any. She told me, 'You ever want to get somebody's attention,'" and Kelly lowers her voice like she is sharing some great secret, "'just set their bed on fire while they're in it.'

"Her name wasn't really Angel, but that's what she called herself. Her real name was Mary Joan something or other, some Italian name. Nobody could pronounce it straight, not even Dr. Rob, who always called her Mary Jo. And she allowed him to get away with that. But nobody else, not even the nurses. Heaven help anyone else who didn't call her Angel. That was her line, her joke, not mine. She told you the first time she met you, 'Call me Angel. Heaven help you if you don't.' It was funny, but then, well, after I found out about her house burning down, then it wasn't. You know what I mean?"

— 78 —

I need a new plan, a better plan. In my old plan I would learn karate or judo, whichever was easier, and grow up to be some kind of crime fighter, a kind of Batman, though that name is already taken and I wouldn't want to be a copycat. Maybe I could be Birdman, and Kelly would be my devoted sidekick, White Canary or Biting Louse or whatever name she wanted. We'd wear slick bulletproof outfits so nobody could kill us, and the fabric would be wash-and-wear so we'd never have to iron them. She'd wear a really tight costume that showed off her cone-shaped breasts and I'd have fake muscles built into mine. And we'd carry all sorts of neat weapons and crime-fighting gadgets in our fat utility belts—smoke bombs, stink bombs, ropes thin as wire—and we'd live in a secret cave down by the Blackstone River, close to downtown, right under the Main Street Bridge—though I don't know if I could sleep with all that racket from the traffic and the waterfall. And even though we wouldn't actually be able to fly, we'd have canvas capes with reinforced steel wires that we could lock into position and turn into huge wings so we could glide from rooftops, soar across busy streets, or catch an updraft and travel far enough to make our escape. We'd have secret identities, but we wouldn't need real jobs. We'd live on the reward money we'd collect for rounding up criminals and putting them in jail, and we'd really only have to work when new criminals rolled into town.

But all of that seems pretty stupid to me now. And I feel sort of retarded for ever dreaming the whole thing up.

– 79 –

Wednesday, June 4, 1969—It's almost suppertime. I'm not hungry, not really, but I think Kelly is. We're in the parking lot of the Red Cross building, on a strip of grass with a single pear tree. Why somebody would plant a pear tree in a parking lot I don't know, but if you climb two-thirds of the way up, onto the thin branches, you can look down past the prickly hedges into the church's parking lot. From there, if you lean far enough north, you can see one corner of our house and part of the backyard where Mrs. K keeps the garbage can and rubbish barrels.

Straight through the hedges is a twenty-foot drop to the church's parking lot so we're not supposed to be up here, period, never mind climb the tree. Once in a while a man or a woman will come out of the Red Cross building and ask us what we're doing. Kelly always says, "Nothing."

When she said that to one of the men, he told us to "go do it elsewhere." Ten minutes later he came back and told us that the tree was private property and not a playground. He came within ten feet of us. We jumped down and ran.

No matter what time of year it is, they say the pears aren't ripe. Last summer, just minutes after a woman came out to tell us we were trespassing, a cop car drove onto the lot. We saw it in time and hid in the hedges. We watched the cop drive around the lot, but he didn't get out.

Now we only visit the pear tree late in the afternoon when there are only one or two cars. Kelly says they belong to the janitor and the cleaning woman. We help ourselves to the green pears which always taste sour, like Sweet Tarts that have gone stale. The pears never taste like the sliced ones that Mom buys in a can. Sometimes we throw the cores in high arcs across the lot, trying to see if we can reach the highway without stepping off the grass. Once we stood at the rail and aimed whole pears at the cars streaming past, but we didn't hit any.

We used to bring pears home, but we don't anymore. Mom's rule is, "Don't eat the Red Cross pears." The last time we brought a batch home—eight or nine of the plumpest, ripest pears we could find—Mom threw every one of them in the garbage. She claims the pears are sprayed with insecticide and if we eat them, we'll get sick and die. But we've eaten hundreds over the years and never gotten more than a bellyache.

Today Kelly walks around the tree bent over like an ape, picking up and examining the fallen fruit. I won't eat the pears on the ground since I picked one up once and found the dirty half swarming with baby ants. When Kelly finds a good one, she washes it with her spit then wipes it on her shirt before biting into it.

While she's hunting, I jump and grab the low branch, then swing my feet up and lock my ankles over the limb. It takes me a few tries to pull myself up and find a position that isn't crushing my balls. I use my arm to keep the sun out of my eyes and look across the highway to the houses on the other side, then I shift around and look the other way, in the direction of our house, but I'm hardly above the hedges and can't see more than a tiny bit of the siding beneath the point of the roof. I'm sure I could hit the chimney with a pear from here. We're close enough that sometimes when we laugh too loud our mother hears us and screams our names.

I watch my sister pick up and sidearm-toss pears one after another until she's traveled completely around the tree. She kicks at a couple, knocking them into the hedges, but they don't make it through. She squints at me and says, "Help me up," and I glare down at her with a cockeyed look just to give her a hard time.

She crosses her arms over her breasts and stares at me with her lips softly pursed. "I'm waiting," she says. She is half smiling, half pouting.

I casually reach up and grab hold of the branch above my head because once she pulled my leg and I nearly fell.

"C'mon. Be my footstool," she says.

I ignore her like she's not even there, then swing my weight forward, landing like Superman with my fists on my hips. "At your service, Miss Lane. What seems to be the problem?"

"Stoop," she says, "so I can stand on your back."

"Don't step on my neck," I tell her, then drop to my knees.

"Closer," she says, so I scoot forward like a little dog.

I lock my elbows and stare at the ground while she lines herself up. I watch my hands to make sure no bugs crawl on them while Kelly steps on my tailbone then hops up. She almost loses her balance, then pushes off. I quickly get to my feet and wipe my hands together, checking for bugs.

Kelly doesn't stay in the spot where I was sitting. She climbs higher, to the next branch, letting her feet dangle. She swings her legs out, then back, hanging by her arms and looking out toward the highway. There's barely any wind, but her hair moves across her mouth so she turns her face into the breeze and looks toward our house. The sun makes blotchy shadows across her breasts. I stare until she catches me looking. "What?"

I pick up a pear and throw a fastball into the hedges. How can she not know how strikingly beautiful she is?

– 80 –

Thursday, June 5, 1969—I go into the kitchen for a drink of water. Mom is seated at the table with a cup of tea in front of her. Her head is down. She pinches the string on the teabag and moves it up and down, up and down. I can feel her eyes on me as I fill a glass with water and gulp it down. When I turn around, she is staring into her cup. "I know what's going on," she says. "I'm not as stupid as you think."

I stand there and pull in a deep breath. Then I hold it in, afraid to move.

"I'm still your mother, you know. Remember that."

My lungs are ready to burst, so I exhale very slowly through my nose.

"I hear you whispering in there, talking about me behind my back," she says, raising the cup. "I don't catch every word, but even when I'm not here, my ears are burning." She sips and nods. "Kelly hates me. I know that. She wants you to hate me too. Both you kids can turn against me, but I'm still your mother. That's never going to change. Even when I'm dead, I'll still be your mother."

"We weren't talking about you," I explain. "We were watching Walter Cronkite."

"Don't lie, Jack. Don't do that. Lying to me only makes it worse."

"I'm not lying to anyone."

As I leave the room, she shouts after me: "Don't put any flowers on my grave when I'm dead. Neither one of you. Because I don't want them."

– 81 –

Friday, June 6, 1969—Even though I'm not supposed to give our phone number out to anyone ever, I give it to Elizabeth in a fifteen-cent card with a sunrise or a sunset (I can never tell the difference) on the glossy cover. The inside of the card is blank—which, I think, is what all cards should be. I print the phone number in big block numbers beneath my name. What else am I going to write? Hugs and kisses? A string of "X"s and "O"s? All of which seems dumb.

I print "To Elizabeth from Jack" on the envelope and leave it in front of her door on top of the newspaper because I'm sure it's the right thing to do. I'd like to believe that by giving out the number, I'm being rebellious and sneaky, somehow disloyal to my mother. But that's not the case. I give pretty Elizabeth the phone number because I know she'll never use it, never call. She'll probably throw the card away soon as she reads who it's from. Why would she keep it? What does she need my number for? Why is a girl who looks like her going to call a boy like me?

Ever.

— 82 —

Saturday, June 7, 1969 —Kelly's at choir practice, though she's really not. Mom doesn't know she quit because we haven't been to church in weeks. I'm eating Cheerios from a plastic bowl with a serving spoon when Mom sits down with her cup of coffee. I don't look up because I'm a giant eating donuts with a shovel, but she fake-coughs and clears her throat not once but twice, so I stop being a giant and look at my mother. She holds the mug with both hands, elbows on the table, and stares. Her nail polish is flaked in spots. There's a tiny Band-Aid covering the pinky nail. "Okay, mister. Give it to me straight. What's going on?"

"With what?"

"You and your sister."

One of my knees starts going. "What do you mean?"

"You know what I'm talking about." She sips and swallows, blinks and stares. "What's with all the whispering lately? You know I don't like secrets." She sets the mug down and waits, but I don't say anything. I use my spoon to scoop up Cheerios like they are life rafts in a white sea.

Two rooms away the phone starts ringing, but Mom doesn't move. "I'm waiting for a straight answer." She stares until the third ring, then slowly gets up. "Don't look at me like I'm the crazy one." She points her finger at me like it's a gun, a dagger, a lightning bolt. "I'm not the crazy one. And I'll find out what's up with you two. You know I will."

She's almost through the bedroom when the ringing stops. "Where there's smoke, there's fire." She keeps going. The phone starts up again. Half a ring.

"Hello?" Her voice is flat, dull, creepy, like someone about to die in a scary movie.

– 83 –

Sunday, June 8, 1969—The phone rings, but I'm alone in the apartment so I ignore it. I'm kneeling on the couch watching a white spider climb the lacy curtain. The ringing doesn't seem to bother the spider and I can't remember if spiders have ears. No one ever calls for me and I don't feel like writing down a message. The spider is climbing an invisible wire and I'm wondering whether shining the emergency flashlight on it would blind it. Spiders have eight eyes. But the phone doesn't quit, and I'm thinking it could be Elizabeth, so on the ninth or tenth ring, I pick up. A man says, "Who's this?" so I say, "Who's this?" even though I recognize the voice. It's Slim, Grandpa Rudy's friend.

Slim says, "Jack? That you, boy?" Behind him I hear music, a woman singing. I think it's Tammy Wynette.

I say, "Maybe. Who's this?" because Slim is a tall, stupid bastard with a Southern drawl and when I talk to him, it's like talking to Gomer Pyle.

"Jack, this is Slim. I need to talk with your Ma."

"My Mom's not here."

The music stops and there's a silence. I think he's hung up. He says, "Man, oh man, where is she at? Is she at work?" and I tell him I don't know, which is the truth.

"Damn," he says. "That's no good. No good at all." The music starts again, the same song, more Tammy. "Take down this number," Slim says. "It's important. I'm over at the hospital."

"Are you sick?"

"Me? Hell, no," he says. "Write down this number for your Ma. It's important. It's about Rudy."

— 84 —

After she fits the chain on the door, my sister peels her shirt up until it's inside out, then pulls it over her head. "Get your pants off," she says. "Hurry up."

I unbuckle my belt and unzip my fly, but before I can get my pants down past my ankles, she wiggles out of her jeans. "Try taking your sneakers off," she says.

I'm bent over tugging at my cuffs, while she stands there in her white bra and her yellow panties, which have a tiny rust-colored stain in the crotch. My pants are bunched and tangled, twisted inside out. I pull them back up so I can get to my sneaker laces. She waves my hands away. "Stop. Let me do it. God, you're helpless."

While she's tugging, I notice she's wearing the necklace Grandma gave her. It's a tiny silver heart that opens up so you can hide a picture inside, though far as I know, Kelly keeps nothing in there. "Take that off," I say.

She tugs at my sneaker, thinking that's what I mean.

"Your necklace. Take it off."

"Why?"

I look at my feet trying to think of a reason. "So that it doesn't get tangled in your hair."

"Good idea," she says, reaching both hands behind her neck.

But the real reason is I don't want to see that necklace or think about my grandmother while we're touching one another.

– 85 –

When our mother is home there are a half-dozen good places we can hide: neighbors' basements, garages, attics that aren't padlocked. Some spaces are cleaner than others. My favorite is the loft above the Peterson's garage because there's a heavy trapdoor and we keep all our weight on it. We take off our jackets, our shirts, sometimes our jeans. Kelly usually removes her bra, but we never get completely naked like we do at home. We make a bed of our clothes and dry hump, then take turns touching. We don't kiss a lot. I'm not allowed to touch Kelly's hair anymore since I made snarls, and now I never know where to put my hands when she kneels in front of me.

After each time, while we fix our clothes, my sister warns: "You can't say anything about this to anybody, not ever, not even after I'm dead, or they'll lock you up and throw away the key."

I never ask who she means by "they."

Sometimes, after all the good feeling fades, a bad feeling follows me around like a dark cloud for days, though usually it lasts only a few hours. And other times I'm frightened, because there is no bad feeling at all.

– 86 –

Monday, June 9, 1969—It's the last week of school. It's been an okay day except I didn't bring a lunch and now I'm hungry. After the second period bell, not a soul around, I roam the corridor like I own the place. I walk up to a locker with no lock and open it. But there's no lunch, just books and papers and a red canvas jacket. I quickly close that locker and sidestep to another. Bingo. Right on the top shelf.

I grab the bag, close the locker, and walk casually down the hall and around the corner to my own locker. I work the combination lock, open the door, and a few papers fall out. I dump my books and the stolen lunch into the bottom, then pick up the papers that fell. A girl runs down the corridor toward the stairwell and I pretend I'm looking for something. When she's gone, I peek into the bag. There's a sandwich wrapped in wax paper. Nothing else.

Some days I get lucky and snatch a lunch with a nice dessert—Yodels, Ring Dings, a bag of cookies, once a fat slice of blueberry pie with the flakiest crust I've ever tasted.

I wonder what the sandwich is. I shove my face into the bag and sniff, but I don't learn anything. I hope it's not olive loaf. Or peanut butter and jelly. Or tuna fish. I'd settle for baloney. I make some room, push the bag onto the top shelf, lock the door, and hurry to second period.

The class is World History, the teacher Mr. Jacques. When I close the door he fake-coughs then clears his throat and says, "Glad you could join us, Mr. Fisher."

I nod at Jacques, who is a slick old goat always teasing the girls (rumor is, he's screwing a couple of them), then I turn to the class and bow swinging my head down low, then up quickly, like a maestro after a concert. My hair whips my eyes. No one applauds.

– 87 –

In grades one through six I wasn't allowed to go outside for recess period with the other children. Every September my mother wrote a note to the teacher requesting that I be excused from "strenuous activities" like playing in the schoolyard because I was "under strict doctor's orders."

My teachers didn't particularly like that I remained behind. During recess period several of them met for coffee and chitchat in one of the empty classrooms. I was frequently left alone, instructed to remain at my desk in nap position with my head on my arms. If the teachers met in a classroom close by, I would listen to their chatter and their laughter. Without students around, they acted almost normal. If they were well out of earshot, I would get up and walk around, amazed at the emptiness and the silence. I would peek in other kid's desks, sift through their belongings, sometimes work up enough nerve to sit in the teacher's chair or stand at the blackboard with a piece of chalk in my hand and pretend I was instructing a class of idiots.

Jenks Junior High was a whole other story. There was no more recess, but there was gym class. Physical education three times a week. On the first day, when I presented my mother's note, the gym teacher said, "You look all right to me. What's wrong with you?"

I told him it was a private matter.

He sent me and my note to the principal's office. The principal was a man named Mr. Monahan who studied my mother's note as though it were a first-rate counterfeit. He asked me the reason I was under a doctor's care. I said I didn't know for sure but believed it was probably because of the hole in my heart. Mr. Monahan was a thin man with a face like a painted skull. "What kind of hole?" he said.

I shrugged and told him I had never seen it. He asked if it was a large hole, and he formed an O with his thumb and forefinger.

"Smaller," I said.

He closed the circle. "Like a bullet wound?"

"Oh, no," I said. "It's much tinier than that. Like what a hat pin would make."

"A hat pin?" he said, and mulled that over for a while as he studied the note some more. Then he asked for my home phone number. I said I couldn't give out that information.

"I can look it up in your file," he said.

I explained that any number he might have on record had been changed because of frequent annoying phone calls. "My mother doesn't allow us to give out the new number."

"Us?" he said.

"My sister and me."

"I see," he said. He picked up the phone and dialed the operator. He gave my mother's name and address, wrote something down, then he hung up and read the number to me. "Is that your new number," he said.

I nodded, and he got on the phone with my mother. He told her he would require a signed note from my doctor if I needed to be excused from gym class.

That afternoon my mother used her red belt on me, and the next day I began my physical education. The gym teacher called me "Ticker." He showed me where to stand and how to dodge and when to duck. Then he loaded up the other boys with volleyballs and soccerballs and basketballs and blew his whistle to signal them to begin.

– 88 –

Tuesday, June 10, 1969—We're racing up the stairs. I'm winning until I trip on the second-floor landing and bang one side of my face into the banister rail. Kelly squeezes past without checking to see if I'm dead or bleeding. She reaches the third floor first. The air is thick, though not that hot, but Dean Martin has his door wide open and his window fan blasting. He's down on both knees behind his TV, looking at something. The bottoms of his white socks are black. Kelly's already on the landing when he turns his face toward us. Dean's wearing glasses, which I've never seen before. The frames are black like Clark Kent's, and the lenses make Dean's eyes look buggy. He takes them off and squints at us. "Hey. You two. Hold on a second."

I stop where I am on the next to top stair, but Kelly keeps moving, wiggling her rump. She's in front of our door with her key already in the lock as Dean steps into the hall. His sleeveless T-shirt shows off his two tattoos; there's a huge brown stain beneath his heart. "Either of you kids know anything about fixing TVs?"

Kelly works the lock and inches the door open. "He does," she says. "He's a frigging TV genius."

"What's wrong with it?" I say.

Dean keeps his eyes on Kelly who has to jiggle the key to get it out of the lock. He presses his lips together into a flat line and shakes his head. He doesn't look at me until she's slipped inside and closed the door to within a couple of inches. "Picture keeps flipping," Dean says. "It's crazy. Every time I adjust it one way, it starts rolling in reverse."

"Vertical hold," I say.

"No shit. It's driving me nuts," says Dean.

Up close I notice the stain on his T-shirt is actually a hole showing a patch of hairy chest. Dean doesn't seem drunk, but it's too early in the afternoon for him to be home and I wonder if he's sick or if he got fired for drinking on the job.

"I keep fiddling with the button but it won't hold. It goes up, it goes down. A guy I talked to says there's an adjustment in the back."

"For fine tuning."

"Yeah," Dean says. "But I can't find any damn button."

"It's inside."

"Inside?"

"You have to take the back off."

"Shit," Dean says. He steps back into his room and frowns at the TV. "I was hoping it was something I could reach on the outside."

"Nope. It's inside."

"That's a dumb place to put it."

"They put it there so nobody will know."

"Sons of bitches," Dean says and shakes his head at the TV.

"I can try and fix it for you. Do you have a screwdriver?"

Dean considers me for a moment. "Flat head or Phillips," he says.

"Flat," I say, and he goes into the bedroom.

Everything I know about TVs, I learned from watching Grandpa Rudy. Most people don't realize there's only about thirty tubes in the average TV and ninety percent of them can be pulled out and replaced in a couple of minutes. Basically, you don't need a repairman and you don't need to know what you're doing as long as you're not afraid of electrocuting yourself. Rudy pays no attention to the high-voltage warning label on the backs of sets. He unscrews the board and sticks his head inside, sniffing for burned tubes. He says the warning labels are put there by the manufacturers to keep people like him from fixing their own sets. He says the manufacturers have a sweet deal worked out with the repairmen.

I learned what I know by watching Rudy work on the old sets he hauls away from in front of people's houses on garbage day. He swaps tubes and makes working sets and sells them. One thing to watch out for and never to touch inside a TV is the cathode-ray tube, which is the long piece that sticks out into the cup holder of the backboard. Rudy's gotten zapped a few times because the CRTs hold a charge even when the set is unplugged. They are like high-voltage batteries. I never go anywhere near them.

"You know what you're doing?" Dean says.

I've got the back off and I'm sniffing for dead tubes. "Smells okay," I say. "I think it just needs adjusting."

"Yeah, well, I better do that. Don't go poking around in there. Just show me the button."

I'm looking, but I don't see any buttons. "What kind of set is this?"

"RCA," Dean says. "Where's the button I want?"

"There should be three of them."

"Just point them out," Dean says.

I tilt my head in closer and feel the heat on my face. I find a row of tiny black buttons that look like screws.

"Careful there," Dean says.

There's a V and an H and a D printed on a yellowed label beneath the buttons. I tell Dean to stand in front and tell me when the picture flips. Then I push the tip of the screwdriver into the V-button and give it a full turn to the right.

"Shit," Dean says. "What did you do? The thing's going haywire. It's worse than ever."

"Which direction?"

"Up. Going a mile a minute."

I turn the button the other way.

"No good. Now it's flipping down."

I use the screwdriver to twist the button back to its original position. "Tell me when it stops."

"It's slowing down. Getting slower. It's barely moving," Dean says. "Hold it. Now it's stopped. Nope! There it goes, sliding up again."

My hand slips and I strike the cap of the picture tube with the shaft of the screwdriver. A blue arc jumps at me like a bolt of lightning.

"Fuck!" Dean says.

My hands are empty. I pick up the screwdriver and look at Dean over the top of the set. His face is white. "You all right?" he says.

I don't answer. My arm is tingling like I struck my funny bone. I'm listening to my heart race.

"Whatever the hell you did, you fixed it," Dean says. "The picture's holding. It's not rolling at all. Son of a bitch," he says, scratching his head. "How much do I owe you?"

– 89 –

Wednesday, June 11, 1969—Mom is downstairs having her weekly meeting with Mrs. K. They write out rent receipts and discuss the deadbeats and gossip about the neighbors while they drink coffee and smoke the Turkish cigarettes Mrs. K brings back from Syria. Mom's been down there almost an hour and I've been on the phone practically the whole time.

I should hang up and go do my route, get it over with, but Elizabeth won't stop talking about her stepfather who wants to legally adopt her now that her real father, who divorced her mother when Elizabeth was two, has come back into the picture. Her real father keeps calling to invite Elizabeth for ice cream. It's complicated and hard to follow. My ear is numb, so I switch the phone to the other side of my face, which doesn't feel right at all, but I'm only half-listening, chewing on a piece of cuticle that I've torn off my thumb. Then Elizabeth stops talking, she just stops, so I walk with the phone and stretch the cord all the way to the dead TV. I turn around and lean my hip against the set, almost sitting, my arms folded across my chest, the phone trapped beneath my chin. Elizabeth sounds like she might be crying, or getting ready to cry—it's that kind of silence. I swallow the tiny piece of skin and work my lips like I'm a fish, a dumb fish, while I listen to the sound of Elizabeth breathing. I should ask her to a movie, ask her something, try to cheer her up, tell her she has nice skin, nice hair, nice lips, say something, anything. No matter how dumb.

Instead, I perform a circle dance, a jittery little series of twirls, letting the cord wrap around my chest as I reel myself in, because I have nothing, absolutely nothing to say to Elizabeth that would comfort her.

"So, anyway," she says and I know she's ready to hang up, so I say, "Hey, want to hear a joke," and she says, "Okay." Then I tell her the dumb joke Grandpa Rudy told me, how a nun falling down a flight of stairs is just like a newspaper. I pause for a three count then deliver the punch line: "Because she's black and white and read all over. Red, get it. R-E-A-"—and I hear a cough, then a bump. Elizabeth mumbles something that sounds like a string of swearwords and a curse at God.

I grip the phone with both hands like it's a slice of watermelon I'm trying to eat down to the rind. Still tangled in the cord, I say, "Hello? Elizabeth?"

Nothing.

A split second before my heart flatlines, she says, "Yeah, I'm here," and my lungs manage to pull in air. "But I need to hang up now." And the air wheezes right out of me. "You made me laugh," she says, "and I had a mouthful. I spilled Fresca all over myself. My shirt is a mess."

I tell her I'm sorry. My stutter makes it sound like "so, so sorry," which isn't the case. I picture Elizabeth in her wet T-shirt and I wait for her to say it's not my fault.

"I'll call you back," she says, "after I change. I'm all sticky."

I wait twenty minutes by the phone. After forty minutes I decide I'll wait one hour, then leave to do my route. I go to the kitchen to check the clock and drink a glass of water. Then I pee. On my way back to the parlor, I get my canvas bag and loop it over my shoulder, so I'm all ready to go. Then I sit by the phone and think about dialing her number. In my mind I see myself dialing. I imagine her mother answers. Her mom is nice and tips me ten cents every week. But in reality, her stepfather could pick up and think I'm Elizabeth's real father calling to take his little girl for ice cream. Or Elizabeth might answer, and I wouldn't know what to say. I try and think of another joke I can tell her, a better joke without nuns or anyone falling down stairs. When the hour is up, I lift the phone and listen for a dial tone just to make sure it's still working, then I go to do my route.

– 90 –

Thursday, June 12, 1969—I've got my bag and my green book and I'm all set to go when Dean carries his phone out into the hallway. He stretches the cord all the way to the window, the receiver trapped beneath his shoulder and ear. "There are three and a half billion people on the planet. Two-thirds of them are starving. You think you're important? Think again, pal."

He's talking into the phone, but he's looking at Kelly who is sitting on the floor, her back to the wall, one leg out, one knee bent, making a gate across the top stair. Today she's wearing high-cut jean shorts, frayed at the edges, and her shirt is tied in a knot above her pale belly. She's only been waiting five minutes but she looks like a bored Elly May Clampett. Today Kelly's agreed to help with my route because I promised to feed her. We don't know where Mom is, haven't seen her since she left for work this morning.

"Yeah, well, you call me back when that happens," Dean says, and hangs up the phone. "Everybody thinks I'm a bank," he says, moving forward. He holds the phone close to his chest in two hands, like he's presenting a gift to my sister. "You look nice today. Dressed for the heat."

I don't know if he's making a statement or asking a question. Kelly ignores him, looking everywhere but at him as she gets to her feet.

"Where you going?" Dean says.

She hides behind her hair, leaning on the rail, then skips down a couple of stairs. "Out," she says.

"Need a ride?"

"Nope."

I squeeze past Dean without saying "excuse me" and go down two stairs, but Kelly doesn't move, so I go around and skip down to the landing. "Let's go," I say.

"Hot day to be walking," Dean says. "You going far?"

Kelly is grinning, hugging the rail. "Nope."

Dean yanks the phone's cord tight as a clothesline. "You change your mind about the ride, you let me know." At the edge of the top stair, he waggles his head and smiles. His lips and teeth are yellow. "Stay out of trouble?"

"I will."

"And don't get lost."

"I won't," Kelly says, and she rolls her eyes at me.

When we get to the first floor landing, she tells me she's changed her mind. She's not coming. She says it's too hot, then she turns around and heads back up the stairs, clutching the rail, dragging her ass like a cripple. I remind her I'm going to buy her dinner and she says, "Tomorrow, maybe."

I watch her climb until I can't see anything but her hand on the rail, then I say, "What are you going to do?" I say it loud enough that the words echo, so I know she heard. But she just keeps walking.

– 91 –

Friday, June 13, 1969—It's after supper, though we haven't eaten yet. We're at the hospital again, just Mom and me. When we asked Kelly to come along, she moaned from the couch and shook her bottle of Midol. She's faking her period so Mom will give her money to buy Tampons.

Normally Mom visits Grandpa every other day unless her varicose veins are acting up from being on her feet all day. Kelly never goes. Yesterday Mom walked over by herself, and today I came along so that she won't have to walk home alone in the dark. It's not a long walk, but the hospital is in a bad section and the lighting isn't good.

The main reason for today's visit is that the phone company made the switchover this morning. Every few months, Mom changes the phone number to stop the prank calls and the bill collectors. We're not allowed to give out the new number except in an emergency. My school doesn't get it. The church doesn't get it. On the way in, Mom gave it to a woman at the main desk who at first didn't seem to want to write it down.

I'm hungry and bored, sweating in a chair by the window. I'm wearing cutoffs and when I move my legs stick to the chair's vinyl. The view sucks—it's the visitors' parking lot. I watch cars come in and park and people get out or people get in and drive away. Mom and Grandpa talk in low voices, exchanging secrets. Mom does most of the talking. I'm not in a spying mood, so I pay no attention. Now and then I stare at the clock. I watch the big hand and try to tell when it moves.

When visiting hours are nearly over, Mom swings her bag up onto the bed and rifles through the middle compartment. She lifts things out and puts them on the bed. "Here's my new number," she says and hands Grandpa Rudy the phone number written on the back of a business card.

Rudy is lying down more than he is sitting up. His big stomach makes a mountain beneath the sheet. He hasn't said anything for over five minutes and I'm hoping he's asleep so that I won't have to kiss his sandpaper beard goodbye. He jerks and snatches the card. "What's this?" The long tube stuck into the back of his hand swings like a jump rope.

"My new number," Mom says. She loads her junk back in her bag a handful at a time. She keeps her eyes on Rudy, smiling like it's a great gift she's handed over.

Grandpa holds the card a mile from his face and blinks at it. Then he moves his chin around like that's going to help. "I can't read a damn thing."

"You don't have your glasses on."

"Is that a seven or a one?" Rudy says.

"Which number?"

"Jesus," he says.

"Where are your glasses?"

"I shouldn't need my glasses."

My mother moves some things on the little bedside table. "Oops," she says, but I don't know what she's oopsing at. "Sit up, put your glasses on."

"I don't want to sit up. I've been sitting all day." He pushes her hand away. It's a gentle push, but she pulls back like he punched her and folds her arms across her chest. She pretends to sulk. When that doesn't work, she taps Grandpa's eyeglasses against her ribs and works the muscles around her mouth. She shakes her head at him, then she leans in and sets the glasses on his face.

"Here. Sit up."

"I'm not sitting up. All I goddamn do is sit up or lie down." Then he shifts, just a little, and the sheet moves with him. One foot emerges. His toenails are yellow. "I don't know why you just don't call the cops and put an end to it. Changing the number every week is nuts."

"It's not every week. I had my old number six months."

"Report the bastard." The thick black frames sit crooked, too far down his nose. His eyes are milky and his hair sticks out at odd angles. He looks like a fat comedian trying to be funny.

"I'm not a troublemaker," Mom says. "I don't call the cops on anyone."

"Somebody threatens your life, you call the police."

"Nobody threatened anything."

"A threat is a warning, plain and simple. That's intimidation. I can't read this," he says. "What are you giving me this for? Suppose it was an emergency for Christ's sake. I gotta go hunting for my glasses before I can dial."

"It's an easy number to remember."

"I've got enough things to remember." He extends his arm over the side of the bed and lets the card fall, but it flutters and lands on the sheet. My mother picks it up.

"Take these things off of me," my grandfather says. "They don't work worth a damn and they're pinching my nose."

– 92 –

Saturday, June 14, 1969—Big, black, puffy clouds move in from the west. The air has a spooky feel. I walk downtown to the corner and the stink of the Blackstone follows me the whole way. When I load up, the papers feel damp and sticky. I don't waste time talking to Huey. I don't dillydally or stop for collections. If people leave the money out, fine. Otherwise I don't bother knocking or ringing doorbells. I race from house to house, stop to stop. My sack loses weight in no time.

After dropping the last paper at the white Victorian, I don't report back to the corner. I head home—straight down Exchange, then up past the high school, then down Broadway. No point in meeting up with Sam. I haven't collected enough to pay half my weekly bill and I don't feel like hearing him whine about how much I owe. I'll deal with him on Monday.

I sprint from Lumb Motors to my house. The sky is heavy and dark. The church tower dongs as I enter my yard. It's high noon and the rosebushes are sagging. I hurry up the stairs and use my key. The parlor has a murky gloom, like it's already night. I hear thunder, then a low rumble. The church tower stops clanging. I'm glad to be home. I drop my empty sack on the big, blue chair.

In the kitchen the air holds a chemical smell, like paint thinner or the kerosene Grandpa Rudy burns to heat his stove. Kelly, in short, pink pajamas, sits bent forward, putting red polish on her toenails. She's sitting in one chair with her right foot flat atop a sheet of newspaper on another chair. She doesn't look up when I come in. "What's that stink?" I say.

"Your sister," my mother says. "She needs a bath."

"No it's not. It's the polish," Kelly says.

At the stove Mom empties soup from a can into a saucepan. I tilt my head to read the label: Campbell's Vegetable Barley. I'm not happy. I don't like vegetables. "What are we eating?" I say.

"Are you blind?" my mother says. She holds the can up with the label upside down. The polish on her fingernails is the same color Kelly is painting on her toenails.

"What's barley?" Kelly says. "Is it anything like rice?" She stretches forward until her head is past her knee. She blows steadily across her toes.

"You've had it before," my mother says. "You ate it and you loved it."

"But is it like rice? I can't remember."

"It's like rice, yes," my mother says. She stirs the soup, adjusts the flame. There are three bowls on green vinyl place mats and a box of Saltines in the center. I sit at the head of the table and reach for the crackers. "Make any money today?" my mother asks.

"I didn't add it up yet," I say. I tear open a fresh sleeve and remove four crackers. I put one in my mouth and three in the bowl.

"Why didn't you add it up? How you going to know what you earned if you don't count your money?"

"I don't like rice in soup," my sister says. "I like rice, but not in soup." She dabs at her pinkie toe. She still hasn't looked at me.

I chew on half a cracker. "I don't think I want soup, either."

"What are you going to eat?" Mom says. I don't know if she's talking to me or Kelly, but before either of us can answer, she says, "Don't eat, then. Either one of you. And it's not rice, it's barley." She stirs the soup. "I never said it was rice."

Kelly winces and points the tiny brush. "You did. You just said it was just like rice. You said that." Then she points the brush at me. "Didn't she, Jack? Didn't she say it was like rice?"

Mom squints. Lines form on her brow. I look at my bowl, then at my sister, then at her. "You did say it was like rice. You did. You always say that. Every time we have vegetable barley."

Mom carries the pan to the table and sets it down on her place mat. "Well, it is. A little. But not enough where you'd notice."

"I don't want any," Kelly says.

My mother spoons soup into her bowl. Then she sets the pan in front of me. The broth is steaming and there's little green specks floating in it.

"I only want a little," I say. I can feel Kelly's eyes on me.

"What am I supposed to eat?" she says.

"You're on your own. Jack and I are eating soup. You don't want soup, you can starve for all I care." She dips her spoon. "And put the cap on that damn polish while we're eating."

Kelly mumbles, then squeaks her chair on the linoleum. She gathers up her polish and the sheet of newspaper and limps out of the room, walking on her heels.

"Only a little," I say. "I'm not really hungry."

"Did you eat?"

"No."

"You haven't eaten anything?"

"No."

"You can't go all day without eating, " my mother says.

I dip in a cracker, soaking up the broth. The nice thing about Campbell's is that the vegetable chunks aren't big and they're soft, almost like mush. Nearly every mouthful slides past my tongue with no taste at all.

— 93 —

Sunday, June 15, 1969—Mom is frying baloney in the black cast-iron skillet that used to belong to Grandma. She uses a ton of butter, like Grandma did. If Rudy weren't in the hospital, we'd all be at his house eating a big Sunday dinner. If my grandmother were still alive, we'd stop at her place on the way there and again on the walk home.

"Mayonnaise or mustard," Mom asks, but I don't answer. I'm reading a Superboy comic, the one where Lex Luther saves Superboy's life by using a bulldozer to shove a meteor of Kryptonite off a cliff. This is before Lex gets pissed off at Superboy for making him bald.

"Hey! Mayonnaise or mustard?"

At the bottom of the cliff is a lake where the Kryptonite will sit in muck until Lex Luther decides to become a supervillain and goes fishing for it. "Mustard," I say. "I don't like mayonnaise."

"Since when?"

"Since forever. I hate mayonnaise."

"You didn't use to," my mother says.

"I've never eaten it in my life." In the skillet the baloney spits grease as it curves into a dome. I close the comic book. "Why does it do that?"

"Do what? What are you talking about?" my mother says. She pushes with her spatula and I watch the baloney slide around the pan.

"Why does it puff up like that?"

She shrugs. "Heat, I guess. I don't know. Ask a scientist." She uses the spatula to shovel the baloney onto two slices of white bread laid out on a plate. "I'm not a scientist." In one smooth motion she spins and slides the plate in front of me. "Fix it and cut it yourself. I'm not your maid." She slaps down a jar of French's mustard and a butter knife.

I roll the comic book into a telescope to look at my dinner. The baloney looks like a whoopee cushion, like a monk's cap. Like the diaphragm Kelly found in a little pouch hidden in Mom's underwear drawer.

"And put that damn thing away while you're eating."

"I'm reading it."

"You should be reading a real book," Mom says. "You'll rot your brain reading that crap. Then where will you be?"

– 94 –

Monday, June 16, 1969—In the checkout lane Mrs. Brown, who goes to our church, aligns her cart behind my mother, then squeezes around the side. She bends slightly forward across the narrow space, almost touching me. She says, "Excuse me," then extracts a *TV Guide* from the rack above my head. My mother doesn't notice. She's busy unloading.

Our cart contains eight items: bananas, milk, a pound of baloney, a few cans of Campbell's soup, and a box of Kotex. Mrs. Brown's cart looks like she won a contest, and I wonder if she's rich on top of being beautiful. All I really know about her is that she's married to a lawyer and that she teaches Sunday school at the First Congregational Church. Kelly had her there for sixth grade, but the next year, when it was my turn, I quit Sunday school after a month. I complained to my mother that Mrs. Brown was a crazy woman and a bad teacher, a nut case who was too strict about which crayons I was allowed to use when coloring the Lord Jesus.

Twice I colored Jesus' face a dark brown. Once I made his face yellow and his robe purple. At the last supper I colored him and Judas the same bright red as Mrs. Brown's long, manicured nails. Mom doesn't like anyone screaming at her kids except her, so I said that Mrs. Brown had scolded me about my color usage.

"Scolded you how?"

"Screamed her head off in front of everyone. I was scared. I thought she was going to belt me."

Mom mulled that over a few seconds then said she had never heard of such a thing. "Jesus is Jesus, no matter what crayons you use."

That was the first and only time my mother let me quit anything just because I wanted to. The truth, though, is Mrs. Brown never said an unkind word to me, never raised her voice. The reality is I found her too beautiful to look at her. Sitting in her classroom gave me a stomachache. And in those moments when I dared look her way, I always stared too long, which usually resulted in an overwhelming urge to pee.

In the checkout line she holds the open *TV Guide* to her face and I watch her eyes. I look, then look away, waiting for her to recognize me. My stomach warms a little. She flips through the pages too fast to be reading and I wonder if she's hiding, if Mrs. Brown has already recognized who she is standing behind and is simply snubbing us.

I decide I should alert my mother who hates snobs, but I don't move or say anything. I stare at the Pall Mall ad on the back cover of *TV Guide,* waiting for Mrs. Brown to peek. Her hair is high and tight like my mother's. Her earrings are small white balls, probably real pearls. I move my gaze down her chest to the flare of her hips. I'm all the way to Mrs. Brown's ankles when my mother nudges me. "Help unload," she says.

I lift a couple of soup cans onto the conveyor belt. I put the bananas up there too. My mother lines up the rest. The clerk punches the keys, rings us up in seconds, then gives the total. My mother rattles things in her purse. "How much?" she says, and the clerk repeats the amount.

While Mom fishes for the money, digging out the exact change, I sneak another peek at Mrs. Brown who is patiently waiting her turn, her red lipstick neatly confined within the borders of her mouth. She is around my mother's age, a pretty woman with auburn hair and a snobby manner. What gets me, what bothered me from the start, are her nails. Long and curved, slick with red varnish, more than twice the length of my mother's nails. I want her fingers inside my mouth, the sharp tips dancing on my tongue. Some mornings in Sunday school, while coloring the robe of Christ, I got dizzy dreaming of how those nails would look wrapped around my cock.

– 95 –

Tuesday, June 17, 1969—I'm walking through the front door of our apartment, not looking where I'm going, when I bump into Kelly coming out. We almost smack heads. She's barefoot, in faded jean shorts and a rainbow shirt, carrying Mom's shiny black heels, one shoe in each hand.

"Hello Jack, goodbye Jack," she says, squeezing past. She almost takes my eye out with one of the heels.

"Where you going with those?"

"Dean's. He bet me five bucks I couldn't walk in high heels."

"That's a stupid bet."

"No shit," she says.

"How far do you have to walk?"

"Just around his apartment. Don't go anywhere. I'll be right back."

"Where am I going to go?"

Twenty minutes later I knock on Dean's door. I have to rap my knuckles hard a few times, before Dean says, "Yeah? Who is it?"

I try to keep my voice from shaking. "Is my sister in there?"

After a long silence I knock again. "All right, all right. Hold your horses," Dean says.

The lock clicks, then the door opens and Kelly slides out before the door shuts behind her. Her face is flushed and the center part in her hair is all screwed up. She's a few inches taller in Mom's shoes.

"What took so long?"

She uncurls her fist, shows me a crumpled five-dollar bill. "Pizza money," she says, but her voice isn't right and her breath smells like beer. She seems dazed, confused. As she steps past me, wobbling on the thin heels, I notice her rainbow shirt is on inside out. "I need to go to the bathroom," she says.

– 96 –

Wednesday, June 18, 1969—After my route I sneak along the Marshall's high hedges, which shield their yard from the street. I'm spying on my mother who is sitting on the cement steps with Mrs. K, our landlady. They are smoking cigarettes in the shade the house makes. Mrs. K lives alone on the first floor and has a name that no one can pronounce because there aren't enough vowels. She was born in Syria where she met and married a Greek businessman who later moved her to the United States. Now she is a widow. She owns the house mortgage-free, my mother says, but I don't know what that means. One time when I asked if Mrs. K was rich, Mom said, "Richer than I'll ever be."

I stare at them through the hedges for a long time, but I can't hear what they are saying except when one of them, usually my mother, gets excited and starts waving her cigarette around. Then the volume on her voice goes up.

"All he wanted to talk about was his dumb dog humping his leg while he watches TV or how his other dog got in a fight and now has one funny eye. No, thank you, I said. See you later." She tosses her cigarette at the rosebushes that stick out past the fence. The head of the cigarette explodes like a sparkler. "The son of a bitch wouldn't stop calling, so I left the phone off the hook until I changed the number." She makes a face like she just swallowed a mouthful of dirt.

Mrs. K nods, then says something I can't hear and I wonder what the Syrian words for son of a bitch sound like. Most of the time my mother addresses Mrs. K as Mary, which she says is the American version of Mrs. K's Syrian name, though Kelly says that's a lie, because she's read Mrs. K's mail and her real name is Yalda, which means "longest night of the year." Mom says Mrs. K is her best friend, a good listener, and a smart businesswoman who understands more English than she speaks. Mom's name is Rita but when Mrs. K pronounces it she stresses and stretches the syllables so that it sounds like two words.

The prickly ends of the hedges brush at my forehead. I move back a step so that I don't get a bug in my hair like the time a brown spider started a nest in my mother's high, pinned-up swirl that the hairdresser said made her look like Audrey Hepburn. I could spy a whole lot better if I had binoculars or a telescope. I asked for both last Christmas, but I didn't get either. Most of my gifts were school clothes, plus a couple of boring board games and a 400-piece jigsaw puzzle I never put together. When I sulked, Mom said I was lucky to get anything because we were all close to living on the street. When I told Kelly we were moving to the street, she said, "Good. Any place is better than living here."

Since January my mother has been working for Mrs. K, helping run the house, collecting rents, handing out receipts, calling repairmen when something needs fixing. She has her own set of keys, which she keeps on a hook behind the stove. She shows the empty apartments to people when Mrs. K puts her "For Rent" sign in the window.

Kelly says Mom doesn't get paid, but that Mrs. K gives her a break on the rent. Every summer Mrs. K flies back to Syria. This year when she goes, she'll leave Mom in charge. She used to go for a week, then two weeks, but this time she's going for the entire month of July. She always brings back crappy gifts—small wooden camels with glass eyes, ugly earrings that weigh a ton, little jewelry boxes in the shape of a coffin. Mom always acts like her gift is the most beautiful thing she ever saw, then sticks it in a drawer or a closet and we never see it again. On her last trip, Mrs. K brought back a tiny vase too small to hold a single flower, and my mother called it "absolutely adorable" then wrapped it in pretty paper and gave it to my aunt Sally for her birthday. That would have worked out okay except Kelly squealed to my aunt, then Sally called up and had a big fight with my mother, and now they don't talk on the phone hardly at all.

– 97 –

Wednesday, June 19, 1969—Before I leave for my route, I watch Kelly roll a fat one and I marvel at how evenly she spreads and packs the crumpled weed and the smooth way she tongues the gummed edge before twisting the ends. She's better at making them than Grandpa Rudy's friend Slim, who always smokes hand-rolled cigarettes. When she has the thing lit and streaming smoke, I tell her she's one step away from becoming a junkie.

"Giant step or baby step?" she says, and I don't have an answer for that.

She stares and puffs, then draws hard until the tip glows red and makes a little crackling noise. She blows a long stream of smoke into my face. It forms a little cloud between us. The smoke smells better than a real cigarette, but it stings my eyes, so I close them.

My sister coughs. "Don't breathe or you'll get a a buzz, a contact high. Do you know what that is?"

I have no idea, but I tell her. "I'm not stupid."

– 98 –

Friday, June 20, 1969—It's after supper and Mom is gone. I don't know where she went; probably downstairs to smoke Turkish cigarettes with Mrs. K and complain about her life. Kelly and I are doing the dishes. There aren't many. Mom made grilled cheese sandwiches and Mrs. Grass' Chicken Noodle Soup for supper. Kelly's washing and I'm drying. She hands me a cup and tells me she is running away again, just not today. "Maybe tomorrow," she says. "Depends on how I feel."

When Grandma was alive, Kelly would sometimes pack a bag and go live there for a while, which in my book wasn't really running away.

"When are you leaving," I ask and she says, "Soon."

"Where will you go," I ask, and I expect her to say Sacramento.

She hands me another cup. "Not sure. I haven't made up my mind. I might just pick a direction and start walking."

I work the towel on the inside of the cup, then the outside. "Not much of a plan," I say.

"Don't need a plan. I'll keep walking until I get some place."

"Where will you sleep?"

"Different places."

"Outside?"

"Maybe."

"You won't have any blankets."

"So."

"Suppose it rains?"

"I'll camp under a tree." She hands me a dinner plate but there are suds on the rim so I drop it back in the rinse water.

"What if it pours buckets and there aren't any good trees to sleep under."

She fishes a butter knife out of the water and hands it to me, handle first. "It won't kill me to get wet."

"It might. You could catch pneumonia and die."

She watches me dry the knife. "Beats living here."

"You won't get far walking."

"Maybe I'll hitchhike."

"If you run away Mom will send the police to look for you."

She shrugs and hands me a spoon. "We'll see."

"They'll put you in handcuffs."

"They'll have to find me first."

"They'll bring you back in a straightjacket."

She hands me another dinner plate. In the center is a small blob of melted cheese. It looks like a big yellow teardrop.

"If you run away Mom will lock you up again."

"No," my sister says, wagging her head, showing me her pink tongue. "That won't ever happen again."

– 99 –

Saturday, June 21, 1969—Kelly is stomping around in her rubber flip-flops killing ants, but I'm not counting. I'm sitting on the hot cement steps doing exactly nothing. Above the church's steeple a streaking jet too tiny to see drags a perfectly straight white line across the sky. I hold my hand against the sun and squint at the jet's long stream, wondering if it's loaded with bombs headed for Vietnam. I watch until the end of the line breaks apart into puffs of tiny white clouds that look like popcorn.

When I look at my sister, she is no longer doing her crazy dance. She's squatting barefoot with a flip-flop in each hand, using them like paddles to squash ants. Her shoulders are pink with sunburn. I think about asking her which way is Vietnam. Instead, I swallow hard and taste my own spit in the back of my throat. I think about how thirsty I am, whether the landlady left the faucet on the outside spout where she hooks her garden hose, how I haven't eaten anything all day but a bowl of Rice Krispies. I wave my arms above my head like I'm stuck on Gilligan's island.

"He can't see you," Kelly says.

– 100 –

Sunday, June 22, 1969—After church we stop at home so Mom can change into her walking shoes and Kelly can go to the bathroom. Then we hike all the way up Broadway to Grandpa Rudy's house. Mom leads us on a shortcut through side streets so we don't have to pass the house where Grandma died. Rudy rents the first floor of a two-story cottage, and even though he's in the hospital, his rent has to be paid. My mother unlocks the door and tells us to wait inside and not to touch anything while she goes upstairs to see the landlord. All the shades are down. The kitchen smells like cigar smoke even though no one has been living there for weeks.

Grandpa Rudy's World War II rifle hangs on the wall above his fake fireplace, which is still decorated with Christmas lights. The rifle has been there forever, but I don't know if it is the same gun he used to point at my grandmother and at my aunt Sally. Grandma used to tell stories about how he would come home drunk and get his gun and touch the muzzle to my grandmother's head and tell her to make him something to eat. Sometimes she would get out of bed and cook something and other times she would just roll over and go to sleep. Sometimes he would poke her repeatedly in the back of the neck with the gun and tell her to get out of town before the sun came up.

When we hear Mom talking in the hall upstairs, Kelly drags a chair over to the fireplace and climbs up onto it. I tell her to get down before Mom catches her, but she lifts the rifle off the wall, then almost falls as she spins to point it at me.

"Better not play with that," I tell her.

"Who's playing?" she says. She holds the rifle level with the butt in her armpit and looks down the barrel at me like she's Annie Oakley. She squeezes one eye. Her face has that expression that I can never describe because it is a look that could mean anything.

Grandpa Rudy's gun makes me nervous, but I'm sure it's not loaded because Mom says he doesn't keep bullets in the house, so to show my sister I'm not afraid I put my hands on my hips and step toward her like I'm Superman walking into a room full of gangsters.

168

"Don't come any closer," she says, but I keep walking until the barrel of the rifle is just inches from my chest and I can see the rust spots. She raises the gun slowly until it's pointed at my nose. I hear the click. After a heartbeat, she says, "Now you're dead. Are you happy?"

"Now you're a murderer," I say.

"Better than being dead."

"Only until they fry you in the electric chair."

"They'll never take me alive. I'd shoot myself first. Like this," she says, and lowers the rifle's butt until it is resting on the chair and the barrel is pointing straight up. She tilts her face and presses her eye to the barrel.

"Bang," she says, and jerks her head back. "Right though the brain. Now are you happy?"

"If you kill yourself you go straight to hell," I tell her.

"That's only true if you're Catholic."

I point at her like I know what I'm talking about. "Protestants too. Grandma said."

"Not always. Not every time."

"Eternal damnation," I say, though I don't know what that is.

"You can still get into heaven if you kill yourself. You just need a really good excuse."

"You'll burn forever."

"God always forgives the poor."

"He won't forgive you."

"He might. You don't know."

"Why would he?"

She spins half around on the chair and bangs the butt of the rifle against the Christmas lights. For a second I think she's going to fall, but she doesn't. She stretches up on her toes and sets the gun onto the two long nails in the wall. "Grandma would defend me," she says. "She'd get God to change his mind about sending me to hell."

"God wouldn't care."

"He would after she told him the whole story."

"What's the whole story?"

"None of your business," she says.

"What's Grandma going to tell God that he doesn't already know?"

Kelly looks at me with her mouth open. Our mother makes a lot of noise coming down the stairs. Kelly jumps off the chair then plops her ass on the seat. She crosses her legs and looks at her nails like she's bored. Mom stops dead in the doorway. "What are you two doing? Why are you sitting over there?"

"Warming my hands by the fire," Kelly says and turns her face away.

– 101 –

Tuesday, June 24, 1969—We sit on opposite ends of the couch while our mother paces back and forth in the hall. The door is open and she keeps peeking in, going from door to window, window to door. We're all waiting for some guy to pick her up. Mom won't tell us his name. Whoever he is, he's over twenty minutes late. After a while, Mom shuts the door so we can't spy, which we can still do anyway the minute she leaves.

Two of the floorboards beneath the linoleum in the hall creak. We listen to Mom pace for a while, then a horn honks twice and she says, "Okay. I'm going. Remember what I told you."

My sister and I don't move. We sit like a couple of statues watching the dead TV.

"Did you hear?" Mom says through the door.

She can't see us, so we make goofy faces.

"Answer me!"

"We heard you. Okay. Bye-bye. Have fun," Kelly says, then wiggles her middle finger at the door.

Today Mom's going on an afternoon date, but she won't tell us where she's going or who the guy is, which means he's new, somebody she just met, somebody she said yes to. A lot of men come into the Blackstone Diner. My guess is he's some customer who gave her a big tip and begged for her phone number, another loser who after a couple of dates Mom will not speak to again, not even on the phone, and eventually the man will quit calling her and stop coming into the diner altogether. More lost business.

The horn toots again, but I don't sneak out to see what kind of car is picking my mother up. I stay on the couch and listen to her heels clip-clopping on the stairs as she hurries down, and then everything is quiet again.

Kelly stretches and yawns. It's almost time for me to do my route, but I don't feel like moving. We sit side by side, our hips and shoulders touching. After a minute she brings her legs up and slides down, curling on her side. She puts her head on my lap, trapping one of my arms. She sighs a great big sigh. In a small voice she says, "You're the only one who gives a shit. Nobody else in the world cares what happens to me."

I use my free hand to sweep the hair away from her face and tell her that's not true.

She says, "Name somebody."

"Grandma."

"Dead people don't count."

"She's watching you from heaven. Just like she promised."

"Big deal."

"It is a big deal. It's a very big deal."

She shifts or shrugs; I don't know which. "Name somebody else, somebody who's not dead."

While I'm thinking, Kelly untucks my shirt and works her hand underneath. She rubs a finger around my belly button, tracing circles, then she moves her hand up across my chest and slides her palm across my nipple. A tingle goes all through me. She tells me I have very smooth skin for a boy.

"It's because of all the milk I drink."

"You don't drink any more milk then I do." She takes her hand away and shifts her weight so that her elbow is pressing hard against my groin.

"You better let me up."

She shifts again, digging her elbow in.

"Really, I need to go."

"You should quit that dumb route. You said you hate it."

"I'm keeping it until Christmas. Sam says people tip big at Christmas."

"How big?"

"I don't know."

"What kind of money are we talking here?"

"I don't know. Move, please."

She yawns, or maybe it's another fake sigh. "Nope. Sorry. I'm comfortable. Your customers will have to wait."

Two seconds later she lifts her head off my lap and sits up. "Bring back something," she says.

"Like what?"

"I don't care. Something good."

I get my sack and check to make sure the green book is in it. I ask Kelly if she wants to come along. "I'll get done twice as fast if you help."

She makes a sour face. "Too much walking. I'm too tired."

"I'll buy you something to eat."

She touches a finger to her nose like she's seriously deciding. "Can we sit in a restaurant?"

I nod. "Times Square Diner has booths."

"What kind of food do they make there?"

"Everything."

"I don't know. It's a lot of walking. What would I have to do?"

"Just bring the paper into the places I tell you."

"Do I have to talk to anyone?"

"Nope. You just drop it in the hall or stick it inside the screen door. Depends on the customer. But it's not hard."

"And you'll pay me."

"I can't give you any money but I'll buy you dinner."

"Can I order whatever I want?"

I touch my finger to my nose, imitating Kelly, pretending I'm doing the serious thinking now. "As long as it doesn't cost too much. I usually get an apple turnover and a hot chocolate. That's forty-five cents."

"I'd rather have the money," my sister says.

> Why not show Kelly on the paper route?

– 102 –

Wednesday, June 25, 1969—Tammy Wynette is singing "Stand By Your Man." The volume is high, but I can hear my mother's voice too. She's singing along with Tammy, drowning her out. I drop my empty sack in front of the dead TV and peek through the doorway. My mother waves from the kitchen, then hurries toward me. We meet in the bedroom which looks neat and clean. I know someone is visiting because Mom is wearing her rose-print dress and her red high heels and too much lipstick. And she's smiling like the cat that ate the canary.

She runs her fingers across my bangs, then places her hand on my back and guides me into the kitchen. "You remember Bill," she says.

A man in a suit and tie puts a stupid smile on his face. He's seated on the bathroom side of the kitchen table. He pushes himself up and stands at attention, chest out, eyes front, like he's presenting himself for inspection. I don't know him.

"The taxi ride in the snow," my mother says.

I stare, but nothing about him is familiar.

"The hospital. Remember? The time we went to pick up your sister," my mother says.

I nod, though I'm still not sure it's the same guy. Bill sighs heavily, jerking his elbows back. He straightens his chair and plops down like he's exhausted.

"I told you he'd remember," my mother says. "My Jack never forgets a face."

"Thank God," Bill says and clasps his hands together, elbows on the table. He bows his head like he's saying grace. "I meet a lot of people, and the worst thing in life is not being remembered when you bump into them again."

My mother puts a hand to her throat and giggles like she's twelve. Like she's retarded. Like she never laughed before in her whole life.

– 103 –

Kelly's hand is on my belly. It stays there forever. I can feel the warm sweat on her palm. I'm wondering if she's fallen asleep. Then her fingers start moving, crawling like a giant spider, slipping under the top of my shorts. I squeeze my eyes shut and concentrate very hard. I pretend it's Elizabeth's hand.

Little by little the warmth becomes a heat—intense, unbearable. The rest is quick, fierce. I'm forced to open my eyes. Kelly's face is right there, just inches from mine. She stabs her tongue into my mouth while I'm sucking air. She licks beneath my teeth while my body completes its spasms. Some days I am in love with my sister and some days I hate her.

− 104 −

Thursday, June 26, 1969—Mom drags her feet, taking baby steps in her high heels, acting like she's scared, but she's smiling as Bill pulls her toward The Mansion of Terror, which used to be The House of Mirrors until some kid fell and broke his stupid arm. Neither one of them invites me to come along and that's fine. The mansion doesn't look like it would be any fun. If Kelly were here, I'd ride with her, though I'd probably fall out of the little bumper car and break my arm.

They're on a date pretending they're not, because Bill is still married and he might run into somebody who knows his wife. I'm a stooge, a prop, a decoy. If Bill starts talking to anyone I'm supposed to hold my mother's hand and walk the other way. He promised me dinner in exchange for being her chaperone, but I'm not stupid. I know why Bill wants my mother in a dark and scary place.

Soon as they get in the ticket line, I turn my back on The Mansion of Terror and head toward The Nickel Arcade, which the last time I was here was The Penny Arcade. I'm looking at all the booths on the midway, games that no one is playing. One is a basketball game with a sign that says Hot Shots, so I walk up to the counter to get a better look. There's no roof, just a high beam that supports the backboards, and I wonder what they do when it rains. Where do they put the prizes? A few of the stuffed animals hanging by their necks are bigger than me. On a shelf beneath them is a badminton set, a Zippo lighter in a wooden box, cartons of Marlboros, a set of aluminum mixing bowls. But what really catches my eye is a yellow snorkel attached to a skin-diving mask like the boys on *Flipper* use.

"Three for a quarter," the kid shouts. "The more you sink the bigger the prize." He's not talking to me. He's yelling at the adults walking by.

The hoops appear to be smaller than normal, but they're lower than ten feet, and the balls look smaller too. The distance from the counter is about the same as a foul shot.

"Sink one ball and win," the kid says.

"What do I win?"

"One makes you a winner."

"What's the prize?"

He glances at me, then back to the crowd. He's got a Band-Aid beneath his ear. "You make a basket you take anything you want from the bottom shelf. Make two and win a prize from the top shelf. Sink all three and walk away with anything you see in the booth."

"What about the snorkel set?"

He turns, checks his inventory. "Swim mask and snorkel are three."

I hand him my quarter and he looks at it like maybe it's fake. Then he sets three balls in front of me. I pick one up. It's feels like a volleyball and it's low on air. I turn it in my hands. The black seams are painted on. The kid stares past me, studying the crowd, while I line myself up in front of the center basket. "You've got to play to win," he shouts. "Three shots for a quarter, folks!"

I imagine everyone has stopped to watch. All eyes are on me. I set my stance, belly against the counter. I take a deep breath, cock my elbow, aim and shoot. The ball hits the backboard then caroms off the front of the rim and drops near the kid's feet. He kicks it aside. "Two to go," he says.

The second ball has less air than the first. My shot hits the side of the rim and dies there, balanced for an instant, then falls off.

"Close," the kid says. "Thought that was going in. One more."

My third and last shot looks way short then drops cleanly through the center of the hoop. I hold my arms in the air, signaling a touchdown.

"Hey, hey! Another winner! Everybody's a winner," the kid says.

My choices are a Hawaiian necklace, a bracelet made out of candy, or a Jetfire balsa wood glider powered by a rubber band. I pick the glider. He doesn't give me the one hanging on a wire from the shelf. He reaches beneath the counter and hands me one in a plastic sleeve with a label that says ten cents. I have to assemble it myself.

"Another winner," the kid shouts. "If he can do it, anybody can. Step right up! Three shots for a quarter!"

Clutching my prize, I run toward The Mansion of Terror feeling like a champion, a winner, like a real hero.

– 105 –

Saturday, June 28, 1969—Hiding behind her library book, Kelly sings: "I know something you don't know." She moves her eyebrows up and down like Groucho Marx. The book has a black castle on the cover. It's almost eleven weeks overdue so she already owes a big fine.

"Where's Mom?"

Book to her chin, she says, "Don't know. Don't care." She's wearing ice-blue eye shadow but no lipstick. Her hair is pulled back tight and she looks pretty enough to kiss.

"I was short again," I tell her, and she turns a page without looking.

My sack's in the hall but I've got my green book because Sam says I need to check my numbers, add up what all my customers owe, no rounding off. He wants a total right to the penny. My insides are still shaking. "I'm sick of being short."

"So put lifts in your sneakers," she says.

"It's not funny. I was short another ten."

"Ten bucks?" She closes her eyes and tries to look sorry for me, but it doesn't work. Her eyelids look like robin's eggs.

"Nine dollars and eight-five cents," I say, shaking my head.

"Is that what people owe?"

"They owe ten times that."

She sets the open book on her head, like a hat, like a roof. She holds it with two fingers and smiles like a monkey. "Do they really?" Her shirt doesn't cover her belly. She's not wearing a bra. I stare at the floor and shrug. "That's like a hundred dollars," Kelly says.

"I know how much it is." I don't tell her that I haven't been marking the book. I shake my head, dragging my feet as I go through the bedroom. Grandma's cast-iron skillet is in the dish rack, which is wrong, because Mom says we're not supposed to let it air-dry because it'll rust. I open the fridge, looking for something, anything, to drink. Mom hasn't bought groceries in a week. I lift a carton of milk but it feels empty, barely enough for a cup of coffee. I take out the jug of ice water and drink from the bottle.

Kelly comes in and drops her book on the table. I'm about to ask her what she cooked in Grandma's skillet, when she says, "Wipe your germs off before you put that back."

This from the girl who puts my dick in her mouth. "Fuck you," I say.

"Don't be a jerk," Kelly says. "You're not supposed to drink from the bottle."

I tilt my head back and swallow more water. A little bit dribbles down my chin but it feels good.

"That's how you catch polio," she says. "You'll end up a cripple."

I give her a slanted look.

"I'm not kidding." She raises her hand like she's swearing an oath. "I read it in a book."

"You can't catch polio if you've already had a vaccination shot."

She leans against the refrigerator like she's waiting for a bus. "Want to hear the gossip?"

"Who died now?" By the look on her face I'm already sure it's Rudy. Mom's someplace right now picking out his coffin.

"Nobody died, but Bill's wife threw him out."

I gulp more water. "Good for her."

"They had a huge fight. Somebody called the cops because they were screaming so loud, but nobody went to jail. But she had the locks changed and now Bill's keys don't work and he can't get his clothes or his record player or anything. He's so fucking pissed."

"She should let him have his clothes," I say.

"She told him she's giving them to the Salvation Army and he can buy them back if he wants them."

"She sounds like a nut."

"He says she's getting a lawyer and from now on he has to talk to the lawyer if he has anything to say to her."

"Sounds complicated."

"He's pretty pissed off about his clothes."

"Does he have a TV?"

She shrugs. "I don't know."

"If he's got a TV, she should let him have it."

"Why?"

"Because he probably paid for it." I put the jug back in the refrigerator without wiping any of my germs off.

"You got any money?" Kelly says.

I tell her no, but I'm lying. Right before I left the newsstand, Sam stuffed two dollars in my pocket, then he wrote plus two in his little book.

Kelly looks at me like I'm far away. "Empty your pockets," she says. "I smell a fib."

— 106 —

The air is buzzing. Something's up. Whatever it is, I'm sure it's not good news. Mom's been on the phone since I got home. She's talking in whispers, and by the look on her face, I'm guessing it has something to do with Grandpa Rudy, though it might be about Kelly and me. My sister's not in the kitchen; nothing is cooking on the stove. I'm flipping through my green book, crossing out names of people that moved, when Mom comes into the kitchen with an unlit cigarette in her mouth.

"Why can't I ever find a match?" Her eyebrows are knotted. "Who keeps taking all the goddamn matches?"

She turns a knob on the stove and bends over. She tilts her face dangerously close to the flame and puffs her cigarette. I know hairspray is flammable because it says so right on the can. Mom's beehive is an accident waiting to happen. I close my eyes and imagine her running around screaming, a human torch, until I smother her head with a wet towel. But that doesn't happen. When I open my eyes, she's leaning against the stove, posing with the cigarette like she's Bette Davis plotting a murder.

I go back to adding up the amounts people owe. Sixty-five cents plus sixty-five cents plus sixty-five cents. I include the customers on Saint Mary's Way even though they've already moved.

After a minute, Mom says, "You and your sister sleep in the parlor tonight."

I look at her, waiting for more information. I stare like she's the creature from the black lagoon. "How come?"

"Because I said so. Roll your cot in there and set it up next to the couch."

"There's not enough room."

She goes over to the sink and drops her cigarette into the bucket we use to wash dishes in. "Then make room."

I ask her who gets the couch and she says she doesn't care. I ask how come I have to sleep in there and she says Bill is going to be living with us for a few days.

"How many days?"

"I don't know. Until he gets a few things straightened out."

I ask if he will be living here more than a week, and she says, "Until he gets back on his feet." She says she doesn't know anything right now. She asks me if I'm writing a book. Then she tells me my nose is going to fall off if I keep asking about things that aren't my business.

– 107 –

At nine thirty Mom tells Kelly and me to go pee but neither of us have to. She asks us if we're sure and we both nod. Then she shuts the bedroom door, sealing us in the parlor. From the bedroom side, she says, "Don't get up for anything."

Kelly says, "Suppose I need to go later," and Mom yells back, "Tough noodles. You had you chance."

I stare at the bedroom door for a minute because I can't ever remember it being closed before. It's very quiet for a while then Bill murmurs something and Mom replies: "Don't worry about it."

I look over at my sister who is scrunched up in one corner of the couch holding her library book. The Mylar cover gleams. I wonder if she's going to keep the light on. Her eyes are focused on the book, but she's turning pages much too fast to be reading them. I wonder if the book has pictures. Then I do a quick internal check, hoping my bladder will hold until morning. I don't need to go right now, but sometimes I wake in the middle of the night with a strong urge to pee. I watch Kelly's eyes as she flips the pages two and three at a time. The cheap wire frame of my cot squeaks beneath me. The rusty springs on Mom's bed are squeaking too. I decide this is what life will be like at the Sockanosset Training School for Boys.

– 108 –

Sunday, June 29, 1969—There's barely any light when Mom wakes us. I try pretending I'm asleep, but she keeps poking me until I twist and sit up. My cot squeaks like an early bird. There are no clocks in the parlor and it doesn't feel like Sunday. While I rub my eyes, trying to get them to focus, Mom tells us to wash and dress and fix our hair.

"Why?" Kelly says "What for?"

Mom shushes her and says, "Church."

We have to speak in whispers because Bill is a lump beneath the covers. I tiptoe past him, but Kelly thumps her heels, aiming for all the squeaky floorboards. When we're dressed and ready, Mom feeds us oatmeal. She lets me go crazy with the sugar. While we're eating, she tells us we're going to church without her. She says she needs to stay by the phone because an important call is coming.

"On a Sunday?" Kelly says.

"Yes, on a Sunday," Mom says. "The world doesn't stop just because it's Sunday." She gets her change pouch from her purse and gives us each a shinny quarter. Kelly looks at hers like it's fake. "Make sure that goes in the collection plate," Mom says to me like she's reading my mind.

On the walk, Kelly says, "You know she's lying, right?"

Up ahead, people are getting out of cars. There's no sun, just gray sky, but I squint looking for Mrs. Brown.

"She's not waiting for any phone call," my sister says. "She just wants us out of the house so she can be alone with Bill."

"Why would she lie?"

"So they can fuck," Kelly says.

The entrance hall has a double staircase, one short curved flight on each side leading up to the doors of the church. We go up one, then down the other, then we hang around at the bottom until the ushers close all the doors, then we go inside and sit in the last pew of the middle section. The ushers are in the second from the last but way on the left. The stained-glass windows, which all show different Bible

182

scenes, look dull, drained of color, like they do at midnight mass on Christmas.

While Father Mitchell gives his sermon I wonder if we should have sat further up. I can't see anyone from here. Father Mitchell is talking about building a house on rock rather than on sand. Kelly has her hand high on my thigh, but she's not rubbing or squeezing and no one can see, so I guess that's okay. The minister says, "And everyone who hears these words of mine and does not act on them will be like a foolish man who built his house on sand." He slaps the pulpit like he's killing a fly. My penis moves a little inside my pants, but I don't push her hand away. "The rain fell and the floods came, and the winds blew and beat against that house, and it fell over. The house collapsed into a pile of rubble!"

I'm confused about whose house he's talking about, but he looks and sounds upset, so I decide it's Jesus' house and I'm wondering if his mother was in it when it fell. I know her name is Mary, but I can't remember if she's the same Mary who gives him a drink when he's hanging on the cross or if it was the other Mary, the whore.

On the walk home, Kelly says, "Stop worrying. Nobody saw us."

"What?"

"There's no God, you know. Not in heaven or anywhere else, so you're not in any serious trouble with him." I'm not even sure what she's talking about.

When we get to our front steps, Kelly stops to look at Mrs. K's rosebushes. I stare at the ground, looking for ants. I spot one dragging a dead beetle. Kelly says, "If there is a hell, which I doubt, we're definitely not going there." She's pinching rose petals and just letting them fall. "You know how angels earn their wings, Jack? They get them after living an ugly life here on Earth."

– 109 –

Monday, June 30, 1969—As I'm heading out the door, Mom tells me to hang on a minute. She follows me out into the front hall. I'm sure she's going to ask me for her ten dollars from last week. "I want to ask you something," she says. "And no lies. I want the truth." She folds her arms and leans down. I close my mouth and breathe through my nose. "Has your sister ever..." She tilts her face at me, then looks away. "Has she ever tried anything weird?"

"Kelly?"

She stares and nods.

"Weird how?"

"With you," she says. "Anything at all?"

I lick my lips and move my head like I'm concentrating. "Like what?"

She shifts her weight from one foot to the other. "Has she ever tried to touch you?" She uncrosses her arms and lets them drop. "Anywhere."

I shrug. "You mean hit or pinch?"

She stares at me hard. Her mouth is tight. I try not to blink. "Never mind," she says. "Go. Do your route. Run along now. Go about your business."

– 110 –

Tuesday, July 1, 1969—On the narrow one-way street behind the *Times* building all of the loading dock's green doors are rolled up. Deep inside the presses are rolling and the sound pouring out is deafening, a steady rush of whooshes, bangs, clicks, and grinding thumps, all combining into a deep hum. I walk up the four cement steps and stop at the red line painted across the loading dock. There are signs posted between the doors. One says, "Ring bell." The next says, "No vendors beyond the red line." The next says, "Employees only." My legs are vibrating. The whole place is shuddering like we're having an earthquake. I put my hands over my ears but the noise squeezes through. I can't stop blinking.

In the maze of machinery above, overlapping sheets of printed pages slide past too fast to read. The wide sheets stream down into an enclosed area where they are somehow cut and folded and come out in a long row of perfect newspapers. Right in front of them, going the other way, neat bundles wrapped in a plain yellow sheet and bound by wire ride a conveyor belt. Before they can fall off, a man in gray overalls lifts them from the belt two at a time and builds a wall around himself.

I'm wondering if he's building a fort when he catches me staring. He freezes in mid-turn. He nods his head as if to say, "What do you want?"

I raise my hand and give him a short how-do-you-do wave.

He looks at my feet, checking to see if I'm over the red stripe, which I'm not. Then he swings two more bundles atop the pile and goes back to work, lifting, stacking.

The huge cylinders above gradually slow. A long chain connecting two giant gears is thick with sludge. No more printed sheets are coming. The noise softens until there's only a hum, but the conveyor belt keeps rolling, click-clacking like a racing heart. A few more bundles emerge before the conveyor belt stops and the man wipes his hands on an oily rag looped around his belt. My ears are ringing. The air hums and the heat holds the smell of sweat and oil and ink.

"Help you with something?" he says, leaning against the wall of newspapers that he built.

I tell him I'm supposed to pick up two bundles for Sam.

"Who?" the man says. He uses the rag to wipe his neck.

"Sam Goldberg," I say. "He got shorted two bundles today. The driver told Huey to pick them up from the loading dock."

"What driver?" the man says.

I shrug because I don't know. "Huey can't leave the corner."

"I don't know what you're talking about," the man says. "I don't know any Sam or anybody named Huey." He folds the rag into a neat square and looks at it. "You can't pick up papers here. Only vendors." He moves the rag down along his chin. "You check with the office?"

"Huey can't spare any papers."

"Is he the vendor?"

"Huey works for Sam. He needs the two bundles before I can start my route."

"Look, kid, you're talking to the wrong guy. I'm just a chump." And he looks around like he just fell down a rabbit hole and ended up here. "You need to see somebody up front."

"Okay," I say. "Can I get there from here?"

"No way. Can't you read? Nobody past the line. A person could get killed walking around in here. You see those gears. You could loose an arm in those gears. You have to walk around. Just go inside and talk to the first person you see."

I'm backing away when a man in a white shirt and a loosely knotted tie comes out through a side door. He's bald, but he looks too young to be bald. He heads straight for the chump with the rag then stops when he spots me. "Who are you?" he asks, but before I can open my mouth he says, "Frank, why's this kid on the dock?"

He reminds me of the cat-loving villain in *You Only Live Twice*.

The other man says, "I told him," and puts his rag away.

"Okay. Scoot," says the bald man. "Take off before I call a cop." I start down the steps. "You know what trespassing is?"

The one named Frank says, "Kid's complaining we shorted him two bundles on a delivery."

"Wait a second. What delivery," says the bald man. "Who sent you over here?"

"Sam." I say.

His face brightens as he steps toward me. "Goldberg?"

I nod.

"There's a name I haven't heard in a while. Sam Goldberg. Jesus. You work for Sam, do you?"

"Yes, sir."

"You work his corner?"

"Sometimes."

"You don't look old enough. What happened to Huey? Sam fire his ass?" I shake my head no. "He's crazy you know. Huey, I mean. You know he's crazy?" I nod, though I don't agree. "He's been crazy since the fire. You ever see him take one of his crazy fits?" I nod again.

The bald man throws his head back and waves his arms like he's drowning. "Sam fucking Goldberg. Hell. Excuse my English," he says. "I guess I haven't seen Sam in ages. How is the old goat? Still dressing like he's a beggar and squeezing every nickel?" I shrug. "So what's the deal? Sam get shorted a bundle, did he?"

"Two," I say.

"Frank, do me a favor, stop what you're doing and get this young man two bundles. Make sure you mark it on the board."

"Will do," the man named Frank says.

"Scribble my initials next to it. Frank's going to get your bundles," he says to me. "You tell Sam we took good care of you. Okay? You tell him Bobby Russe was asking for him. He'll remember me. Tell him Bobby is still waiting for him to stop by with coffee and donuts. Don't forget now."

"I won't."

Frank slides two bundles across the red line. He gives me a sour look. I fit my fingers under the wires. They're hard to lift.

The bald man says, "Tell Sam I told you he better be paying you extra for doing his pickups. Tell him I'm going to complain to the child labor union." And he laughs. "Tell him I called him a cheap prick, too. He'll get a kick out of that." He put his hands on his hips and he laughs again. He laughs really hard while I struggle down the steps with the bundles.

On the walk back to the newsstand, I decide I'm not going to tell Sam any of those things. Or Huey either.

– 111 –

I'm always the last to hear the news about anything, good or bad. I remember when JFK was shot. I was at home, in the bathroom. My mother had let me skip school because I had diarrhea, what my grandmother called a case of the collywobbles. After almost an hour of sitting on the toilet, I came out and found Mom standing in front of the TV with this horribly dumb look on her face. Her arms were hanging awkwardly at her side, like a gunslinger ready to draw. "They shot him," she said.

I thought she was watching one of her stupid soap operas where husbands were always shooting their wives or someone else.

"They've got him at the hospital, but it's bad. It's real bad."

Walter Cronkite was talking, so I shut up and listened. Whenever Walter Cronkite came on in the afternoon it was important.

Always the last to hear—same when Mom locked Kelly up. I found out hours too late to do anything, though I don't know what I could have done to make Mom change her mind. She calls me the man of the house but she never listens to me.

It's the same with the news about Saint Mary's Way. Today, on the bottom of the front page, I find out the entire block has been condemned. The city needs all the land that runs between Blackstone Avenue and Exchange Street. By next spring the whole street will be bulldozed flat, all the houses, good and bad, demolished; then the city's going to put up a huge housing complex, an eight-story building just for old people to live in. Which is crazy. It's just nuts. More than half the houses on Saint Mary's Way are in better shape than the houses on other streets. A few are in really rough shape—rundown rattraps, two-alarm fires waiting to happen. But nobody lives in those houses and I don't think anyone has for a very long time. Maybe bad tenants are to blame, people who didn't pay their rent on time, and lazy landlords who just let their houses go to hell.

When I tell Sam, he says, "That's old news." He tells me to just hang in there, do my route, and write down the names of the people who stiff me. He says if I play my cards right, in another year, I'll have a ton of new customers, sweet old ladies who always pay on time and hand out weekly tips like Halloween candy.

– 112 –

Sixty-nine Saint Mary's Way is a red brick two-story house with a slanting porch surrounded by high grass. The boarded-up windows give it a menacing look. There are two huge trees with branches that resemble giant claws reaching toward the roof. In the narrow driveway is a rusted yellow Volkswagen without any wheels resting on cinder blocks. The car doesn't have any doors. There's no steering wheel, no dashboard, just a snarl of wires. I squeeze between the car and the house and walk around to the back. The windows are boarded up there as well, but the back door has been kicked in.

I walk into a small bare room with peeling blue wallpaper and a broken chair in the corner. The floorboards creak. I go into the kitchen. The sink has been ripped out and there's an empty place where the stove and the refrigerator should be. There are plates and cups in the cupboards. The other rooms are mostly empty or too dark to explore. In the room with the front door, what was probably the living room, shoes, clothes, and newspapers are strewn about. There's a wooden dresser with all the drawers pulled out. On one wall is a huge spot where the plaster has fallen off or been torn away. The opening shows that the wall is constructed of wooden slats. On the floor the plaster lies smashed in piles of dust. I kick at some of the chunks, which resemble puzzle pieces.

I never delivered here, but I know the house. It's only been a month or so since people lived here, but the place seems to have been abandoned for years. I find the bathroom, which has been stripped of every fixture. I look down into the hole where the toilet should be. I spit into the dark then listen to see if I've hit anything.

– 113 –

She uses her Zippo to get the thing going, puffs a small cloud, then sucks hard, making a faint whistling sound though her teeth. She pinches the middle and hands it to me. I two-finger it like a cigarette and Kelly giggles. Smoke pours out of her mouth.

"What?"

"Nothing," she says.

I pull a short, quick puff but I don't hold any of it in.

"You smoke like a faggot," she says.

"So?" I take a longer puff then drop the joint in the ashtray.

"One more," Kelly says.

I shake my head no, but she fishes the joint from among Mom's crushed cigarettes, pinches it between her nails, and steadies it to my lips. "Just breathe," she says.

I pull another drag and feel the burn all the way down. I explode a cough into her face.

"Ugh! Please don't spit," she says.

The old Kelly, the one Mom locked away, would have spit back, or punched my chest, or clawed both my eyes out. I think about fake-coughing just so I can spit at her again. I suddenly think that would be funny.

"Look," she says. "The ashtray is sending up smoke signals."

Five or ten minutes later, I tell her I don't feel anything. I rock forward and put my arms up, showing her my open palms. "Nothing. Didn't work. I'm the same as ever." Then I ask her what she's grinning at.

"I'm not grinning," Kelly says. "Do you see me grinning?"

I lower my hands and grab at the knees of my jeans. I spend half a minute kneading the rough fabric. "These pants feel weird."

"Do they?"

"You're grinning."

"I'm really not," she says.

I start to get up, then think better of it. "You look really high."

"I am," she says. "I'm wasted. So are you." She's holding the joint, which has gone out. She taps the tip against the ashtray like she's knocking ash.

"I don't think I'm high."

"Of course not. That's how you can be sure," she says.

– 114 –

Kelly sets up her White Album on Mom's stereo, which we are never supposed to touch. I don't mind the Beatles, though I'm not nuts over them like most people. I listen to the beat and stare at the dead TV, suddenly convinced there is some way to fix it. Like maybe it's a simple thing, something we missed. Like maybe it's not plugged in. Like maybe Mom yanked the cord by mistake when she moved the set. I think about getting up and looking behind the dead TV, experiencing the excitement of seeing the plug lying there. But I don't move from the couch. Kelly is singing along with "Back in the USSR." I stare at her mouth. I watch the different shapes her lips make. I keep picturing myself getting up and walking toward the TV, finding the cord and plugging it in, fixing everything. But that doesn't happen.

Two or three songs later, when I close my eyes, there's a storm in my brain. It starts out small, then becomes a winter blizzard. And suddenly the room doesn't feel so warm. I'm chilled to the bone. On the stereo Paul is singing in a high tone, sounding like a girl, or maybe that's John. I'm sure if I looked in the mirror and held the emergency flashlight at just the right angle, I'd see snow piling up behind my eyeballs.

– 115 –

With my eyes closed, I tell Kelly: "You know, if we left tonight, hitchhiked to Florida, got to Cape Canaveral..." I'm working this out as I go along. "Sneak past the gate and the guards, manage to slip into Apollo 11..." It seems rational enough. "Hide in some cramped compartment where the astronauts won't see us, we could rocket to the moon with them."

"Neat plan," Kelly says. "Let's do it."

"We should. I'm serious."

"So am I. Get your hat and let's go," she says.

"No. Really. I'm not fooling. With a little luck we could pull it off. We could actually fly to the moon."

"Eat some sugar, baby brother. It'll bring you down a notch. You're starting to freak me out."

– 116 –

Wednesday, July 2, 1969—It's late afternoon and I'm stuck working the corner. Huey's in the hospital; the Fire Department's rescue wagon hauled him away. He had a seizure, a real thrasher, and I missed it. Sam missed it too, but not by much. He got the story secondhand. He pulled up in his station wagon and found no one working the newsstand. He was pissed. A woman from the bank came out and told Sam what happened.

Seems Huey took another fit and fell off the curb, and people ran over, thinking he was having a heart attack. Traffic stopped. Huey's lips turned blue and he started kicking his feet and jerking like a fish. The lady told Sam how traffic backed up all along Main Street. Somebody at the bank called the rescue squad and the medics came and loaded Huey onto a stretcher and took him away in the wagon. I'm sorry I missed it.

By the time I showed up, everything seemed normal enough except, instead of Huey on the corner, Sam was pacing, breathing like a dragon. He told me about Huey, the ambulance, all of it. He didn't look happy. "Anybody could have swiped a paper or a magazine. Somebody could have walked off with the whole business." He handed me an apron weighted with change. "Put this on," he said. "I've got to go."

"To the hospital?" I said.

He got into his car. "What hospital? Hospital, for what?"

"To visit Huey?"

"To hell with that. All they're going to do is give him a shot of insulin. He's probably home already, tucked in bed. Watch the corner until I get back. I've got a million pickups." He looked at his watch. "Son of a bitch," he said.

– 117 –

After Sam drives off it takes me a couple of minutes to realize I'm just supposed to forget about my route for now. My customers will have to wait. I don't know if Sam is going to pay me for working the corner, or how much he pays Huey. I tie the apron around my waist, but it hangs too low. I look like I'm wearing an ugly, gray miniskirt. The weight presses against my thighs and the change in the pouch clinks when I walk.

I pick up a stack of papers and put them under my arm. I move from rack to rack, jingling like a Christmas sleigh. I try to act like I know what I'm doing, like I'm in charge. I study the comic book rack. There's nothing new so I think about flipping through one of the old issues, but I wonder how that would look to customers and what Sam might say if he saw.

I'm staring straight down at the gutter when I see the wheels of a car pull up. It's Sam's station wagon. He hasn't been gone five minutes. He leans half out his window. "You know what that bitch from the bank said to me?" Which bitch, I'm wondering. "You know what she said?" He focuses on the traffic light, which is red. He adjusts the pencil on his ear then rests his arm across the steering wheel. "That little bitch says to me: 'It's not true that you're supposed to stick a spoon in a person's mouth when they're having an epileptic fit.' She says, 'You're not supposed to stick anything in there, or even go near their mouth. If you do you might loose a finger.'" He shakes his head, looks me over, nods at my pouch. "Don't lose that," he says.

"I won't."

The light turns green and he races the engine. "Before I forget, I'm going to need you to work at the track Sunday."

"This Sunday?" A horn blares. Not Sam's.

"You'll do fine. Make some money for a change. I'll drive you over, set you up." Another car sounds its horn. "Got to run," Sam says and speeds off.

I watch his station wagon climb the hill and I wait for him to toot his horn like he sometimes does for Huey, but he doesn't.

– 118 –

I see the man coming. I watch him cross the street at an angle, almost get hit by a car, then stop at the curb to light a cigarette that's been dangling from his mouth the whole trip. He's twenty feet away having trouble steadying the match. His suit and shoes are dusty and I'm sure he's drunk, but he still looks like he might have some money. I pull one from the pile and fold it in half. I hold it out like I've seen Huey do. "Paper?"

His match burns down and he has to light another. This takes longer than it should. I wait until he's got the cigarette lit. "Paper, mister?"

He drops the match, which is still burning. "What did you call me?"

Before I can say anything, he charges at me, his shoes clapping the pavement. I back up into one of the milk cartons supporting a stack of papers.

"What did you say to me?"

Then he stops, his chest a foot from my face. I put the folded paper back under my arm. His cigarette sticks out of his fist. He points it at my head. His eyes are huge. "Don't call me mister, okay? You don't know me." He tilts his head and pulls back as if, despite the size of his eyes, he can't quite bring me into focus. His lips curl outward: "I hate that. What do you think, I'm somebody you know?"

I swallow hard, try again. My voice trembles: "Did you want to buy a paper?"

He waves the cigarette around between us and retreats another step, smiling, leaning more on one foot than the other. He blows smoke in an upward stream. "Do I want to buy a paper? Well, let me think, maybe I do, maybe I do." He pulls a short drag on the cigarette. "What's your name, kid?"

"Jack," I say.

"Jack, huh? I know a Jack." He turns his head to exhale. "You ain't him." He pulls another drag and looks me up and down. He holds the smoke in his lungs a long time. "I'm very pleased to meet you Jack. You look like a smart boy. You a smart boy, Jack?"

I shake my head no.

"You're not?" He makes his big eyes bulge. "You sure?"

I shake my head again.

"That's funny, Jack, because you sure look smart." He steps to his left, faces the street. "You act smart." He looks down at something in the gutter. "Talk smart. " He pulls another drag, blows it right out, then steps toward me, his gaze aimed high. "I scare you?"

I say nothing.

"I didn't mean to scare you. But you called me mister. I don't like that."

"Sorry," I say.

"I don't like being called mister at all, Jack. Not at all. Do you know what a mister is?"

I shrug.

"Tell me what you think mister means?"

"It's a man," I say.

"No, that's wrong." He seems excited by my answer. He moves the cigarette around. "And some people would agree with you, and you know what—they're wrong. A mister is a thing. It's a nothing, just a device for spraying. Woman use them for perfume. Your mother use perfume?"

"Sometimes."

"She use a mister?"

"I don't know."

"I had a mother," the man says. "She's dead now. My mother died a long time ago. Now I've got a wife who sprays perfume like it's air freshener. And she doesn't buy the cheap shit, you know what I mean?"

I don't, but I say nothing.

"You ever watch a woman spray on her perfume, Jack? You ever do that?"

I shake my head no. And he seems to like that answer. He smiles, showing all his front teeth. "Well, sounds to me like you need to pay more attention, Jack. You've got to keep a closer eye on what's going on around you. Never take your eyes off the women, kid."

He winds up and flings the cigarette at the gutter. "How much is the paper," he says.

– 119 –

The moment I step through the door, I know my mother's not home, because Kelly, who lost her phone privileges again, is pacing with the phone on her ear, stretching the cord so tight all the coils have uncurled. "Don't care," she says. "You're still a piece of shit. I hope you drown at your fucking beach house." She's wearing nothing but a bra and a pair of panty hose. The bra is one of Mom's old ones. It's slightly yellowed, and there are safety pins in the straps. I don't know who she's talking to and I don't care. I watch the phone, which is heavy as a brick. I wait for it to fall and break my sister's foot.

She listens and nods, then she says, "You know what I wish. I wish that your sister and your mother both get breast cancer and die."

Three minutes later, when I come out of the bathroom, I catch her using a nail file to tear at her panty hose. She pinches an inch of the nylon away from her knee before she stabs, then she pulls the nail file upward making a ripping sound like fingernails dragged across a window screen. Each time she bends forward her hair hangs down preventing me from peeking at her cleavage. When she catches me staring, I say, "You better be careful. There are arteries in your legs that'll gush blood so fast you'll pass out and die."

"Good," she says.

– 120 –

Wednesday, July 2, 1969—Kelly says Bill is living with us because he lost his job. She claims she heard him on the phone begging for his job back. "His boss is a prick. They took away his taxi. I don't think he has any money."

"Does Mom know?"

"Don't be dumb," my sister says.

"So what's he going to do?"

She shrugs. "Eat our food, take up space, boss us around, stink up the bathroom."

"We can't afford another mouth to feed."

"No shit," she says.

"He must have some money. A few bucks. Something."

"Nope. I looked. Nothing but papers and cards in his wallet."

"You looked in his wallet?"

"Checked his pockets, too. All he had was three dimes and a nickel."

"You stole money from Bill?"

She flutters her eyes, flashes a crooked smile. "No pictures in his wallet. Not a single one."

"You're going to hell," I say.

"For what? I didn't take his lousy thirty-five cents." She makes a face like she's ready to spit.

"But you were trying to steal. That's just as bad."

"Not really."

"Thieves go to hell. It's in the Bible."

"You never read the Bible."

"Grandma said."

"She didn't own a Bible."

"Still counts."

"Well, she never said that to me."

"Still counts."

"I don't believe in hell."

"Tell it to the devil."
"Oh, who cares?" she says. "I'll be dead before I get there."

– 121 –

We're sitting on the couch minding our own business. Kelly's reading "1984," a book she's borrowed from the library a half-dozen times already. I'm flipping through an old 80-page Giant Batman, the one with "The Secrets of the Batcave" laid out on a two-page map.

Bill walks in and gives us a funny look, a long sideways glance like he's adding things up. "What are you doing," he says.

I realize we're scrunched over to one side, our shoulders and legs touching. There's enough room on the couch for two other people to sit down. My heart jumps into my throat. I'm sure my face looks guilty of something. I'm about to open my mouth when Kelly bangs her elbow into my side. "Get away from me, you creep. You smell."

I scoot over to the other armrest and we pretend fight, slapping at each other's arms, until Bill says, "All right. Knock it off. Get in separate rooms if you can't get along."

– 122 –

Thursday, July 5, 1969—Mom is pretty sick of Bill. Yesterday I caught her giving him dirty looks behind his back. This morning when she left for work, she hurried out while he was having a pee and didn't kiss him goodbye. My guess is she's tired of his excuses. Fed up with his bullshit. Half the time she doesn't answer him when he talks about some job he almost got but didn't, or some prospect he has for tomorrow. Sometimes when he comes home, he slurs his speech. He's friendly enough, but with an almost creepy politeness, especially to Kelly, and he has trouble getting in and out of chairs. He's always asking if anyone phoned for him, if he has any messages, and my mother keeps reminding him she doesn't want the whole world having her phone number.

Kelly avoids him like the plague. She says he's a bum. I know what I have to do. I know Mom isn't strong enough to throw him out. I know it's up to me to get rid of him for her. I ask Kelly if she has any ideas. "We could poison him," she says. "Make it look like an accident."

"How?"

"Put rat poison in the sugar bowl." She delivers this with a straight face, in a flat, even tone. "He puts like five spoonfuls in every cup of coffee. Figure it out. He'll be dead by lunchtime."

"How is that an accident? Who keeps rat poison in a sugar bowl?"

"Nobody. That's what makes it an accident."

"What about Mom?" I say. "She uses sugar."

"Hey, you want to make an omelet, you've got to break some eggs."

– 123 –

Sunday, July 6, 1969—I've got a fever, a legitimate fever, so Kelly and my mother go to church without me. Bill is at the kitchen table smoking, drinking coffee. His teeth are in a glass of water. When he sees me, he pinches them out and fits them in his mouth. Then he brings the cigarette to his lips and stares at me while he makes a kissing face sucking smoke. "Going to work?" he says.

"Yup." I pick up my sack and look inside. There's nothing in it but the green book and a crumpled-up candy wrapper. I didn't tell anyone that I'm working at the track today. My mother thinks I'm covering some sick kid's Sunday route.

"You know, you might think about giving up that lousy route and getting a regular summer job. Make some real money."

I take out the book and flip through it like I'm looking for something. "Delivering newspapers is a real job."

"No, you see, that's where you're mistaken." He drops the cigarette into the glass of water and it makes a short hiss. "A paper route's not a real job at all."

"More real than yours."

He pushes his chair away from the table, but he doesn't get up. I close the book and curl it into a tube. I look at Bill like I'm looking through a short telescope. He crosses his legs at the ankles, slumps down, and crosses his arms. His smile isn't real. "You're a funny guy. You should sign up for the circus." He puffs his cheeks and moves his jaw around like his teeth aren't fitting right. "I hear they're in town, looking for new clowns. You might want to go down and audition."

"Maybe you should go."

"Me?" he says. "Why's that?"

I keep my eyes on him but I don't say anything.

"Oh, I get it. You think I'm a clown," Bill says. "You think I'm funny?"

"No, but I heard they're looking for apes, too."

"Watch it now."

"Big, ugly, smelly ones."

"That's two," he says and wiggles the peace sign. "I'm counting."

I stare at him but I don't say anything.

"Care to go again. One more?"

I drop the green book into my sack and hitch the strap onto my shoulder.

"I didn't think so," Bill says.

My heart is banging inside my chest. "Toothless ape," is on the tip of my tongue but it's not worth dying for.

– 124 –

On the ride Sam says it's "perfect track weather," but the air feels damp and smells like rain. He gives careful instructions, then tells me I'm a smart boy, I'll do all right, not to worry, I'll be fine. Unlike Huey, I've got a brain on my shoulders. He tells me I'm going to make a lot of money. He repeats all of it a dozen times.

Soon as we get there, Sam slips a bib-apron over my neck. The canvas is stiff and heavy, a filthy gray worse than the bag I haul my papers in. The double pockets are weighted with coins. The pouch bangs against my stomach and thighs as Sam jostles the apron into place. "Turn around," he says.

I face the sun. We're standing beside his dusty station wagon in the gravel lot at the far end of the Narragansett Race Track. It's early, but already hot. Sam's door is open and the engine is running. We're a long walk from the grandstand entrance. The sun sits low over the building like a heat lamp.

"You're going to make a lot of money today. A lot of money." He pulls the strings around to my back and knots them. The apron bites like a girdle; the weight of the coins presses against the front of my jeans. "That's not too tight, is it?"

I don't say anything. I look out at the people hurrying across the lot toward the entrance. Some of them are almost running.

"Stand up straight," Sam says.

I'm standing up as straight as I can, but I pull my shoulders back. I turn around slow, trying not to jingle.

Sam's hair sticks out beneath one side of his cap. He looks older in the harsh sun because he needs a shave. "Not bad, not too shabby," he says. "Okay, you've got eight dollars in there. Nickels, dimes, and quarters. That should be plenty, more than enough. If for some reason you run out of change, you go up to one of the parking lot attendants and buy more."

I look at Sam like he's crazy.

"What's the matter?" he says.

"Buy it with what?"

"With your cash. You'll get paid in bills—dollars, fives, maybe some tens." He reaches into his side pocket and pulls out a thick stack of folded bills. "Just about everybody is going to hand you a bill. They're all big shots, so they don't carry change. Anybody hands you a twenty or anything larger, you tell them to go get screwed."

He counts off seven one-dollar bills then ruffles the stack and tugs at a five. "Here. Put this in your pocket."

I take the bills and fold them twice and slip them into my back pocket.

"Twelve plus eight makes twenty. That's your bank. Twenty bucks. Be careful giving change. Take your time. Count slowly and don't let anybody rush you. And keep all your bills together, right in your pocket, not in the apron, you understand?"

I nod.

"You get low, you find a parking lot attendant and give him a five or a ten and ask for more change. Tell him you want quarters, dimes, and nickels. Get ones too if you need them, but I don't think you will. Count whatever they give you. They're all good guys but any one of them gives you lip or tries to pull anything, you tell them you work for me. And get their name, you hear?"

More cars pull in, bunching up, then turning off in all directions. People are walking fast. Where are the horses? I'm wondering.

"Look at me," Sam says.

"Where do they keep the horses?" I ask.

"Out back in the stables. Don't worry about the horses," Sam says. "You're here to work. You're going to make a lot of money today." He looks me over. I can't tell if he's happy or disappointed. "Stay sharp now. Be alert. You get all kinds up here. All kinds. Don't let anybody gyp you. What's the matter? Why the puss?"

I shrug my shoulders. The coins in my apron jingle. "I thought I'd get to see the horses," I say.

"Yeah, well." He goes around to the back of the station wagon and drops the gate. "You'll see the horses another time." He puts one knee up and leans in. He shoves some things around, then backs out with a bundle. He uses pliers to clip the wire. "You've got fifty programs. I'll be back before you run out."

I nod. "What do I do if you're not?"

He tilts his head like I've asked an important question. "You sell fifty before I'm back and, well..." he looks off, toward the entrance to the track where people are pouring in. "That's where you want to be, right up close to the door. You see that guy in the hat selling programs? He's an asshole. Don't get too close to him."

I look toward the crowd in front of the grandstand but I don't see anyone in a hat selling anything.

"Don't even talk to him," Sam says.

"Why not?"

"Because he's a jerk. And he's selling the same programs you are. Talk to everyone else, though. Don't just stand around. This place will become a madhouse. You've got to make yourself heard. Let people know what you're selling. That asshole won't give you any trouble but you can bet dollars to donuts he'll be yelling, so you yell, too. Okay?"

"What do I yell?"

"Programs. Same as him. GET YOUR PROGRAM HERE! Remember what you're selling. Programs, not newspapers. "

Two rows down a man in a plaid shirt gets out of his car and angles toward us. He's got a dollar in his hand. "That today's sheet?" the man says.

"Yes, sir," Sam says, "sure is. Here you go, sir." He grabs a program off the stack and holds it out. The man hands over the dollar and starts reading. Sam jiggles the coins in his pocket.

"Keep the change," the man says.

"Thank you, sir. Good luck and I hope you pick a winner."

"Me too," the man says. He doesn't go anyplace. He holds the program between his face and the sun.

Sam looks at me and I wonder if I'm supposed to do or say something. The man with the program starts walking. I step into Sam's shadow to get the sun out of my eyes. "There. See how easy it is?" Sam says. He hands me the dollar. "Put that in your pocket. That's your first sale."

– 125 –

Wednesday, July 9, 1969—When I come out of the bathroom, Bill is yawning at the kitchen table. He's bare-chested and his hair is wild and he needs a shave. He's not smoking but he's got his pack of Marlboros and a clean ashtray lined up beside his coffee mug. I detour around to the stove side of the room. "Hey," he says. "Just the guy I want to see. Sit down, Jack."

I tell him I can't because I'm late.

His face spreads into a huge grin like I've said something really funny, like he's straining not to laugh. "Half a minute," he says.

He lifts the pack of cigarettes and looks inside. I think he's counting how many are in there. I rock back and forth on the sides of my sneakers while he fingers a cigarette and works the lighter. He puffs a cloud and stretches. "Sit," he says. Smoke leaks from his mouth.

I decide what the hell, half a minute, and pull out the chair directly across from him. I lock my ankles beneath the chair and fold my arms across my chest like I'm cold.

"So," Bill says. "Your Mom give you the scoop, did she?"

I don't say anything. I stare at the apples and pears printed on the vinyl tablecloth.

"She fill you in about what's happening with her and me?"

"Not really," I say. The stink of his cigarette reaches across the table.

"She tell you I'll be living here for a while?"

I look up. "She mentioned it."

He puffs and nods. "Good, good. Because that's what I want to talk to you about." Then he stops talking and I sit there like an idiot for ten seconds until he says, "There are going to be a few changes around here. Some of them you'll like, and some you won't."

"What kind of changes?"

"Certain duties, certain responsibilities. A few new rules," Bill says. "Like what people say and how and when they say it. I'm sure you and I are going to get along fine. But your sister, well, that's a girl with a bad attitude. And that's going to end up hurting her in the long run." I push away from the table and get up from my chair. "Whoa," Bill says. "Where you going? We're not finished here."

I keep walking. "I have to go."

"We're just getting started."

"You said half a minute. It's been half."

"Sit down," Bill says.

"Can't. Sam's waiting."

"Fuck Sam. I don't care about Sam. I said sit down!"

I feel my heart speed up. "You're not my father. I don't have to listen to you."

The second I turn my back on him I hear his chair squeak the linoleum. A few thumping footsteps later the side of my skull explodes like he buried a hammer in it.

"Sit down, asshole!"

I turn around and open my mouth to scream but he's right there. His hand clamps onto my throat. I lose my balance. He squeezes hard, like he's trying to lift me. I'm swinging wildly, banging his chest with weak punches. My feet aren't touching anything. I can't breathe. He holds me up and away, then throws me back. I land hard. My head bangs against something. I'm thinking, Okay, I can get away now. I can run. But then he's on me, a knee in my belly, his hand pressing into my shoulder. I see the windup. His arm becomes a blur, then the room explodes blue to black then red. My teeth cut into the inside of my mouth.

"You little fuck. You little smart-ass bastard! I'm not going to tolerate the shit you give your mother. Not from you or that little tramp of a sister."

My throat burns and the inside of my mouth feels enormous. I can't find my tongue. I think I've bitten it off and swallowed it. Then I find it, a tender lump throbbing in my cheek, twice its normal size.

Bill stands over me. He moves his fingers through his hair then extends his hand to help me up. "That's lesson number one," he says. "Learn it. Know it. So we don't have any more misunderstandings between us."

– 126 –

After my 1st stop, the white Victorian, instead of heading home I walk my route in reverse. I go door-to-door, house to house, looking for new customers. Sam says I need to balance my losses, though I'm not sure what he means. I introduce myself to strangers and make my pitch. Nobody wants to listen to me. I don't blame them. My lip is puffed up on one side and my tongue is swollen. I sound like I'm retarded.

At one house a man in a yellow bathrobe asks me what my name is. His legs are bare. He's wearing penny loafers with no socks. I tell him my name is Jack and he smiles at that and repeats my name four or five times to himself, except he says Zack, thinking that's what the retard said. He smiles and nods, looking me up and down. He asks how much the paper costs per week.

"Sixty-five cents," I say.

He blubbers a short laugh. "I could get a pound of pork chops for that."

He has short blond hair, barely more than a crew cut, neatly parted in the middle, and he touches above one ear as he looks me over. Then he opens the door a little wider and asks if I'd like to come in. I say no. He says I look awful thirsty and I tell him I'm not, though I am a little. He asks if I like pork chops and I say not really.

"How can you not love them?" he says, and I shrug. He laughs again, then stares at me like he's waiting for a better answer. I ask him if he wants to take time to decide. He's still playing with his hair. "Decide? Decide what?"

"About the paper."

"Ah, yes. The paper." Creepy smile. "You're one heck of a salesmen, do you know that?"

When I tell him I can come back another time, he huddles forward, like we're sharing a secret. "You could? When?"

I shrug and move my feet. "Tomorrow?"

"Tomorrow's no good. I have a doctor's appointment."

I nod. "Or the next day."

He says, "Sixty-five cents is a lot of money. I'm on a tight budget, you know?"

I say nothing.

"I'm between jobs right now." He stops touching his hair and wrinkles his face like he's concentrating very hard. "That's sixty-five per week?"

"Yes."

"Delivered. By you?"

"Yes, sir."

"Right to my door?"

I nod.

"Okay. Sure. What the hell. Why not? Where do I sign?" He moves his hand through the air like he's writing.

"There's nothing to sign," I say. "I'll start bringing the paper tomorrow."

"Nothing to sign? Well, I gotta tell you, Zachary, this deal just gets sweeter all the time."

– 127 –

Bill is sitting at the kitchen table, holding his face in his hands. My mother stands behind him, rubbing his neck.

"Look at my mouth!" I shout at her. "Look what he did!" I stop rubbing the spot and look at my hand like it's covered in blood.

"Lower your voice. The windows are open and Bill has a headache. I know all about your face," she says. "I got the whole story." She looks down, staring into Bill's hair. He's got a bald spot big as a quarter. "Bill, honey, do you want to talk to Jack now?"

Bill nods his head very slowly. The rest of him starts trembling. "It was this ring. I forgot about the goddamn ring." His voice cracks like a little girl's. My mother works her fingers at the base of his neck. She looks at me with tired eyes, annoyed I'm still here.

I hold my face and breathe like I'm dying.

"He's sorry," she says. "That's what he's trying to tell you."

"What about my face?"

"Case closed."

"What about my face?"

"Put some ice on it."

"We don't have any." I point at Bill. "He used it all."

My mother sighs. "Then fill the damn tray and make some."

– 128 –

For breakfast we eat grape jelly on white toast. We used to have a toaster but it died around the same time as the TV, so Kelly cooks the bread on the end of a fork, holding it over the flame, which is how Grandma made toast every morning. It's not as easy as it sounds. I know because I've wasted a ton of bread trying and one time set fire to the sleeve of my shirt, which left a huge red mark on my arm that eventually blistered and leaked pus like a bad sunburn. Most of the time, the bread falls off or the edges catch fire.

I chew really slow because my mouth still hurts, though there's no mark, no sign that anyone hit me. When I tell Kelly that Bill gave me a slap for doing nothing whatsoever, she says, "Get used to it."

– 129 –

Bill's got money, lots of it. My guess is he robbed a bank, but Kelly says he got lucky playing the horses. I try and figure how much as he peels a five-dollar bill off a thick wad of cash. He tells me to buy myself supper. "My treat," he says.

The five is new and crisp. I hold it up and examine it to see if it's counterfeit, but if it's a fake, I can't tell. Sam once showed me a twenty that he said was counterfeit, but I couldn't tell then either.

"Don't blow that on junk, now," Bill instructs. "It's not for candy or comic books. That's supper money for you and your sister. I'll take care of feeding your mom." He wraps a rubber band around the wad and shoves it into his side pocket like he's slipping a gun into a holster. It makes a huge bump in his trousers and he moves it around a few times.

My mother comes out of the bathroom. She's all dolled up, wearing a ton of makeup. The colors of her face appear carved. She's smiling, showing her teeth. It's the biggest smile I've see in I don't know how long. She spots the five in my hand and says, "I hope you said thank you."

"No thanks necessary," Bill says. His hand goes inside his pocket and he brings out the cash. He claps his other hand over it like he's performing a magic trick. "What do you feel like eating, baby?"

– 130 –

Monday, July 14, 1969—My mother is packing more clothes than she needs. Something is up. My nose is twitching. Supposedly she and Bill are going on a small vacation, a week at some beach in Newport. Mom says Bill's wife is being "a royal bitch" so he needs time to "sort things out," and she's going along because she deserves a break from "all the bullshit," meaning, I guess, Kelly and me. But Kelly says they're running off together and never coming back. I'm on the bed, watching what Mom puts into the big suitcase Bill stole from his wife, and more importantly, what she leaves behind.

"What's it called again?"

She folds a bra in half and tucks one cup into another. Her hands are noticeably trembling. "The hotel?"

I shake my head wildly back and forth. "Not the place. The thing."

"What thing?"

"The thing. The package."

"Oh, that. It's called a honeymoon getaway package for two." She doesn't so much say the words as sing them. I've never seen her so giddy. "We'll be living like rich people, sleeping in a nice, cool, air-conditioned room every night and eating a complimentary breakfast every morning." She catches me staring. "Don't get any ideas. Newport is only an hour away."

"You hate the beach."

She holds a lacy blouse in front of her and checks her reflection. "That's not true. I hate the heat and the sand and the waves, but it's pretty to look at. Especially at night." She scrunches the blouse into a ball and tosses it onto a pile of Bill's dirty laundry. "I'll leave the phone number, but don't use it unless you have to. It's a five-star hotel. Very fancy. They don't want kids calling up all the time."

"When are you leaving?"

"Tomorrow." She folds and tucks, arranging everything neat. "Sometime in the afternoon."

I count ten pairs of underwear. Why ten, I wonder. "When are you coming back?"

"Next Tuesday." She closes the suitcase which is so stuffed the snaps don't line up. "Checkout is at noon, but we'll probably hang around, do some shopping, grab dinner, then head back. Put your weight on this," she says, and I press down with both hands. She fastens one side, then the other. "If you're really good, I'll bring you back a surprise."

"Like what?"

"I don't know. Something nice, something special."

"Like a new TV?"

My mother fights a smile. "I don't think it'll be something quite that expensive. But we'll see."

She grasps the handle and tugs, but I've still got my weight on the suitcase. "You keep a close eye on your sister. You know the rules. No fighting. You call if she gives you trouble."

"What kind of trouble?"

"Anything you can't handle."

I step away from the bed and pull in a breath, ready to disclose all my secrets, tell her everything. "How will you know if I've been good or not?"

She smiles, but barely. "Oh, I'll know."

"But how?"

She pinches my chin and tilts my face then looks into my eyes like she's reading something there now. "I'm counting on you, Jack. Don't let Kelly ruin this for me. You watch that girl like a hawk until I get back, and don't let her or anybody talk you into doing anything foolish. Okay?"

I nod.

"Last thing I need is some cop at my door telling me my kids fell off a bridge or got run over by a bus."

– 131 –

Tuesday, July 15, 1969—They look like they're going to a wedding or a funeral. Bill has on a pale blue suit that shines when it catches the light, and our mother is wearing the plain black dress she wore to Grandma's wake. Her face is made up thick, especially her eyes. I can see the line on her neck where the putty color ends, and she's wearing way too much lipstick, but otherwise she looks nice, and her hair, which my sister helped wash and set, is almost hairdresser pretty. Bill makes me carry both suitcases out into the hall, then he takes over from there. I watch him lumber down the stairs. He doesn't look up, doesn't say goodbye or offer me any advice like a father would. Back in the parlor, Mom writes down a phone number on the flap of an envelope. She puts the envelope on top of the dead TV and weights it there with an empty ashtray so the window fan doesn't blow it away.

"That's for emergencies only," she says. "It's long distance, so remember."

She kisses Kelly on the forehead and says, "Don't tease your brother while I'm gone." Then she bends to kiss me. I lean away, but not fast enough. She plants one on my cheek. "Please," she says, "I'm begging you both, don't ruin this for me. Behave yourselves."

Behind our mother's back Kelly sticks her tongue out and makes goofy faces while wiggling her hips.

"Okay, then," Mom says, and grabs her pocketbook. Kelly freezes, becomes a statue. Mom holds the pocketbook in both hands like it's a football. "For the next week I'm going to be living like a queen." She lets out her breath as she glances at her shoes, then looks around the room like she's forgetting something. Her lips are tight, her eyes wide, shining.

After she leaves, Kelly slips the chain on the door. There's a fuzzy print of our mother's lips centered above her eyes. She shakes her head; the ends of her hair sway. "This joker could be the one, Jack."

– 132 –

After we strip bare we get down on our knees and line up like we're playing leapfrog. Kelly calls it doggy-style, but I don't see the connection. She reminds me *not* to forget to breathe. I can't see her face, but I have a good view of her hips and the small bones in back. She crouches on her elbows, head bowed, like a monk in prayer. I do all the work while she hums her mmm-hmm song.

"Mmm-hmm mmm-hmm, mmm-hmm, *mmm-hmm...*"

Now and then she lifts her head and tilts her face forward, and a couple of times she looks back like she's checking to see if I'm still there, but mostly she just keeps her head down, buried beneath her hair, chanting one mmm-hmm after another. Grandpa Rudy says people mumble mmm when they're too fucking lazy to say yes.

– 133 –

Twenty minutes later, Slim calls. I tell him my mother left an hour ago. I don't say she's gone on a romantic getaway. I don't tell him I'm talking on the phone naked. He asks if she's headed over to the hospital and I say I don't think so.

"Listen," he says. "Let her know—" He coughs, starts again. "Let her know that Rudy had a heart attack this morning. He's going to have surgery this afternoon. It was a pretty intense attack, but fortunately, no damage to his heart. You got that, Jack? You understand what I'm telling you, boy?"

After I hang up I leave the phone off the hook so that if the hospital calls they'll get a busy signal. I knock on the bathroom door and tell Kelly that Grandpa Rudy had a heart attack.

"Is he dead?"

"They're operating on him this afternoon."

She doesn't say anything, so I open the door. She's sitting in the tub, bubbles to her boobs, working a brush through her hair. I lower the lid on the toilet and sit. "What should we do? Do we call Mom?"

The brush stops. "Call her how? She's in a frigging car."

While I think about that, she brings one knee up above the sudsy water. It breaks through like an island being formed by a volcano. Then she starts up again, working the brush in slow strokes through her hair.

"We could call the number of the hotel and leave a message for when she gets there."

"And ruin her vacation the second it starts. For what? Nobody died yet."

"Suppose he does die. Suppose he dies on the table."

"Then we'll call," Kelly says. "Then we'll have to call."

"Maybe we should go over there. Maybe we should go to the hospital and wait."

"Wait for what?"

I give her a hard look, but she misses it. She examines the brush a moment and rakes it with her fingers, clearing a few strands of hair.

I tell her I don't know what to do. I tell her I think we should go over there. "So he'll have someone there, someone that he knows when he wakes up."

"If he wakes up," my sister says. Then she says, ""You go. I'm not waiting around a stupid hospital."

I tell her I don't want to go by myself.

"Then don't. Nobody's asking you. Nobody's making you go. So just forget about it until something happens." She hands me the brush, handle first. "Do the back, just the bottom. Don't let it touch the water. I don't want the ends to get wet."

I take the brush and go to work. Twenty strokes later, I say, "Do you think he'll be all right?"

"Who?"

"Rudy." She tilts her head so I can get the other side. "I mean, what do you think? Do you think he's going to die?"

"Sure," she says.

"You do?"

"Eventually," she says.

– 134 –

Wednesday, July 16, 1969—After breakfast we wash our dishes in the sink. She wears our mother's green Playtex gloves and I dry. She leaves the gloves on while we do it on the floor in the parlor. I watch our reflection in the dead TV. Then Kelly uses our mother's spare set of house keys to let us into Dean Martin's apartment. There are four empty Narragansset beer bottles on top of the TV. The screen takes forever to warm up.

I tell Kelly we're missing it. "Hold your horses a minute," she says.

"Two, one, zero. We have a liftoff," the TV announcer says. He sounds really excited. "We have a liftoff and it's lighting up the area. It's just like daylight here at Kennedy Space Center. The Saturn Five is moving off the pad. It has cleared the tower."

I do a little dance, wiggling my hips like I'm doing the twist, as the Saturn rocket, the most powerful rocket ever made, pushes out fire. My insides feel like I'm flying, like I'm traveling with it.

Kelly giggles. "It looks like a stiff peter."

I give her a sour look.

"What? It does. A dong. A prick." She waves at the TV. "Bye-bye little zipper snake."

I tell her the Saturn Five is as big as a thirty-five-story building. "That's seven times taller than the *Times* building." On the TV, the rocket is just a fireball, no bigger than my thumb.

My sister stands bowlegged in front of the set. She's holding her fist in front of her crotch, jerking her hips and pumping like she's whacking off. "Look out moon. Here we come."

– 135 –

Thursday, July 17, 1969—We drink Folgers Crystals instant coffee without milk because there isn't any. It tastes bitter, but neither of us feels like mixing a batch of Carnation instant milk. I sit at the table wearing only my socks and underwear. After five minutes of hunting through cupboards, Kelly finds where Mom hid the sugar bowl: beneath the sink, behind the Drano and other poisons. "Maybe she mixed rat poison in," Kelly says, sniffing the bowl.

I spoon in a ton, and after I drink the coffee, the bottom of the cup has enough sugary sludge to make a second cup taste just as sweet as the first.

"Let's take our cups into the parlor and sit like adults," Kelly says, imitating Mom. She leads the way, but we never get there. We end up sitting on the bed, watching one another making faces in the mirror, holding our cups with both hands so we don't spill a drop on the sheets.

When we get around to kissing, Kelly's mouth tastes like stale coffee syrup, so I don't kiss her again. Not on the mouth. I think about my mother, not during, but afterwards, with my sister still sitting on my chest like she's riding a pony.

"Your turn now," she says, reaching between my legs.

I close my eyes. I can still taste coffee in my throat. I feel jittery and sticky. I think about telling Kelly I'm not in the mood, but I wait too long.

– 136 –

Friday, July 18, 1969—We're stoned. At least I think I am. Kelly mixed a few pinches of marijuana in with the scrambled eggs she cooked in Grandma's cast-iron skillet. A few small sticks and seeds got mixed in too, but they tasted okay. Now, she is sitting on the floor of Dean's apartment, her back against the wall. I'm in Dean's puffy chair, which has a row of cigarette burns up and down both armrests. We're watching the moon mission on Dean's TV and we're getting good reception, no horizontal flips, but they're not showing anything good, just two guys talking behind a desk. One of them is Walter Cronkite, who reminds me of Captain Kangaroo. Right in front of Walter are a couple of neat models—one of the Lunar Lander, one of the Apollo 11 capsule. They must have been hard to glue together and paint, but neither man is paying these neat toys any attention.

I ask my sister if she's hungry.

"We just ate," she says.

"When was that?"

"A few hours ago."

I ponder that a minute, then ask if she's hungry now. She shakes her head wildly and the ends of her hair do a dance. "I think I could be hungry again," I say.

"So eat something."

"I'm going to. That's my plan," I say, but I don't get up.

After a while she says, "There are some Fritos left. You want those?"

I nod, but she's not looking at me and I have no idea where the bag of Fritos is.

We watch Dean's TV for a while, waiting for something to happen. The man sitting beside Cronkite talks about the millions NASA has spent, and Walter seems pretty amazed. I think about all the money I owe Sam. I try and do some math, figure out the amount I've collected so far plus how much my customers still owe, but the numbers crowd together until they drop off a cliff.

"Look at those model rockets," Kelly says, pointing at the TV. "Those are cool. I want one."

I try standing, but my knees won't straighten and I sink back into Dean's chair. "I think I better eat something. I'm feeling a little sick."

Kelly bounces up. "Okey-dokey. Let's see what Dean's got in his fridge."

— 137 —

Saturday, July 19, 1969—No sign of Dean in days. I'm thinking maybe he died in a car accident or got thrown in jail for stealing cigarettes from the man who stocks the gas station's cigarette machine. Kelly doesn't even knock before she unlocks his door and lets us in. We go right to the kitchen and she puts four of Dean's eggs in a pot of water and sets them on a burner. She ignites the gas with a match because Dean turns off his pilot light whenever he's going to be away for a while. She twists Dean's plastic timer to ten and the thing starts to tick like a time bomb. There's bread, but it's moldy.

"Fuck toast," Kelly says. "Let's watch TV."

It's early. There's nothing to watch except *Bozo the Clown*.

I sit in Dean's chair while Kelly flips through all the channels, past snowy screens and test patterns, twisting clockwise before ending up back with Bozo. She looks at me and makes a face. "Take your underwear off."

"Why?"

"Because it's disgusting. You've got piss stains in the front." She points at my groin, wiggles her nose like Samantha on *Bewitched*. "They smell like shit."

I look down at the yellowed spots but they're not too bad. "I can't smell anything."

"I don't want that stink in the same room while I eat."

She moves to Dean's dresser, opens a drawer, closes it, opens another. "Here," she says, holding up boxer shorts. They're pale blue with a wide waistband and enough creases to show they've never been worn.

"Too big," I say.

"Don't be dumb. They'll stay on fine when you're sitting. Drop those. I'll soak them in a bucket of bleach."

I arch my back and pull my underwear down to my knees without getting out of the chair. There is a shit stain but it's tiny, smaller than a dime. I wiggle and kick until I'm free.

Quite suddenly, without warning, Kelly is in front of me. She hunches down, gobbles me up, no hands, all mouth. When I arch my spine and lift, her arms slide beneath me and her fingernails dig into my skin. She looks up, catches me staring. "Don't watch," she says.

I tilt my chin up and focus on the TV, but I can still see my sister's head bobbing. Bozo is twisting a long, narrow balloon into an odd shape. Somebody off-camera barks like a dog.

– 138 –

After my route I go to Times Square Diner, which is no bigger than a tractor-trailer: twelve stools, five booths, and a row of porthole windows that don't open. The walls are crusty yellow except near the grill where they're thick with grease. The air always smells of onions. There are no waitresses, no one behind the counter except Ray who does all the cooking. If you sit in a booth, which I seldom do, you can look out the little window while you wait for your order, but you still have to get up and get your food after Ray cooks it. And you need to pay attention because Ray won't tell you twice. There are no menus, just a display board above the grill with items spelled out in red plastic letters, and a chalkboard on the door of the refrigerator where Ray writes the soups and dinner specials.

Ray prints very neatly for an old guy. The lines of his block letters are perfectly straight and all his curves are smooth. I wish I could write like that. I always read the specials and their prices, which seem pretty reasonable, then I always order the same thing—an apple turnover and a cup of hot chocolate. On really warm days when the door is wedged open with a brick and all the fans are whirling, I might order a root beer instead of the hot chocolate. The cost is the same.

Usually when I go in, there's no one in the place but Ray, which gets weird because he doesn't have a TV or play a radio. While I eat he reads the newspaper forward and back. Sometimes he stands with his back against the grill, staring toward one of the windows. I try not to make too much noise chewing, but the crystallized sugar on the turnover sometimes crunches beneath my molars.

Ray says that one day all my teeth are going to fall right out of my head. "Just like mine," he says, using fingers to stretch his mouth, showing me his jack-o'-lantern smile.

– 139 –

Sunday, July 20, 1969—When I reach the top of the stairs, I see Dean's door wide open. Kelly is bent over behind Dean's TV, rolling it toward the door. She straightens up, the electrical cord in one hand, the house keys in the other. "Jesus, you scared me," she says. "I thought you were Dean. Don't do that."

"What are you doing?"

She pushes the TV along on its squeaky wheels, steering it towards the door. "We're borrowing this."

"You're stealing Dean's TV?"

"You want to watch the moon landing, don't you?"

"I'll read about it in the paper."

"Not the same and you know it."

"Better than going to jail."

"Relax, it's cool. Dean's stuck working double shifts because somebody walked out or something. So he's not coming home. He's just going to sleep in his car."

"How do you know?"

"He called me."

"Why would Dean call you?"

"He likes me," Kelly says and smiles. I give her a long, hard look and she says, "He wanted me to meet him. He said he'd take me to McDonald's if I would spend the night with him."

"Spend the night?"

"Yeah. Keep him company. I told him I was stuck here babysitting my little brother."

"You're not in charge."

"I said I wanted to see your face turn ugly when the astronauts crash into the moon."

"They're not going to crash."

"They might."

"They won't."

"Wanna bet?"

— 140 —

Sunday, July 20, 1969—It's a little after four in the afternoon. This is it. The bug-shaped Lunar Module is dropping, coming down fast. I'm on the couch and Kelly is standing close to Dean Martin's TV which is in front of our dead TV. I can only see half her face but I know she's waiting for the module to blow up or crash into the moon.

One of the astronauts says, *"Sixty seconds. Lights on. Thirty feet down. Two and a half... picking up some dust..."* I don't know if it's Buzz or Neil talking. *"Thirty feet. Two and a half down..."*

"Who's talking?" I ask Kelly.

"Shush! Get ready," she says.

"Get ready for what?"

"You'll see."

The TV's picture makes no sense. I don't know what I'm looking at. Some part of the moon? I close my eyes.

"Four forward. Drifting to the right a little...thirty...thirty seconds..."

"Ka-boom!" Kelly says.

I open my eyes. The room is a blur.

"Contact light...okay...engine stop."

"Uh-oh," Kelly says. "Their engine's dead."

"Tranquility base here. The eagle has landed."

I punch my fist into the air and let out my breath as Houston replies: *"Roger, Tranquility. We copy you on the ground. You've got a bunch of guys about to turn blue. We're breathing again. Thanks a lot."*

Kelly moves between me and the TV. She puts her hands on her hips and says, "Well, that was disappointing." She sighs and shakes her head at the set. "I'm going to take a bath."

"They're down," I say. "They've landed. We did it. We're on the moon!"

"Yeah. Well, don't count your chickens before they hatch." She unbuttons her shirt as she walks from the room. "None of us are out of the woods yet."

"What are you talking about?"

"Moon germs," she says. "Bacteria. Microorganisms. Viruses. Wait and see. Even if they make it back, which I doubt, they'll be covered in moon germs. In a few months, we'll all be infected. We'll all be burning up with fevers and puking our bloody guts up."

– 141 –

Sunday, July 20, 1969—There's no wind on the moon, but the American flag, which is on a frame, looks like it's moving and I'm wondering why that is.

The president is calling long-distance: "Neil and Buzz, I am talking to you by telephone from the Oval Office at the White House, and this certainly has to be the most historic telephone call ever made. I just can't tell you how proud we all are of what you—"

"Oh, Christ," Kelly says. "Turn him off."

I tell her to shush and drop to my knees in front of the set.

Nixon says, "For every American this has to be the proudest day of our lives. And for people all over the world, I am sure they, too, join with Americans in recognizing what an immense feat this is. Because of what you have done, the heavens have become a part of man's world. And as you talk to us from the Sea of Tranquility, it inspires us to redouble our efforts to bring peace and tranquility to Earth. For one priceless moment in the whole history of man, all the people on this Earth are truly one; one in their pride in what you have done, and one in our prayers that you will return safely to Earth."

"He is such an asshole," Kelly says. "Turn the channel. Hurry. See what else is on."

I twist the selector, flicking through channels, but nothing is.

– 142 –

Sunday, July 20, 1969—Hours after Neil and Buzz put their footprints on the moon, I wake up sweating in the big blue armchair. The TV is off. Kelly's not on the couch. I stare at the blank screen and let my eyes grow accustomed to the dark. I think about switching on Dean's TV to see if the astronauts are dead yet. Instead I get up and walk into the bedroom. A breeze stirs the curtains, but I can't feel it. The air is too hot for a blanket.

Kelly is sleeping on her back, her short nightgown across her thighs. She looks dead, so I walk around to her side of the bed to make sure that she's still breathing. Even in the dark, she's ten times prettier than my mother.

I watch her sleep for a while, then I look out the window for the moon, but I can't find it. The streetlights cast an eerie haze and the sky isn't anything worth looking at, so I turn around and stand with my knees against the mattress, looking down at my sister. I watch her breasts move slightly with her breath. There isn't much light from the window, but I can see one nipple pressing at the fabric. I bring my face down close, but I don't touch it.

When she shifts position, ruining the view, I go around to the other side of the bed and climb in. I lie on my side, hugging my pillow and watching Kelly's chest move up and down with each breath. I fall asleep looking at her.

"Move," she says, and bangs an elbow into my chest.

I'm in the middle of the bed and she's at the edge. I quickly scoot over, fix my pillow. There's enough space between us for another person, but she stays at the edge. I lie on my back for a long time with my eyes closed, but it's too warm to sleep. My pillow doesn't feel right. I listen to the crickets, and I think about my mother and where she might be. I wonder about the astronauts, not the one orbiting the moon, but the two that are on the surface, Buzz and Neil, and I wonder what they might be doing, and how I would feel trying to fall asleep in a cramped space a quarter of a million miles above the Earth.

My sister starts to make a slight hum on the end of each breath. I stare at the ceiling and watch the shadows. After a while, I get to my knees, moving painfully slow, trying not to rock the mattress. I sit on my heels and stare at her face for over a minute, then I gently lift her gown up onto her stomach. If she wakes, I'll say the breeze did it.

I steady my hand an inch above the bushy hairs expecting to feel heat radiating upward like sunlight off the moon, but my hand actually feels cooler there. I keep my hand rigid and study her face. Her eyelids flutter and there is a faint smile in the corners of her slightly parted mouth.

I lower my hand until my fingers fluff along the hairs, which feel soft and damp like the thick green moss that grows beneath the grape trellis. I rub back and forth, then up and down, but I don't stick my finger in. She shivers, opens her legs a little. I jerk my arm away, but she's got me, digging her nails in. "Don't stop," she says.

– 143 –

Monday, July 21, 1969—Late, late in the night, I wake to the sound of something or someone knocking. It's distant and faint, barely loud enough to hear. At first I think it's rain hitting the roof or a car with a flat tire riding by. Then I understand it's the astronauts, Buzz and Neil, tapping at the window. We're three floors up, but I picture them floating outside, supported by jetpacks, hovering like a couple of hummingbirds. They're taking a short break from their moon mission to visit me, and the good news is they've brought the cure for this unbearable heat: an air-conditioned space suit for me to sleep in. What a relief. Kelly and I can take turns wearing it. We'll sleep soundly; no more humidity.

Problem is the space suit comes packed in a standard NASA lightweight aluminum case too bulky to fit through our narrow windows. They tap and tap, signaling for assistance. I'm about to get up and help them when I hear creaking and I sit up. My heart is pounding. The window is wide open, but there's no breeze and the curtains are still. I stare at the doorway. The room is pitch-black. My heart thumps. After a few seconds, I hear my sister sigh in her sleep.

I nudge her but she doesn't move. "Kelly." I poke her with my elbow.

She shifts away from me while I hold my breath and stare into the dark. My eyes are playing tricks. There's a flickering glow in the doorway. Did Kelly leave the TV on? Then I hear a click, the light fades, and I know someone is there.

I roll against my sister's back and whisper into her ear. "Get up. Mom's home."

She bumps my arm, groans. "Why are you on me?"

"Shush."

"Get off. What are you doing? You've got room."

"They're home. Mom, Bill. What do we do?"

She shoves me away, sits up. My eyes hurt from straining. After a few seconds she says, "You're dreaming, idiot. Go back to sleep."

But I know someone's there. I hear a floorboard creak, then the room explodes with light. "Son of a bitch," says an iron voice. "I'll be damned."

The light stings. I shield my eyes. There's a man in the doorway. He's bigger than Bill. Black spots float around his face. He's half in shadow, split in two, but I know him.

"God help you both if I'm seeing what I'm seeing."

It's Dean Martin in his T-shirt and oily work pants, a beer bottle in his hand.

Kelly yanks the sheet up to her neck. "What are you doing? Get out," she says. "How'd you get in?"

She yells so loud the echo hurts my head, but Dean appears amused by her outburst. He shakes his head really slow, grinning at us like Fred MacMurray on *My Three Sons* or Robert Young on *Father Knows Best*. "Get the fuck out of here before I call the police!" Kelly shouts.

Dean makes a dull clicking sound with his tongue. He lifts his arm, the one not holding the beer. He raises it like Hitler. His hand is a fist. When he uncurls his fingers, Mrs. K's spare set of keys drop down. He makes them clink and ring like a little bell, like it's a magic trick.

"Those aren't yours," my sister says.

"They're not yours either," Dean says. He raises the bottle to his mouth and drinks without moving his head or taking his eyes off us. His Adam's apple moves like mice are running down his throat.

"You can't walk in here like you own the place." Her voice is level, strong. "Get the fuck out. Now!"

Dean clenches the keys and brings his fist down really fast, punching himself in the leg. Then he leans a shoulder into the doorframe, tapping the top of the bottle to his chin. His lips are moving, but he's not saying anything.

Kelly's face is red, but she doesn't look scared, just angry. She holds the sheet to her neck like that's going to protect us. "I said get out!" Her voice finds a new pitch, higher than our mother's. "Now!"

Dean frowns but doesn't move. He looks at the keys in his hand, then he tosses them into the dark parlor. They must land on something soft because there's no chime, no sound.

Kelly bangs my hip. "Get up."

Crazy talk.

"Go, move," she says. "Call the police."

I look at her, then at Dean, then at her again. She bumps me with her knee. "Tell them we're being robbed."

"Pfft," Dean says. "Who the hell is going to rob you? You've got nothing to steal."

"Give them our address and tell them a drunk broke in while we were sleeping."

"I didn't break nothing," Dean says.

"Go on, Jack. Tell them you're a kid and your mother's not home."

Dean steps away from the door. He leaves just enough room for me to make it. He's daring me to try. I swing my legs over the side of the bed. My insides are moving faster than the rest of me. As soon as my feet touch the floor, Dean says,

"Go for it, Jack. Dial the operator. Have her send the cops over. The more people who witness this the better."

"Last warning," Kelly says.

"Tell them to send a newspaper photographer, too. I want somebody to take a picture of this."

"Do it, Jack. Do it."

"Shut up." Dean says. "You ate my food and stole my TV. You're the thieves! Both of you."

"We only borrowed it," I say.

"Tell it to the cops."

"Don't talk to him, Jack. Don't look at him. Just go to the phone and—"

"You took my beer, too," Dean says and points his bottle at me. "I'm sure that's not all you stole. And that's not the worst of it. I see what's going on here. You ought to be ashamed of yourselves. Both of you."

"Take your stupid TV," Kelly says. "It's a piece of junk anyway. Just get the hell out." Dean swigs another drink and Kelly puts a hand on my back. "He's not going to touch you. Don't worry, Jack."

I push off the edge of the bed and get to my feet, but I'm dizzy. Something starts throbbing behind my eyes. I sit right back down again.

"What are you doing," Kelly says. "Go and call."

Dean takes a couple of steps toward me. "So how long has this shit been going on?"

"Don't talk to him, Jack."

"Hey," Dean says, pointing the bottle at her. "Shut the fuck up. I'm all done talking to you. I'm speaking with the boy."

Kelly says, "Dial the operator. Tell her it's an emergency. Make sure you—"

The bottle shatters against the wall. Beer and glass rain down, splashing onto the bed.

"Are you crazy?" Kelly yells.

"I said, shut up! I'm not playing with you."

"Fuck you!" Kelly says, and tosses the sheet off. "You can't come in here, scream at us, and throw bottles around. Are you out of your mind?" She swings her legs off the bed, pulling the sheet with her. Her hair is wild and she looks small standing there, holding the beer-soaked sheet in front of her, glaring at Dean.

He moves forward a step. "Where do you think you're going?"

He spreads his arms, ready to catch her if she runs. Instead, she climbs back onto the bed, stepping over broken glass, then hops off the other side. "Wait here," she says to me, then goes into the kitchen. She doesn't run.

Dean tilts his head. He looks confused for a moment, then points his finger at me. "Don't move." He steps slowly across the room. "Hey!" he yells. "Get your ass back in here. I'm not done with you."

"One second," Kelly says from the kitchen.

Dean moves past me but stops at the doorway. "You want to play," he says. "I know a game we can play." But he looks puzzled. He squints at the darkness. "Turn a light on in there!"

"I'm in the bathroom," Kelly says. "One minute."

There's a glazed look in Dean's eyes. It's something more than drunkenness. "Get your ass back in here." His speech is a little slurred but firm, loud, commanding.

I'm holding my breath, listening for the back door. I expect Kelly to run. I want her to get away. When Dean chases her, I'll lock him out and call the police.

He leans into the dark. "That girl's trouble," he says. "I know trouble and she's a bucketful." He steadies a hand on the doorframe, turns his eyes to me.

I can't control my knees and I'm sure he sees them twitching because he says, "Relax, Jack. I'm not going to hurt you. I'm not like that. This isn't about the TV." He looks toward the kitchen. "You see the moon landing?" I nod my head and Dean nods his. "Between you and me, I don't care about the TV. Nobody needs to know you stole it."

"We didn't steal. We just borrowed it."

"I know," Dean says. "And I bet she put you up to it, too. Am I right?" He moves his head, dipping like a boxer, trying to see into the kitchen. "You sit tight and do what you're told and we'll get along fine. But that one...that little lady's going to get a lesson in good manners. And she better not give me any grief either. Okay," he shouts. "Your time's up, missy! Piss break's over."

He steps forward through the doorway into the dark, then quickly comes back. I hear the clunk, but I can't see Kelly and I don't know if Dean hit her or what he hit her with. Dean staggers, inching backwards, twisting his torso as he stumbles. I can't see his face. Then I can. Blood spurts from his nose and mouth. His eyes flutter, then he slumps and falls straight back like he's doing a reverse dive into a pool. The room vibrates like a plane struck the house.

Kelly leaps into the light, screaming, "You fuck! You fucker!" She's swinging Grandma's cast-iron skillet like it's a tennis racket, moving the skillet through the space where Dean is no longer standing.

"Jesus Christ. What did you do?"

Kelly hitches and swings, barely missing my elbow. I step away and try to avoid tripping over Dean's arm. One of his legs is twitching but the rest of him looks dead.

"What did you do? Why did you do that?"

"Piece of shit," Kelly says. She raises the skillet high in a two-handed grip.

The front of Dean's hair is damp, dark with blood oozing out like oil from a well.

"Did he touch you?"

"Why'd you hit him? You didn't have to hit him."

"Are you okay?"

"All he wanted was his TV."

She lowers the skillet, turns it upside down. "That's not all he wanted."

"You didn't have to crack his head open."

She bumps Dean's hip with the side of her foot. He makes a gurgling sound. "Fuck him," she says.

"I'll get a towel. You call the police."

"No."

"Tell them to send an ambulance."

"We're not calling anyone." She squats beside Dean, nudges him with the skillet. One of his eyes is slightly open, but he's not moving. "Put some clothes on, then start packing."

"What am I packing?"

She plucks Dean's wallet from his pocket. A couple of scraps of paper fall out when she opens the fold.

"What are you doing?"

She pulls out money, but I can't see how much.

"We need to get out of here," she says. "So get moving."

"Where are we going?"

She tosses the wallet onto the bed. "I don't know, but we're not coming back."

– 144 –

Every light in every room is on. My head is buzzing and it feels like daytime, except the windows are black. The clock above the refrigerator says quarter to four. I get my canvas bag and fill it with food from the cupboard. I put in cans of peaches, pears, fruit cocktail, B&M baked beans, Campbell's soup, a box of Uncle Ben's minute rice. It doesn't add up to much, so I throw in food I don't like, clearing the shelves. Kelly loads her red suitcase with candles, toilet paper, soap, toothpaste. She puts in two plates, two cups, spoons, and forks, like she's packing for a picnic.

We don't speak. I'm jumpy. Now and then I see my sister freeze and stare through the doorway, listening for some sound from Dean. I don't look at him. I can't tell if he's breathing. Any minute I expect him to get up off the floor and kill us both.

I grab the emergency flashlight off the refrigerator. I drop it in the bag with everything else. Then I pull the strap to test the weight. I can lift it, but it's a strain. I slide the strap onto my shoulder. It feels like I'm carrying a thousand papers. I nearly jump out of my skin when Kelly taps my arm. "Can opener," she says. "Don't forget it."

– 145 –

The moon is a slice, a sliver. It looks like a crazy clown's crooked smile. Kelly walks twenty feet ahead of me, moving up Broadway like she knows exactly where she's going. She's got a pillow under one arm, her suitcase under the other. There is no traffic, not a soul in sight.

My canvas bag feels like it's gaining weight. The strap digs into my collarbone, the bad one, the one Mom broke, so I shift it to the other shoulder. I tell Kelly to slow down and I hurry to catch up. In front of Lumb Motors she puts down her suitcase and uses her Zippo to light a cigarette. I look back at our house. The moon is following us.

I stop five feet behind my sister and shift the weight of the bag onto my back. The strap presses into my forehead. The warm air pricks my skin. I walk slightly bent, balancing the weight. Kelly smokes the cigarette hands-free. The tip dances like a firefly. Her face looks wet. She's sweating worse than me, though she might be crying. I don't stop to find out. I move past her, take the lead. "C'mon," I say. "I know a place we can live."

— 146 —

An hour later we're drenched with sweat, still huffing from the long hike and from dragging an old mattress from one of the upstairs bedrooms down into the room that we're camping in. There's dust in the air. When the specks float in front of the emergency flashlight, they look like gnats or mosquitoes. Kelly lights a candle. She's smoking another cigarette; her fourth or fifth since she brained Dean and left him to die. The windows are boarded with plywood and there's no air. I'm sure we're going to suffocate in this heat.

"I fucked up," she says.

"No kidding."

"I wasn't thinking straight." She paces from the boarded window to the spot where I dumped my canvas bag. Smoke leaks out one corner of her mouth.

I use one candle to light another. "You shouldn't have hit him so hard. Not in the head."

"Fuck that. I'm not talking about that. I should have grabbed his keys."

"Huh?"

"I wasn't thinking. We could have taken his car."

"What for. You don't have a license."

"It's a fucking automatic with power steering. A monkey could drive it."

"Where would we go?"

I'm expecting her to say Sacramento. Instead, she blows smoke at a candle making the shadows lean. "I don't know," she says. "But look where we are."

– 147 –

Tuesday, July 22, 1969—It's dark and dirty. The air feels thick, damp, sticky, and there's a definite odor of cat piss though I haven't seen or heard any cats, but I've counted a dozen spiders. I need a bath. We've been here two full days, almost two. Kelly's got one candle burning, which doesn't give much light, not enough to see a spider until it's already crawling up my leg. One candle is less to worry about when we hear a car coming or someone passing outside. We haven't eaten since breakfast when we finished the last of the powdered donuts and split a can of warm cola, but I don't feel hungry. I've been smoking too many cigarettes, more than Kelly. She slept most of the day. Every time I close my eyes, I imagine spiders are crawling on my face.

I use her Zippo to light another Marlboro. I do it quick so my sister doesn't say anything about wasting lighter fluid. I puff and pace. Smoke streams from my nose as I walk to the boarded windows and back.

After a couple of trips back and forth, she says, "How many of those are left?" She's on the mattress, sitting yogi style, working an emery board across her nails. Shadows dance across her chest and face.

I open the pack and shake it like I'm counting, but I know there's only four. "Four," I say. "But there's another pack."

"Full?"

"Unless you opened it."

She concentrates on her nails, which seems dumb, while I play with the lighter, snapping the lid on and off as I pace. I flip and click in rhythm with my step and wonder if I should mention food. In two or three days there'll be nothing left.

After a while, she says, "Stop doing that."

"What?"

"Clicking that thing. You're going to break it."

"How am I going to break it?"

"Somebody could hear you."

"Who?"

"Can you quit it? Please. It's annoying."

I stop pacing and stare at her with the cigarette in my mouth. I squeeze the lighter in one fist and the pack of Marlboros in the other and wait until she tilts her face up enough to break through the curtain of hair. Her skin looks pasty and yellow, and there are dots of white flame in her eyes.

"You hungry," she says.

"A little."

"I'm starving," she says. "All I had was that donut."

I watch the light play on her face while she stares.

"We should go to a movie," she says. "Eat there."

I take the cigarette from my mouth and drop it into an empty fruit cocktail can. "Waste of money. Somebody might see us."

"Not if we're cool. We'll hide in the balcony like secret agents."

"No. A movie is a bad idea."

"It's only a dollar to get in. Something really good could be playing."

"There's two of us, two tickets. That's two bucks."

"Not if we buy just one. I'll let you in through the fire exit."

"The ushers have flashlights. We'll get caught and go to jail."

"They sell hot dogs," she says, like that's a big deal.

I hear a car passing so I move a couple of steps toward the window. There's a pinhole in the plywood but I can't see anything, so I turn and look at my sister. "Kelly, why do you think nobody loves us like Grandma did?"

She smirks and looks down, working the emery board against her thumbnail, then she holds her hand at arm's length, fingers spread. "Think about it," she says. "Why would they?"

– 148 –

In the dream Kelly gets screamed at then slapped by our mother for being naked, but I don't. That's not the weird part. The weird part is Kelly has a penis and I don't. There's nothing between my legs except smooth flesh. Not even any body hair. While I'm feeling around, finding nothing, my mother says we're moving to Kansas to live on a farm that Bill bought. She doesn't say anything about Kelly's penis, but she looks at me and shakes her head. "You know what this means," she says. "This means you have to take control of your life."

– 149 –

Kelly hands me ten dollars of Dean's money. I check it for blood, but there isn't any. I don't ask her how much cash she took from his wallet. I go for food. I run to the end of Saint Mary's Way, then head downtown. I walk past city hall and the police station. I go into the Blackstone Diner and order four weenies, no onions, and four Cokes. My mother's boss Rocky is standing on a chair, changing a light bulb above the door. The kid who bags my order has four pimples big as warts on his forehead and a pathetic moustache. I tell him to keep the change and he says, "Really?"

When I get back, Kelly's got candles burning. Four of them. Their glow pushes shadows into the other rooms. She holds one of the candles like she's making her First Communion. Her mouth is closed but she's breathing into the flame, making the walls appear to lean as she advances toward me, taking baby steps. The flickering light paints shadows beneath her eyes making her look older. She starts whispering something about darkness being her old friend, about darkness coming to talk to her. It takes me a few seconds to understand what she's saying. The words are from the Simon & Garfunkel song, except she isn't singing them. She moves toward me like a zombie, reciting the lyrics like we're having a normal conversation.

I sit down on the broken chair we're using like a table and she gets down on her knees and shuffles across the mattress. She aligns the candle between our faces. "Go on," she says.

"Go on what?"

She sets the candle on the floor between the wall and the mattress. "Finish," she says.

"Finish what?"

"The song." She slides forward and props an elbow on the broken chair, her face close enough to kiss. "Say the last part."

"No."

"Go on. It'll be our prayer."

"Eat your dinner," I say.

She pouts like she's going to cry. "You're no fun. You know that?" Then she drops onto her back, lets out a long, fake sigh. She asks where I bought the wieners and I say Times Square. She bites into one. Then it's quiet for a while, except for the sound of us chewing and the wind moving through the house carrying some faraway traffic noises.

— 150 —

Long after I think she's asleep, my sister asks if I believe her father and my father are the same man. "I mean, think about it," she says. "What are the odds the same guy knocked Mom up twice?"

"Could happen."

She snorts a laugh. It sounds fake. "Not too many men are that stupid."

And I think about how stupid some people are, especially men, and how when I grow up I'll probably be one of them.

"Besides," she says. "I have a pretty good idea who my father was."

"You do?"

She nods.

"Who?"

"Not telling."

"Is he the man in the picture?"

She shakes her head. "If anything, that's your guy."

"Why do you say that?"

"Because he looks like you. That picture has always looked like you, even when you were small. You look like one another."

"You can't see a face."

"Yeah, but I can tell by the rest of him."

I close my eyes, trying to see the picture in my head. "He's just some guy standing in a pile of leaves. He could be anybody."

"You wait," she says, "someday you'll own a suit like that and be holding your hat in your hands and you'll walk into a pile of leaves near a fence and someone will snap your picture."

"Who's going to take my picture?"

"Anybody might. Maybe your girlfriend or your wife. Or some newspaper reporter. Then you'll see. Your picture will look just like that."

"Then who's your father? What's your guess?"

"Not saying."

"Because you don't know."

"If I told you what I think, you wouldn't believe me. You'd call me crazy."

I look at her like she's crazy now. "What difference does it make if I believe you?"

She drags a hand through one side of her hair making a comb with her fingers. "Tell me who you think."

"Nope. Sorry. Promised I wouldn't."

"Promised who?"

She shakes her head. "Sorry. That's part of the deal." Her eyelids flutter as she slowly drags pinched fingers across her lips like it's a zipper.

"What deal? You don't know anything."

Her sigh makes her shoulders slump and her breasts rise. "I wish I didn't, brother dear. Wish I didn't. But it's all water under the bridge now. None of that even matters. How anyone gets born is such a small part of nothing." She uses both hands to push her hair into a heap on top of her head and holds it there. Her elbows stick out like she's getting ready to do sit-ups. "Grandma used to say life is a gift. No receipt, no returns." She's smiling, her mouth tight. If she put on red lipstick she'd look like our mother, a younger version. "Let's eat something, fill our bellies, and be glad we're alive."

– 151 –

It's too hot to sleep. The air feels damp, like a heavy rain is coming. I'm on the bare mattress with my jeans pushed down to my knees. Kelly's on top, resting on my thighs. Her skirt covers us both. The hem reaches halfway up my chest. She slides one hand beneath the skirt and I watch the bulge of her arm move across the fabric until her fingers find me, then she shifts and wiggles and that quickly I'm inside her. I close my eyes. My jeans trap my legs. She's dead weight and centered. I can't do more than jerk my hips a little. She does most of the work. She rocks slow, front to back, side to side. I concentrate on the sensation of her hard muscles moving beneath her soft flesh. Then she starts lifting and landing hard, pumping with a frenzy, causing a slippery slapping noise, and I have to hold on to something, so I grab at the fabric around her hips.

She huffs and moans. "Careful. You'll rip it."

I don't know if she means the skirt or something inside her. Either way, I don't care. I take my hands away. I let her ride. I call her names in my head. Nasty names. Things I would never say to anyone, especially a girl. Then I roll her onto her back and push into her hard. I hold her ankles in the air and pretend to be a jackhammer, trying to make her squirm, make it hurt, but I don't think she notices.

– 152 –

Wednesday, July 23, 1969—There's no wind that I can feel, but the candle is making the shadows bend and stretch. I'm staring at the flame, thinking about the astronauts, wondering whether they'll burn up on reentry. I decide they will. They're all going to die and somehow it's my fault.

Kelly says, "Rudy."

"Rudy what?"

She uses one hand to hold back her hair.

I lean on my elbow and try to see her eyes. "What about Rudy?"

"Never mind."

"What? You're worried about Grandpa Rudy now?"

She shakes her hair, which needs washing.

"Then what? What about Rudy?"

After a silence, she says, "I think he's my father."

"No way. How is that even possible?"

"Think about it."

But I don't want to think about it. "Why would you say something like that?"

"Because I'm pretty sure it's true."

"No way. That's crazy talk." I go back to staring at the candle for a few seconds, then I look over at Kelly. I stare at her hard. "Now you're just making stuff up. You're trying to be mean."

She meets my stare for a second, then arches forward and ducks behind her hair. "Ask Aunt Sally if you don't believe me."

"I don't believe you. Nobody would ever believe that."

"Call her up and ask what it was like growing up in that house. She'll tell you stories you won't believe."

I roll onto my side facing the shadows, trying to get my mind to stop.

"Call her," Kelly says. "Don't take my word for anything."

"Shut up."

"Don't tell me to shut up."

"Then stop talking. I'm not calling Aunt Sally. And I'm not listening to another word you say. I'm going to sleep now."

"Good night," my sister says. "Sweet dreams."

It's the "Sweet dreams" part that makes me want to punch her. I make a fist and hold my breath. I'm still watching the shadows dance when she blows out the candle.

I'm straining my eyes looking for spiders, when she says, "Why don't you like her?"

"Who?"

"Aunt Sally. She's always been good to you."

"I never said I didn't like her."

"She gives you money on your birthday. She's taken you tons of places."

"She's not so nice."

"Nicer than Mom."

I squeeze my eyes shut, then open them trying to adjust to the dark, but I still can't see anything. "Remember that time she took us to Rocky Point and a fake pirate pretended to cut my throat."

"Yeah, I remember that," Kelly says. "She took your picture. That was a fun time."

"Maybe for you, but I still believed in pirates then."

– 153 –

After Kelly falls asleep I pull on my sneakers without untying the laces and go outside to pee. I can't find the moon and the streetlights seem too bright. I walk past the condemned houses on Saint Mary's Way, then up Blackstone Avenue. I stop looking for the moon and climb the hill like I'm doing my route. I walk right through the gate of the White Victorian. I step into the hallway and pull the string on the overhead light. The click sounds like a gunshot. I grab yesterday's newspaper off the stack. I don't know if Sam delivered it or if he made Huey do it, or if he's already hired some new kid to do the route.

Someday I'll get a job and mail Sam all the money I owe him. Right now, I just want to know about the astronauts, if they're alive or dead, but I don't look at the newspaper until I'm at the corner. Then I unfold it beneath the streetlight.

My hands are shaking, but I'm relieved. The astronauts are A-okay. The headline spells out their glory. The mission is a success. Apollo 11 is headed home, all systems go.

Back at 69 Saint Mary's Way instead of lighting a candle, I use the emergency flashlight. The batteries are low, but I read everything there is about the moon mission. I study the pictures, which look like ghosts, then I find this on page two:

> TWO LOCAL CHILDREN REPORTED MISSING
> Pawtucket Police are concerned over the disappearance of two children who have been missing for three days. The children were identified as a Kelly Fisher, aged 15, and her brother, Jack Fisher, aged 14. They were last seen Sunday afternoon and were reported missing by their mother. Anyone with information as to their whereabouts should call the Pawtucket Police Department.

– 154 –

I wake up out of breath like I've been running. I'm sweating and my stomach hurts. I think I'm in my mother's bed until I see the melted candles, one small flame flickering about a foot from my face. Then the room filters through. The place might be hell. The shadows give it that kind of power.

It's never a good idea to fall asleep with candles burning. I think about waking Kelly up and screaming at her, then I remember that I lit these; they're my responsibility. I stare at the one still burning. Its wick is so low, it might go out by itself. All the others did. I make a wish, then blow out the last candle.

I'm staring at the darkness above my head, thinking about what my sister said about Grandpa Rudy, when a siren blares, growing louder by the second. I stretch my legs, ready to jump up and run. I'm waiting for flashing lights, footsteps, yelping police dogs. Our mother will burst in with them. She'll pull me by my hair back to my life. I decide that the minute she walks through the door, a policeman on each arm, I'll ask her about Rudy. I'll deliver the question point-blank and know by her face, by her eyes, what the truth is.

But the siren gradually fades, moving off, unwinding until it's barely a hum. I close my eyes, listening. Kelly shifts on the mattress. She bumps my elbow. Somehow she finds my hand in the dark and fits her fingers between mine. "Not for us," she says and squeezes. "Maybe the next one."

– 155 –

I doze for a minute or an hour, then wake with a terrible feeling. At first I think my heart has stopped and I'm not surprised. Then I'm sure someone is in the house. Kelly is a lump beside me. Her faint snores sound like a squeaky bicycle with a rusty chain. I'm sweating but I feel cold, and there's a dull throbbing behind my eyes like a bad stomachache in my brain. I hold my breath and listen, but I can't hear anything except Kelly's snores. Maybe I fell too fast out of whatever dream I was having. I can't remember the details or anyone that was in it. Though I'm sure I must have been. Can you even have a dream you're not some part of?

– 156 –

Moon Report, Past Due
by Jack Fisher

The moon is a cold rock one-fourth the size of Earth. It generates no light of its own. There is no atmosphere, no air, no water, and no sound. The surface is always too hot or too cold. The daytime temperature reaches 225 degrees and at night it drops to 245 degrees below zero. The gravity is about one-sixth the gravity of Earth, so if you weigh 100 pounds on Earth you'd weigh about seventeen pounds on the moon. This is good news if you're wearing a heavy space suit and carrying a lot of junk.

The moon travels around the Earth at a speed of 2,288 miles per hour, completing one full orbit (a distance of one-and-a-half million miles) every 29-and-a-half days. The word month is derived from this 29.5-day period.

As it circles the Earth, the moon keeps changing position, reflecting different amounts of sunlight, moving through a cycle of phases:

- *New Moon*
- *New Crescent*
- *First Quarter*
- *Waxing Gibbous*
- *Full Moon*
- *Waning Gibbous*
- *Last Quarter*
- *Old Crescent*
- *and back to New.*

When the moon is full, it rises at sunset then stays visible all night long. Many people consider this phase related to love and romance. They say a full moon affects people's minds and makes them act crazy, and they call those people lunatics.

I think my sister might be a lunatic. My mother too, probably. I'm not sure about me yet.

A couple of thousand years ago, people thought the moon was a god, or the eye of a god, so they sang songs to it and said prayers and made sacrificial offerings of dead animals. Goats, cows, lambs, pigs, chicken. People too, I think.

If you stare at the moon, it's easy to imagine you can see a face, supposedly a man's face, but that's just the sun reflecting off the dark and light areas, all the bumps and craters. There isn't any man in the moon. At least there wasn't until we put one there.

People like to make up stories about things they don't understand, so there are over a thousand myths about the moon. One legend claims that on the surface is everything that was wasted here on Earth: misspent time, squandered wealth, broken vows, unanswered prayers, useless tears, all the leftover bits and pieces of countless shattered lives.

If you believe in that sort of thing.

Just before Neil Armstrong stepped down from the ladder, he described the lunar dust as "fine and almost like a powder." He and Buzz didn't hang around long or walk very far, but they left behind a mess of footprints just like kids do after playing in new snow. But snow melts and lunar dust doesn't. And because there is no erosion, those footprints will remain visible for at least ten million years.

Unless someone takes a broom and cleans up the place.

– 157 –

It's not quite dawn, still dark and quiet, when they find us. I'm curled on my side listening for early birds when a shadow crosses through the beam of a flashlight. I think it's a dream or some trick my eyes are playing. Then a skinny cop is standing there, a tall silhouette in the glow of the doorway. I can't see his badge or his uniform, but I know it's a cop because he slashes his light across my eyes and says, "They're in here. Both of them."

Then everything speeds up. My heart. Thumping footsteps. Voices everywhere. The room fills quickly. There are four. Our mother is not with them. The glare hurts my eyes as four beams dance about the room like overlapping searchlights. Kelly quietly snores through all of it.

One of the cops kneels in front of me and illuminates his own face. Maybe it's the glare or the angle of the shadows or the fact my eyes are stinging, but he looks enough like Sam to be his twin. He keeps asking me my name but my sense is that he already knows it. I make two fists and extend my arms, waiting for the handcuffs, expecting to be dragged away, but I'm not afraid. This is my chance to finally be the hero. I'll tell them it was me who hit Dean Martin with Grandma's skillet. I'll confess to everything, explain how there's not even any need to wake my sister.

I only close my eyes for a couple of seconds, but when I open them, the cop has turned his attention elsewhere. He is squeezed in with the others. Together they form a wall, a human blockade, surrounding my sister's side of the mattress. Their combined shadows shift and loom. One of them kneels, one of them whispers, one makes a sound that could be anything.

There is something ridiculous about four uniformed police officers crowding around an old mattress, shinning their flashlights into a pretty girl's face. It seems so God-awful silly, I put my hand on Kelly's hip and nudge her.

"What?" she says.

Resources

RAINN: The nation's largest anti-sexual assault organization.
Website: www.rainn.org
The Rape, Abuse & Incest National Network is the nation's largest anti-sexual assault organization. RAINN operates the National Sexual Assault Hotline at 1.800.656.HOPE and the National Sexual Assault Online Hotline at rainn.org, and publicizes the hotline's free, confidential services.

Child Help USA
Website: www.childhelpusa.org
Childhelp programs and services are designed to help children from any situation and let them experience the life they deserve-one filled with love. The principal theme is to provide these children with an environment of love and kindness and with the best possible treatment services so they will see how special they truly are.

Child Help USA Hotline
National Headquarters
15757 N. 78th Street
Scottsdale, Arizona 85260
Phone: 1-800-4-A-CHILD or 1-800-2-A-CHILD (TDD) (24 hrs)

ASCA
www.ascasupport.org
Adult Survivors of Child Abuse (ASCA) is an international self-help support group program designed specifically for adult survivors of neglect, physical, sexual, and/or emotional abuse.

Bradley Hospital
www.lifespan.org/bradley/
Emma Pendleton Bradley Hospital provides a range of family-focused, high quality mental health care to infants, children, adolescents and young adults with emotional disorders and/or developmental disabilities.

Bradley Hospital
1011 Veterans Mem. Pkwy.
East Providence, RI 02915
401-432-1000

Acknowledgments

This book is dedicated to the very large memory of my maternal grandmother, Frieda (Stricker) Thurber, who, by the time I was fourteen, had saved my life and the life of my sister an incalculable number of times.

Secondly, and pretty near equally, I am grateful to my loving wife Colleen whose support and faith in the value of my work still sustains and still amazes.

And I'd be a thoughtless old coot if I didn't acknowledge my son, Sam, for his reliability and friendship over these past few years.

In addition, I am deeply indebted to my agent Jack Scovil for his confidence and his endurance; my dear friend Andrew Wilson for his willingness to read everything I've ever put in front of him; and the wonderful people at Casperian Books LLC.

CPSIA information can be obtained at www.ICGtesting.com
Printed in the USA
BVOW041657280212

284022BV00002B/58/P